"Jamey," Rue whispered. "I've wanted to hold you all day, to get you in my arms and love you. I want you like I've wanted no other woman and have since I first saw you . . . you with your flashing eyes and raven hair."

Frightened now of the unfamiliar sensations as her body clamored for fulfillment, she pulled slightly away from him and whispered shakily, "No, Rue, this is wrong. We hardly know each other and—"

"What does time have to do with us?" he replied as his mouth discovered her cheek and earlobe, finally sliding down the slender column of her throat, blazing a hot, fiery trail of kisses. . . .

Dear Reader,

It is our pleasure to bring you a new experience in reading that goes beyond category writing. The settings of **Harlequin American Romance** give a sense of place and culture that is uniquely American, and the characters are warm and believable. The stories are of "today" and have been chosen to give variety within the vast scope of romance fiction.

"I can't really remember when it first occurred to me that someday I wanted to be a writer, but I do know that since my early teens I've been collecting thoughts and impressions that felt as though they should be written." Caron Welles has indeed made an impression with her first novel, *Raven's Song*. Caron and Jamey Marsh, her heroine, share a common occupation, and *Raven's Song* will leave you enlightened and encouraged by the talent of young songwriters.

From the early days of Harlequin, our primary concern has been to bring you novels of the highest quality. **Harlequin American Romance** is no exception. Enjoy!

Vivian Stephens

Vivian Stephens
Editorial Director
Harlequin American Romance
919 Third Avenue,
New York, N.Y. 10022

Raven's Song

CARON WELLES

Harlequin Books

TORONTO • NEW YORK • LONDON
AMSTERDAM • PARIS • SYDNEY • HAMBURG
STOCKHOLM • ATHENS • TOKYO • MILAN

For Jan Hicks,
who believed

Published July 1983

First printing May 1983

ISBN 0-373-16013-5

Chapter One

Jamey sometimes worked with only her desk light on as the room lights were a dead giveaway of her presence, almost a guarantee of interruptions. This morning was one of those times. It was important that she complete the apportionment of the school's budget in time to meet with Mac before lunch to review it. If she could pull it off, she would still be free in time to take Steve into Nashville this afternoon.

She was engrossed in translating budgeted dollars into teachers and textbooks when she realized her foot was tapping in time to a catchy, familiar tune. Flicking back the curl of long black hair that had fallen over her shoulder as she worked, she looked up and checked the time before leaving her office. It was five past ten. Moving with an unconscious grace, Jamey walked across the room and turned down the hallway that led to the music room.

"Sounds good, Steve," she said softly from the doorway. "I might have known it would be you."

The music died abruptly as the young guitarist swung around in surprise. "Oh, Jamey, I didn't think you were here! I thought you had already gone to meet with the Super. We'll still be able to go, won't we?" His eyes jerked to the wall clock, the grim expression on his face giving away his apprehension.

"I'm working on the budget now, Steve, and if I can

get enough peace and quiet to finish it, I should be through in time for us to leave right after lunch." Jamey walked across the room and placed her hand on Steve's shoulder. "But you'll have to go back to the main building. No more practicing."

"But, Jamey—"

"No, Steve. I think this is best, anyway. You've played that song until it's running out both our ears, and all you're going to do now is make yourself more nervous."

Steve nodded, but his glance fell away from Jamey's direct gaze as his shoulders slumped dejectedly.

"Hey, how many times have you told me how good you are? And how you're going to make it in music?" Jamey deliberately lowered her already husky voice to make it gentler, more soothing. "Well, you're right. You *are* good, and you probably will make it, but it's going to take time. Nobody gets there in music without paying their dues."

Steve looked up, a shy smile brightening his youthful features. "I know. I'll make it. And I'll make you proud of me on the way! Thanks, Jamey."

"Okay. Now off with you," she quipped as they both turned toward the door. "I've got to get this budget finished or today won't be the day you start your road to fame and fortune."

As they reached the doorway Jamey paused and added seriously, "Steve, you really are good...and I'm already proud of you. I wouldn't be fighting for you in this if I didn't believe in you."

It was eleven fifteen when Jamey wrote in her final budget figure. Quickly reviewing her totals, she reached for her phone and called Mac, Tanasie Basin's superintendent, on the interoffice communication line. "Mac, I've got those budget figures worked out. Will you have time to meet with me before lunch?" Receiving an affirmative answer, Jamey hung up and hastily gathered her papers.

Mac McCormack crossed to his office window. The tall, solid bulk of his large frame was reflected in the glass as he stood, watching Jamey move across the open field that separated the school building from the administrative and dormitory section of Tennessee's newest juvenile institution, Tanasie Basin State School. He thought, not for the first time, that she was awfully young to be in a position of such responsibility. He had opposed hiring her at first on the basis of her youth, and because her consulting experience was somewhat limited, but was glad now that his opposition had been overcome by the other members of the administrative committee assigned to screen the applicants. At twenty-six, she was proving to be one of the best educational consultants he had worked with. She seemed to have an innate understanding of the delinquent mind—which was almost laughable, when she was so strait-laced herself. But the understanding was there, and with it, the ability to coordinate educational programming for delinquent youth. He was well pleased with her work so far.

He was also, he thought, falling in love with her, though he didn't seem to be getting anywhere with her. She was so independent, so busy standing on her own two feet, that she just didn't seem to see him as a man. And she would be leaving soon anyway, unless he could convince her to stay on as the school's administrator. Still, working with her was almost a bonus, when just looking at her gave him pleasure.

Jamey was almost boyishly slender, which made her look younger than her twenty-six years, but her feminine curves made a definitive statement as to her gender. Even dressed in jeans and western shirt, as she was today, she looked essentially female. Her long, shiny black hair normally fell to the middle of her back in gentle waves, the soft curls framing a heart-shaped face with deep, wide-set brown eyes, upturned nose, and a gamin mouth that was more often than not turned up in a grin. The combination of a light summer breeze and her own movements as she walked briskly across the field fanned her hair into a dark aureole, giving her an elfin look. At five feet four inches, Jamey made a small and charming package, but an energetic one.

Her energy was partially responsible for her involvement in this Steve Carlson business. And that, more than the budget, was on Mac's mind today. He still wasn't sure how he had let her talk him into this project, but knew she would expect him to honor the agreement they had made. Besides, it was true that young Carlson had musical talent, and that he was doing well at Tanasie Basin, but it was equally true that he was a juvenile offender. In fact, at seventeen, his rap sheet had been so long that he had been sentenced to Tanasie Basin for more than a year, less than half of which he had so far served. Damn! The boy had openly admitted his involvement in three burglaries and was suspected in a good half-dozen more, though he was adamant in denying any knowledge of the additional crimes. And here Mac was, with fifteen years' experience in juvenile corrections, agreeing to let Jamey take this kid to Nashville to play for a group of country-rock musicians. He supposed he had agreed partly because he hadn't expected her to find anyone willing to listen to an unknown seventeen-year-old kid...especially a delinquent kid. But he hadn't, at that time, recognized the extent of her determination.

In a gesture that communicated his feeling of resignation toward Jamey's musical project with Steve, Mac ran sun-bronzed fingers through wavy dark brown hair that was just beginning to yield to a hint of silver. A self-deprecating scowl marred the even, still youthful character of his face for a moment as his light green eyes darkened in a reflection of concern. Only the silvering of his hair and the slight webbing of lines that fanned outward from his eyes, laugh lines he liked to think of them, revealed that he was nearing his fortieth birthday.

As Jamey tapped on his office door Mac let his arm drop to his side and moved away from the window, his features quickly schooled into an expression that gave nothing of his thoughts away. "Come on in, Jamey, and let's see what you've got. I'm eager to see how you've dealt with this budget cut," he said, ignoring his greater worry.

Jamey's mouth turned up in her usual grin as she handed him the sheaf of papers. She sidestepped, avoiding the masculine arm that would have enveloped her shoulders, evidence of Mac's more-than-professional interest in the materials she carried, proof of his growing interest in her. "It looks pretty good, really. The cuts could have been a lot worse." She looked up to let her eyes meet Mac's, comfortable with the platonic pleasure she felt in his presence, if not with the feelings he seemed to be making ever more obvious lately. But she had dealt with men's overtures in the past; Mac's she would cope with later, away from the restrictive confines of their work environment, she promised herself.

While Mac perused her work, Jamey took his place at the window and gazed out over the field, allowing her mind to wander as her eyes traced the Tennessee terrain. She traveled a lot in her work and had always found beauty in every place she had been, but had never felt that any of them could compare with her home state of Oregon for sheer majesty. Tennessee was certainly a beautiful state, though, and Jamey was rapidly coming to love this gently rolling land that bumped into a blue and cloudless sky on the horizon, green meeting blue in startling clarity.

She had been here for nearly three months now, but

there had been little opportunity to see much of the state, just a few weekend trips in the local area. Otherwise, her time had been taken up with the details of getting Tanasie Basin ready to begin its school program in September—and with Steve's music. It was mid-August now, and her work was almost done. Another six weeks and she would be returning home to Oregon. Silently she vowed to make more time for visiting the state's many points of interest.

Mac interrupted her reverie as he completed his review of her work.

"Looks good, Jamey. I've just got a couple of questions on these ongoing expenditure items. You've got things pretty heavily weighted toward classroom materials. Do you think we might run into problems later in the year on contract services?"

Jamey had anticipated that question and was prepared for it. As she responded and moved on to answer further inquiries about her apportionment of the budget, she became aware of the underlying tension in Mac. Certain that his edginess was related to her upcoming trip to Nashville, she focused more firmly on budget matters in an effort to avoid any new discussion of her work with Steve.

As she came to the end of the lengthy document, Jamey reminded Mac that he could request a budget revision if any unforeseen problems arose. "But I feel sure this will work just fine as it is," she concluded as she leaned back against the chair cushion.

"Okay, go ahead and submit it to central office. If they want justification on any part of it, be ready." Mac slid the master across the desk to her and kept the copy for his files. Jamey stood up to leave, relieved that there had been no further argument about Steve and his music.

Her relief was short-lived. As she started toward the door Mac halted her movement. "One more thing,

Jamey. Keep a close watch on young Carlson today. We don't need any bad publicity out of this, and if I didn't trust your judgment, I'd put a stop to it right now . . . before you both leave yourselves open to a lot of trouble.''

Jamey turned, biting back a retort that would have revealed her momentary flash of irritation. What did he think Steve might do? Rip off a gold record from a wall in Rue Garrett's home right under their noses?

As quickly as the thought occurred to her, Jamey quelled it. Mac's caution, though she didn't entirely agree with it, was certainly understandable. Tanasie Basin *didn't* need any adverse publicity so soon after its opening.

She sighed before replying. ''I know, Mac. You trust me; I trust Steve. I've worked with him all summer, and I know he's not going to do anything to jeopardize this project. I also really believe he's got talent that he should be encouraged to develop. Anyway, we'll know a lot more after today. The group he's playing for look like they're headed for the top in country music, so I don't think they'll pull any punches with us. They can't afford to waste their time.''

''Can you afford to waste yours?'' Mac gave a half-smile of apology as he asked the question. He knew Jamey well enough by now to know that when she gave her word on something, she followed through. And she had given her word to young Carlson.

Jamey faced him squarely. ''Mac, you know I'm committed to this. You know the whole history of my getting involved with Steve and his music. If I hadn't, he would have been shunted off into some vocational training program that held little interest for him, and told to forget about his music except as a nice way to spend his leisure time.'' Warming to her subject, she continued. ''This way he'll have both. He recognizes that he needs vocational skills to fall back on while he tries to break into music—and will have to have those skills if he never makes it—but the fact that he can still pursue a career in music is really important to him. And if he doesn't make it, at least he will have had the chance."

"Okay. You don't have to sell me again." Mac picked up a paperweight from his desk and turned it idly in his hands as he continued. "I've agreed to let you try to help him. And the fact that you've landed him an audition with any group, let alone a group as good as Mississippi River, is more than any of us expected."

"That's just it, Mac," Jamey interrupted. "You seem to think this is some sort of game. I didn't get Steve this audition. All I did was send tapes of his music to several of the groups in the area, and this is what happened. You better be prepared for it. Steve is good, and there's a good chance that it's not going to go unnoticed."

"We'll see, Jamey," he responded, the placating words proof of his disbelief. "Anyway, what time are you planning to leave today?"

Jamey ignored Mac's doubts about the possibility of Steve's success. Only that success itself would alter his opinion. "We'll leave right after lunch and probably get back around five thirty or six. If anything happens to change that schedule, I'll call and let you know."

Mac returned the paperweight to his desk and turned back, smiling now, as he said, "Well, good luck to both of you. I'll see you when you get back. And I'll pick you up about seven, if that's okay. You haven't forgotten we're meeting Damon Carter and his sister at Sperry's around eight, have you?" he asked, reminding her of their plans to spend the evening with an old college buddy whom he hadn't seen for several years.

He had originally invited her to a quiet dinner for two at Sperry's, one of his favorite restaurants, and Jamey had been secretly relieved when his friend's surprise visit to Nashville had caused their plans to change. She had begun to question the wisdom of accepting so many of Mac's invitations. And she knew the time was rapidly approaching when she would have to tell him they could be nothing more than friends.

Jamey shook her head, her smile hiding the worrisome thoughts that plagued her. "No. I should be back in plenty of time. See you then."

DECIDING not to take the time to go home and change into a dress before leaving for Nashville, Jamey returned to her office to pick up the tan corduroy blazer she often wore to dress up her jeans and give herself a more professional look. She had quickly discovered that staff at Tanasie Basin dressed in a studiedly casual manner, a fact that rather amused her when she thought of the pains she had taken to organize her wardrobe around the demands of her career. Smiling at the thought, she ran a comb through her long tresses and applied a fresh coat of lip gloss, and was ready to go.

During the forty-five-minute drive to Nashville, her thoughts were divided between the audition Steve would soon have with Mississippi River and her own growing worries about what Mac wanted from their relationship. She had been going out with him casually for the past two months, and she valued his friendship, but lately he seemed to want more from her than she was prepared to give. She liked men, enjoyed going out with them and having them as friends, but preferred to keep them at a distance emotionally. She wasn't interested, at this point, in a deeper relationship. Her career came first, and she knew what could happen to a woman's career when a man entered the picture permanently. Her own mother had given up a promising career in photojournalism for what had turned out to be a not-so-promising marriage, but by the time she realized what she had done, there had been two children to consider. She had chosen to stay with the marriage "for the sake of the kids'' and had never returned to her career—a fact she had never let her daughters forget. And Jamey never intended to be caught in that trap! She hoped she would marry someday, but later, when her career as an educational consultant was well established.

She was trying to think of gentle ways of convincing Mac that she was sincere in her rejection of anything more than pleasant evenings that ended with casual kisses, when Steve broke in on her thoughts. "You're awfully quiet, Jamey. If I didn't know better, I'd think you were more nervous about this audition than I am, and I've been thinking about jumping out of the car for the last ten miles," he quipped.

Jamey turned her head and smiled. She had no intention of telling him what she had been thinking. "No, Steve, I know you'll do fine. I was just thinking about work. School starts in two weeks, and I get the jitters too. I've put a lot into Tanasie Basin, and now we're all about to see how well I've done my job." Quickly glossing over her silence, she led him into a discussion of his own concerns. "What are you going to play first this afternoon?"

"Oh, I thought I'd start off with 'Rolling Water.' It's one of their biggest hits, and I think I do it pretty well. What do you think?" Steve had half turned in his seat and was gazing earnestly into Jamey's face.

She glanced over at him. "I think that's a good choice. It's a beautiful song, and you do a nice job with it. Are you going to play any of your own songs?"

"I don't know. It's so hard to know if they're any good. When I play them for myself, I like them...I think they sound good. And everybody at Tanasie Basin says they sound good. But *these* guys are pros! I'm afraid they'll think my stuff is lousy or, worse yet, laugh at me." Steve looked down at his hands, which were clenched tightly in his lap, then away out the car window. "I don't think I could take it if they laughed at me."

Jamey could understand his insecurity but was appalled by his lack of confidence. "Wait just a minute, Steve," she said heatedly, "you have to remember that these guys have already heard some of your music on the tape I sent them, and they were obviously impressed. Otherwise they wouldn't have asked you to play for them in person, and Rue Garrett certainly wouldn't have arranged to hear you in his own home." Exasperated, she continued. "That he's willing to work with us to get around your security status, and to overlook the fact that you've been convicted of several crimes, should tell you something."

"Yeah, I know you're right," he answered quietly. "I'm sorry, Jamey. It's just that I'm so nervous."

"Oh, Steve. Don't look so hang-dog. And you don't have to tell me you're sorry every time I get a little angry. Anger between friends is normal and healthy." Calmer now, she smiled. "And being nervous is okay—that's normal and healthy too—but falling apart is *not* okay. So get it together! Okay?"

"Okay," he agreed, the beginnings of a smile lightening his features. "How much longer until we get there?"

Jamey burst out laughing and, reaching over, ruffled his sandy-blond hair. "You sound like a little kid. 'Mommy, are we there yet?'" she mimicked. "But to answer your question, about ten minutes," she added as she glanced around at the ever-increasing density of buildings that marked their entry into the outskirts of Nashville.

They were still laughing at their shared anxieties when Jamey turned into the entrance of the underground parking garage at the apartment complex Rue

Garrett had directed her to in his letter. Rolling the car
window down as she flicked off the air conditioner, she
reached out and handed to the garage attendant the
pass Mr. Garrett had sent her. He looked at the pass,
then back at Jamey, and said, "Yes, ma'am, go on
down to the end of this row here and park it in one of
those two places at the end. Then go to that bank of
elevators over there on the left and take the express
elevator to the penthouse. That's Mr. Garrett's."

Jamey thanked the attendant and proceeded down
the row, parking her car in the first of the two spaces he
had indicated, next to a sleek light metallic-blue Mercedes. Her Datsun looked a bit out of place among all
these fancy, expensive cars, she thought. She hoped
she and Steve wouldn't feel out of place with the
people who owned them.

Trying not to show the nervousness that had suddenly hit her, Jamey held her head high and pressed
the button for the express elevator. Waiting for it, she
remembered something her mother had told her once
when she had picked Jamey up at the airport. "I can
spot you from a mile away in an airport, Jamey," her
mother had said. "You're the one who walks as though
you own the whole darn place." Smiling at the memory, Jamey thought that it was her own special trick to
keep the rest of the world unaware of her basic shyness.
If you moved with an air of confidence, she had
learned, it kept most people at bay. They would stand
back almost in awe, afraid to get in the way of such
obvious purpose.

As it turned out, Jamey need not have worried about
feeling nervous or out of place. Embarrassment was a
much better word for what she should have been worried about. The man who greeted them at the door of
the penthouse was nearly naked. He answered the door
wearing only a towel draped around the lower half of

his body and dripping water. It was obvious that he had just stepped out of the shower.

Jamey blushed and stammered, "Oh, I'm s-sorry! I thought this was Mr. Garrett's apartment." Stepping aside and indicating Steve, she rushed on. "We have an appointment with him. Can you tell me where he *does* live?"

Grinning at her discomfort, the man answered, "Yes, ma'am, I'm Rue Garrett, almost literally in the flesh, I'm afraid. And don't back away; you're expected. I'm just running a little late today. We had a long session at the recording studio."

Grasping her arm as Jamey would have backed farther away, Rue pulled her through the door and into the foyer of the apartment. "You too," he said to Steve. "Come on in and close the door. If you'll just go on in the living room and make yourselves at home, I'll get dressed and be with you in a few minutes."

Jamey's focus traveled upward, moving across the expanse of his tanned chest and registering his broad, muscular shoulders and arms. Gray-blue eyes twinkled down at her as Jamey stared angrily into the face of this stranger, her blush becoming deeper by the second. She refused now to let her gaze fall any lower than the tanned column of his throat.

Rue laughed. "Lord, I didn't know there were women around anymore who blushed. Haven't you ever seen a man before?"

Twisting her arm from his grasp, Jamey sputtered, "Of course I've seen men before...and in less than you're wearing now," she tacked on unnecessarily, thinking that she had been around men in swimsuits lots of times, but not about to share that modest thought with him. "But most of those weren't strangers! And they certainly didn't grab me by the arm and start yank-

ing me around the first time they saw me!'' she added
acidly.

Rue was laughing heartily now, his eyes narrowed in
interest, which only fed Jamey's embarrassment and
frustration. ''I could do more than that, if that's what
you want, lady,'' he drawled lazily.

That sent her backing away as fast as she could
move, until she bumped into a solid object behind her.
Steve! What must he think of this? she wondered. She
had forgotten he was even there.

''Please, just go get dressed,'' she begged, trying to
regain her dignified image. ''This is really embarrassing—for you as well as me, I'm sure—and we only
have a limited amount of time this afternoon. I have to
have Steve back at Tanasie Basin by six.''

''Embarrassing?'' he queried, ignoring her comments about time. ''Not for me, honey. I learned a long
time ago that this old shell I live in isn't anything to be
embarrassed about or ashamed of. Looks like you
could use a few lessons on that subject, but I'll let you
off easy this time.''

Looking over her head, he said, ''Steve—that's your
name, right?—why don't you take our blushing friend
on in the living room and help her calm down. I'll be
back with you shortly.''

As he moved down the hallway he called back over
his shoulder, ''And if the doorbell rings, go ahead and
answer it. The rest of the guys stopped off for lunch
and should be getting here any time now.''

Jamey stood, unable to move, watching his retreating form. Her arm still tingled where his hand had held
it, and she rubbed it idly. She wasn't sure whether the
tingling was from the strength of his grip, her embarrassment, or just what the cause might be.

Steve brought her back to awareness of her surroundings as he touched her shoulder from behind.
''Jamey,'' he whispered, ''are you okay? He was a little

rough with you," he added resentfully. Steve had come to feel protective of Jamey as their friendship had deepened over the summer months, and Jamey was well aware that he exerted a lot of control over the other residents at Tanasie Basin when it came to gossip about her. She also knew that most of the residents were curious about her life away from Tanasie Basin. That was normal. A young and attractive single woman working in an institution was always a source of speculation, no matter how circumspect her behavior, and more often than not any resident who felt he had a special relationship with a woman staff member behaved protectively toward her.

"I'm fine, but I think we better find the living room," she answered, hoping to divert his attention from Rue Garrett's behavior. She didn't understand it herself, and didn't want to analyze it. "I suppose it's through here, since he went that way." She indicated an archway to their left.

As they entered what was obviously the living room, a room done in earth tones complemented by the addition of leather and wood furnishings, Steve continued in the same vein. "I still don't like the way he treated you, and I don't think Mr. McCormack would either."

"What does Mr. McCormack have to do with this, Steve?" Jamey asked, stunned. She hadn't realized any of the residents were aware that she had been going out with Mac. She had been so careful to keep their outings quiet.

"Oh, come on, Jamey! Everybody at Tanasie Basin knows he's nuts about you. All you have to do is have your eyes open. You should see the way he looks at you when he knows you aren't watching!"

Jamey stared at him, openmouthed. "Steve, Mr. McCormack is not 'nuts' about me, as you so inelegantly and inappropriately put it," she denied. "It's true that we've gone out a few times, but we're just friends, and I'd appreciate it if you would make that clear to the rumor mill. Normally, I wouldn't even dignify such a statement with an answer, but I can't have that kind of talk going on at work. I hope you can understand that.''

"Sure, Jamey, I understand it. But I know what I see too. Still, I'll tell the guys they're wrong, and maybe it'll shut them up,'' he finished.

"Tell the guys they're wrong about what?'' asked a deep, masculine voice from behind them.

They spun around simultaneously, surprised to see Rue Garrett standing in the doorway. Neither of them had heard him enter the room.

Jamey felt the shiver ripple down her spine as she saw him for the first time in clothes, and wondered why he should have this effect on her. His jeans and blue-and-brown striped shirt, which was open to three buttons down, did nothing to hide his aura of male sexuality. He was tall, she thought, well over six feet, as she raised her brown eyes to meet the steady gaze of his gray-blue ones. Her eyes played over his face, taking in the strong, straight lines of his jaw and nose, and the wide, sensual mouth. His brown hair, glinting with auburn in the sunlight streaming through the huge windows that comprised one wall of the room, was styled to medium length and slightly curly. It came down just over his collar and framed the ruggedly masculine contours of his face. As she studied those masculine features, he returned her scrutiny boldly.

Steve recovered first from Rue's intrusion on their conversation. "Just that Jamey and our superintendent have a thing going,'' he stated triumphantly, as though it gave him some sort of victory over the older man. "They're dating, and all the guys know Mr. McCormack is crazy about her, but she wants me to tell them they're wrong,'' he supplied.

"Steve,'' she hissed. "Will you be quiet? Mr. Garrett is *not* interested in the rumor mill at Tanasie Basin, and it's not true, anyway," she affirmed, her eyes moving from Steve to Rue and back again.

"On the contrary, I find it very interesting. And call me Rue, would you? I'm not a very formal person." Something she couldn't recognize flared in his eyes as he continued in a low voice. "I've never been in an institution before, but I bet there's some real interesting talk that goes on about a pretty lady like you. As prudish as you seem to be, though, I'm amazed you do the kind of work you do. I'd have thought it would be much too real for you."

Insulted, Jamey retorted, "Look, both of you, I'd really like to change the subject. For starters, my personal life is none of your business; secondly, I love my work; and, to end this discussion, I am *certainly* not a prude," she stated angrily, focusing on Rue as she finished.

"You could've fooled me," he laughed, "with that blush you gave when I answered the door. Or was that just an act?"

As Jamey started to reply, the doorbell rang. "Saved by the bell," Rue growled, "and just when this conversation was starting to get interesting."

She was still seething with temper when he returned with five other men, presumably the members of his band, Mississippi River. Rue confirmed her thought as he made the introductions, all business now. "Boys, this is Miss Jamey Marsh, and this is the young man we're all here to listen to, Steve Carlson. Jamey, Steve, this is Mississippi River—Bob, Tom, Randy, Jim, and Hank." He indicated each man in turn. "Let's get to work."

"Hang on, Rue!" The man he had called Hank was speaking. "Wowee! No wonder we're all gathered here today. If I'd known Miss Jamey Marsh was going to be such a pretty little thing, I'd have skipped my lunch so I could get to know her without all the rest of you yahoos around." He grinned. "I'm going to write you a song, ma'am," he quipped, moving toward her, "sort of a takeoff on an old but much-loved number, and I'm going to call it 'Shall We Gather at the Marsh.'" He winked at her, and Jamey felt her face go red all the way to the roots of her hair.

The room was a sea of laughter as Rue interrupted. "Okay, that's enough, Hank. Down, boy! Can't you see you're embarrassing the little lady?"

Jamey was surprised by his protective attitude. He had been attacking her ever since she walked through — or was yanked through! — his door, she thought.

He turned to her and continued, "Pardon his exuberance, Jamey, but he's the clown of the group. Never lets a chance slip by."

"Clown? You crush me, Rue," Hank wailed. "I'm dead serious," he intoned, making it perfectly obvious that he wasn't. "Don't you believe a word he says, Miss Jamey. I think I'm falling in love," he added as he went down on one knee before her.

"Okay, let's get down to business." Rue pulled Hank back, giving him a look that said play time was over, then sat down on the couch close to Jamey. Indicating a stool in one corner of the room, he ordered, "Go on over there and set up, Steve, and let's hear you play. Just take your time setting up. Nobody's in a hurry."

Tension charged the atmosphere in the room. Jamey wasn't sure if the taut feeling was hers alone, or if they all felt it as they waited for Steve to play. Perhaps, she thought, it was merely her own nervous response to the fact that Rue Garrett was sitting so close to her, proprietorially close.

She tried to edge away from him, but was too near the end of the couch to get very far. He noticed. She could tell that by his amused expression as he turned and raised his eyebrows mockingly. She almost stuck her tongue out at him, but stopped herself just in time, unaware of the seductive picture she made as she ran her tongue over lips that seemed suddenly dry. She swallowed, unable to look away and break the locked gaze of their eyes.

Steve unwittingly broke the tension between them by announcing that he was ready to begin. Turning to look at him, Jamey gave him a tremulous smile of encouragement and nodded slightly. He didn't seem nearly as nervous now as he had in the car, thank goodness. She was sure he would play well.

As Steve started to play, the sound of the music carried her away, as it always did. "Rolling Water" was one of her favorite songs, with its gentle melody and steady, rhythmic beat. It touched a responsive chord in her subconscious. Closing her eyes, she sank back into the cushions and let the music have its way with her. She could feel it moving over and around her, the way water did when you floated on your back, eyes closed, on a hot and sunny day.

When the last strains of music died away, she opened her eyes, only to find Rue staring at her. She smiled, still affected by the music, but a little embarrassed that she had let it carry her away to her own private world. He returned the smile, and it was as though he had been there with her, floating in the rolling waters of her mind. His eyes sparkled with the same indefinable emotion she had noticed before, and she wanted only to escape. She didn't want to define the emotion. Something deep inside her sensed the danger of definition, and she shuddered.

Rue turned slowly away and said softly, "That was nice, Steve. Keep going."

Steve swung into another of the tunes that Mississippi River had made popular, and Jamey was careful this time to keep her eyes open and stay in the room.

She didn't like it that Rue seemed to have been able to follow her mind to its private places, even if he was only able to go because he had written the haunting melody that took her there.

Steve played several more songs that were on the group's latest album before Rue requested that he play some of the other music that had been on the tape Jamey had mailed to the group's office in Nashville. Grinning, Steve agreed. He was all confidence now. He looked at Jamey as he told the group he was going to play "Sweet Freedom," her favorite of the four songs he had written so far.

As the melody filled the room Jamey sensed that these professionals were impressed that a seventeen-year-old could offer such beautiful musical expression. What they couldn't know was that Steve was wise beyond his years about such things as freedom—wise because of years of abuse and neglect that had ended in his being locked up for burglaries that she sometimes thought he had committed for the sole purpose of escaping his father. Being locked up was the first freedom he had ever known from a man so vile that his acts almost defied description. It hurt to think of the words in Steve's legal file telling of all he had endured. And knowing where his words and music came from made them hurt too. But in a sweet way, for they were the proof that Steve's psyche had survived. Just one Steve, she thought, one gentle soul who overcame the worst life has to offer, made all the hard work and heartache worth the effort. That was why she loved her work, because it *was* real, the very reason Rue had given for being surprised by her choice of career.

There was silence in the room as Steve came to the end of "Sweet Freedom." Reluctantly, it seemed to Jamey, Rue broke the silence. "Where did you hear that song, Steve?"

Jamey was surprised by the question. She was sure

she had written in the letter she had sent with the tape that all the songs other than those done first by Mississippi River were Steve's original work. Leaning forward, she answered for him. "He wrote it—words an' music."

Rue silenced her quickly. "Let him talk for himself, Jamey." Turning back to Steve, he explained. "It's a little hard to believe that a seventeen-year-old could write with such feeling, Steve. Are you sure you never heard that song anywhere else?"

"No, sir. The only place I ever heard it before I wrote it was in my head. The words just seemed to be there, to need saying, and then the music just added itself. They were the only notes that fit the words," he explained. "Why?"

"Because if that song is original, I want to buy it from you so we can record it. It's very rare, Steve, for a kid to write a song that's worth listening to, and that song should only have been able to come from a man who had known total hell for a lot of years. For that reason, I have to question its source. If you agree to let me record it, I have to know that it's original. Otherwise, we could both end up in a heap of trouble. You're in enough trouble as it is, and I sure don't need any."

Jamey could read the indecision on Steve's face as he answered. "It's original, Mr. Garrett, but I'm not sure I want to sell it. 'Sweet Freedom' tells what's in my soul, not yours, and I'd like to be able to record it myself someday. I hope you can understand that I'll have to think about your offer, sir. I appreciate it, but even if I didn't care what happened to my song, I would still need to learn more about how the music business works before deciding."

Watching the frank exchange between these two men—one still young, probably in his early thirties; the other a young-old man of seventeen—Jamey silently cheered. Steve was doing just fine for himself, holding his own in a world he desperately wanted to enter. And Rue Garrett's candid approach, his straightforward honesty, evoked a feeling of admiration in her.

"I'm afraid he's right, Mr. Gar—Rue," she corrected. "Neither of us knows much about marketing his work, and I think we might want to talk with an attorney before we agree to anything."

Rue turned, a look of surprise on his face. "You two really *are* naive about this business, aren't you? Just babes in the woods." His steady gaze encompassed them both as he went on. "If Steve can continue to write songs as good as this one, he'll need both an attorney and an agent. If you trust me, I can recommend some good people, but I think the first order of business is to get his current work copyrighted. You haven't even done that yet, have you?"

Acknowledging Jamey's negative indication, Rue turned back to Steve. "I'll help you with that, son, then why don't you think about my offer for a while? Meantime, I'd like to hear some more of your music. Okay?"

"You got it," Steve replied, grinning broadly.

As Steve returned his attention to the music he loved so much, Rue's eyes returned to Jamey's face. She had been about to thank him for his offer of help, but the look he gave her—was it a hunger of some kind?—stilled her words, and she turned quickly back to stare blindly at Steve, her thoughts a denial of the almost overwhelming urge she felt to turn again toward Rue Garrett.

Chapter Two

"You should have heard him, Mac," Jamey enthused as they drove north toward Sperry's that evening. "He was wonderful! He played beautifully, and he handled himself so well when Rue Garrett offered to buy 'Sweet Freedom.'"

She still had to tack on Rue's surname, couldn't allow herself the familiarity of thinking of him by only his first name. But just speaking his name brought Rue's face clearly into focus and set her pulse racing, and she struggled to dispel his image as Mac turned toward her. Involuntarily she compared the two men. Mac was nearly as tall as Rue, but his added girth made him seem shorter now, as she remembered Rue's lean muscularity. Mac's features seemed almost boyish compared to the rugged handsomeness of Rue's face, though Mac must be at least five years older, she thought.

If her smile was a bit forced and overbright, Mac didn't seem to notice. Smiling, he halted her mental comparison. "What's the next step?"

Carefully avoiding any words that might hint at Rue's persuasive efforts to get them to stay in town for dinner with him that evening, Jamey explained, "I told him I thought we should talk with an attorney before we agreed to anything, and he said I was right. But he's eager to get the rights to 'Sweet Freedom' as soon as possible, so he can include it in an album they plan to cut soon." Pausing—wishing she could avoid telling him, but not understanding why she should wish it— Jamey sighed and went on. "He's coming out tomorrow to go over all Steve's options with us."

"Tomorrow?" Mac asked, obviously stunned. "That is fast! It seems you were right, Jamey. Young Carlson just may have a future for himself in country music," he added musingly. "But we'll have to be careful about the effect this has around Tanasie Basin. It's sure to arouse some envy among the other residents, and I don't want any trouble—for us or the boy."

"Oh, I don't think this will cause any trouble, Mac. Most of the guys are aware of Steve's music, and they knew about today's audition. They're really proud of him, and I think they'll stand behind him all the way."

"Well, perhaps you're right. You've been right about everything else so far," he smiled. "What time is this Garrett fellow coming out, and where are you meeting him?"

Jamey had hoped to avoid that question. She knew Mac wouldn't like her answer. But now that he had asked it, she was forced to respond. "He's coming out about two, and we're meeting at my place." She went on quickly, before Mac could protest. "I told Steve I would pick him up at one thirty and take him to the cabin. They'll have more privacy there. If we met at Tanasie Basin, the other guys would all be trying to meet Mr. Garrett and get his autograph, and it just wouldn't work," she justified. What she didn't tell him—couldn't tell him, she thought—was that Rue had refused to meet with them at Tanasie Basin, making it patently obvious that Steve was a secondary consideration in tomorrow's meeting.

Mac didn't like it, and he wasn't mollified by her explanation. Turning to look at her with narrowed eyes, he asked, "Do you think that's a good idea, Jamey? You're a single woman, living alone in a secluded spot. You don't really know this Garrett fellow, but surely you do know that most show business people have quite a reputation for their *mis*behavior toward the opposite sex. I don't think it's wise for you to let him know where you live, and especially that you live there alone.'' The beginnings of suspicion deepened his voice as he ended a brief silence. "How about if I come over and meet him with you?''

Too quickly, Jamey responded. "No, Mac! I don't think that's necessary.'' The atmosphere in the car was thick with tension as his suspicion found roots, and Jamey groped for the words that would convince him. "Rue Garrett is a professional musician, and all he's interested in is a song that he believes will be another hit for him,'' she lied. If the message in Rue's eyes hadn't been obvious enough, he had made his position clear when she had refused his invitation that they stay for dinner. But for Mac to know that, or to guess at her own body's rebellion against her mental commands as it had responded to the message in Rue's eyes, would be overwhelming. She didn't want to think about it, had been struggling against the unwelcome memory since leaving Nashville this afternoon.

Unwillingly she conceded to herself that she had never felt so alive in a man's presence before. It had felt as though a constant current of electricity had been pulsing through her body. She tried, ineffectively, to convince herself that she was only impressed by his popularity in the music world, as he had claimed other women were. But her heart recognized the lie, even as her mind sought to believe it.

Their arrival at the restaurant interrupted her thoughts, much to Jamey's relief, and precluded any further argument on the subject as Mac was forced to focus on negotiating the cramped spaces of the crowded parking lot. But it was difficult to ignore her escort's tight-lipped stoicism as he offered his hand to help her from the car, then walked in silence at her side toward the building. She could only hope that Mac wouldn't allow his displeasure to spoil this reunion with his friend and that seeing his friend again would take his mind off of her meeting with Rue Garrett.

Mac avoided Jamey's eyes as they stepped into the dimly lit English Tudor elegance that characterized Sperry's, then moved away from her to claim their reservations. The information that the other members of their party had already arrived and been seated seemed to ease Mac's irritation, and Jamey felt suddenly more confident that only she would be aware of the tension that underscored his now smiling facade.

As they were led to the table where Damon Carter and his sister waited, Mac caught sight of the other man. He extended his hand in greeting, his smile becoming steadily more real as his friend rose and met Mac's hand with his own. The waiter moved discreetly away, and Jamey nearly sighed aloud with relief as she realized that Mac truly had forgotten about Rue Garrett, at least for the moment. She wished she could forget him too.

Jamey deliberately pushed the thought away as she turned to assess Damon Carter. She was surprised by his appearance. He was as short and stocky as Mac was tall and solid. The two resembled a sturdier version of Mutt and Jeff, she thought, smiling at the simile. And Damon definitely didn't fit the mental picture she had formed. She had expected a much more athletic-looking man, one whose body was tanned and firm from working on-site in his job as an architectural engineer who traveled the globe, one whose physique was more like Rue Garrett's.

Damn the man! He kept creeping into her thoughts and coming out ahead in her involuntary comparisons. Determinedly Jamey turned back to her survey of

Mac's friend. She had also somehow given the man dark hair in her imaginings, instead of the rather unruly thatch of red hair that topped his ruddy face. Studying Damon Carter's features, Jamey became so absorbed in her self-enforced assessment that it took her a moment to realize that he had been introduced to her and had offered her his hand. She offered her own quickly, embarrassed by her absent behavior.

"And this," Damon said with a grin, releasing Jamey's hand as he turned toward the woman who had remained seated throughout the exchange, "is my sister, Margaret."

Jamey and Mac turned simultaneously to focus their attention on Damon's sister, each prepared to offer a polite acknowledgment. The familiar face that smiled up at them stopped them cold, and they stood frozen for a moment in astonishment. Their mutual interest in her brother and the candlelit environment had diverted them, keeping the woman's identity a temporary secret.

"Meg!" Jamey exclaimed as she recovered her poise, recognition and pleasure blending in the single word. She would never have linked the lovely woman before her to Damon Carter, she thought. Meg was easily as tall as her brother, at least five-seven, but slender. Only her shoulder-length red hair gave away any family tie between the two.

"Well, I'll be darned!" Mac expostulated. "Why didn't one of you tell me?" he asked accusingly, glancing from sister to brother and back again. His amazement answered Jamey's unspoken question of whether or not he had ever met his friend's sister before the day of her interview for a position at Tanasie Basin.

"And miss this reaction?" Meg teased, an impish grin lighting her attractive features. "Not on your life!"

"And also because she refused to allow our friendship," Damon assured Mac with a hint of pride, "to have any effect on her chances of getting a job at Tanasie Basin.''

Meg Carter flushed at her brother's implied praise, the added color lending her face a lovely glow. She laughed to cover her momentary discomfort. "You three had better sit down before the management accuses you of creating a public nuisance," she taunted lightly, neatly changing the subject.

As Damon moved to take the seat beside Meg, Mac held Jamey's chair, then seated himself next to her, leaving his arm casually draped across her shoulders. The action was possessive, triggering Jamey's memory of Rue Garrett's unexpected behavior, and she didn't like it. Didn't like either Mac's action or her thoughts.

Unaware of Jamey's reaction, Meg resumed the conversation. "Speaking of Tanasie Basin, what ever became of the young man you were helping with his music, Jamey?''

Mac's reaction to the innocent question was instant. He tensed, then withdrew his arm quickly, as though remembering his anger of only a few moments earlier.

Jamey's reaction had been immediate too, but she paused and took a steadying breath as she searched for words. It had been inevitable that the subject would come up during the course of the evening, she supposed, though it wouldn't have happened so quickly had fate not made Meg a sister to Mac's friend, as well as one of the group of teachers Jamey had so recently hired. At that moment she regretted more than was imaginable that she had told the other woman of her musical project with Steve, but Meg's eager interest in everything about Tanasie Basin had been so inviting.

She avoided looking at Mac as she haltingly brought Meg up-to-date on the youth's progress. But he made his presence felt, if only by his physical withdrawal.

"And all Steve's hard work was rewarded today by his first audition with a working group," Jamey finished lightly. Her omission of the band's name had been intentional. She didn't even want to say the words Rue Garrett or Mississippi River, let alone be forced to describe again the events of her afternoon. Not only was it tantamount to waving a red flag in a bull's face as far as Mac was concerned, it was also a subject she dearly wanted to avoid. She was trying so hard to forget her own unexplainable reaction to Rue Garrett.

"What group?" Damon Carter's query killed Jamey's hope that the topic could now die before she had even finished thinking it, but she was granted a reprieve as the waiter arrived to take their orders.

Moments later, as the waiter moved away from their table, Damon leaned forward in his chair. A wayward lock of red hair fell across his forehead as he repeated his earlier question.

Mac turned in his chair, his eyes almost cold as he watched Jamey's face, waiting for her response to a question she apparently didn't want to answer. She felt as though she had just been pushed into the center ring at the circus and told to perform as she plunged into a discussion she wanted no part of, her only conscious intent to use it as an opportunity to kill Mac's suspicions...and to end the show as quickly as possible.

"Mississippi River," Jamey said a little too rapidly. With any luck, she told herself, they had never heard of the group. Not everyone was a country music fan.

"You're kidding," Damon said incredulously. "I've heard them in concert, and they're extremely good. Rue Garrett has as smooth a tenor as I've heard in years," he vowed, "and tremendous range and power. You and your young friend are moving in an exalted musical circle if you're in with Mississippi River," he stated.

"Damon's right, Jamey," Meg agreed enthusiastically. "I believed you when you told me Steve was talented, but this is something else. If he's attracted Rue Garrett's interest, he must be *very* good!''

"He is," Jamey responded shortly, irrationally angered by what she had decided was the typical gushing response to the news that Rue Garrett was interested in Steve's music. The staff at Tanasie Basin had reacted in much the same way.

Jamey didn't bother to remind herself that she had been almost pleased by other people's reaction before she had actually met the man. But she did make a mental note of the fact that she wasn't the only one who felt irritation at their response. Mac's tight-lipped visage promised further inquisition later, when they were alone, unless she could somehow convey an attitude of being unconcerned about Rue Garrett's attention toward herself...and Steve, she tacked on as an afterthought.

Somehow she managed to get through the conversation—and half of what should have been a delectable salad, but wasn't because of her agitation—without revealing her own attraction to the popular singer. At least she did until Meg inadvertently changed the tenor of their discussion. "When will you know more about Steve selling his song?" she asked, her green eyes sparkling with interest in the soft candlelight.

Mac leaned forward, breaking the strained silence he had maintained throughout Jamey's description of Steve's audition. He answered for her, and she felt the sting of irritation. "Tomorrow. This Garrett fellow is coming out to talk about options with Jamey and Steve. Maybe you two can help me convince her that it's not a good idea for them to have this meeting at her place," he appealed, his suspicions apparent to all of them.

In a flash of insight Meg responded indignantly, "For heaven's sake, Mac! Either you've been paying too much attention to the gossip columns or you've worked in corrections so long that you just don't trust anybody anymore." she said tartly. "If Rue Garrett ever wanted to schedule a meeting at my house, you better believe I'd let him," she continued, purposely digging at him, "but I suppose you think they should meet at Tanasie Basin where all the boys would be flocking around the man, making it impossible for them to accomplish anything."

Mac fairly bristled at Meg's caustic, but accurate comments. "That's exactly what I think," he snapped. "Jamey doesn't need some two-bit singer with an inflated ego hanging around her home."

His response angered Meg, *really* angered her, and she attacked in an amazingly calm manner that all but excluded Jamey and her brother. "I hardly think," she said haughtily, "that you can classify Rue Garrett as 'two-bit' or his intention to go over options with Jamey and Steve as 'hanging around.' For your information," she added, her eyes flashing fire, "Rue Garrett is an extremely handsome and talented man who could more than likely have most any woman he wanted, but is probably too busy to even think about such things at this stage in his career."

Jamey didn't know whether to laugh or cry. Like Meg, she had felt a rush of fury at Mac's uncharacteristically insulting comments, and she silently applauded the other woman's impulsive defense of Rue Garrett. Though she might have gone a bit too far, Jamey thought, deliberately baiting Mac as she had. And anyway, unlike the red-haired woman, she had to ride home with Mac, alone, and suffer the consequences of this unfortunate mess. She reminded herself that she had no reason to defend Rue Garrett, that, in fact, the opposite was true. Her soft laugh came out sounding more nervous than she realized as she tried to retrieve the situation.

"That's something like what I tried to tell him, Meg, but he seems to have this idea that I'm some sort of

femme fatale that Rue Garrett won't be able to keep
his hands off of.'' She felt a twinge of regret for her
deliberate deception, but decided that it was too minor
to worry over. Why then did she feel this nudge of guilt
as some internal demon drove her to carry the little
white lie a step further? ''Can you imagine anyone as
famous as Rue being interested in someone like me?''

Her question, lightly intended, had been a mistake.
It made the discussion too personal. She recognized
that immediately. Mac's eyes were bright with renewed
suspicion, almost accusing her of the attraction she denied so blithely.

Mac opened his mouth to speak, whether to defend
his feelings, to tax her for hers, or to apologize for his
uncustomarily spiteful outburst Jamey couldn't say, as
Damon responded first.

''Whoa...wait a minute. I forgot to warn you that,
unlike her delightfully even-tempered brother, Meg
has a disposition that can be a true reflection of her
flaming locks,'' he said teasingly, ''but now that you've
found out the hard way, I think it's time we straightened this conversation out. I'm not sure fame or talent
or the man's apparent attractiveness to the fairer sex,''
he continued, a twinkle in his eyes as he glanced at his
sister, ''has much to do with any of this. What I imagine is that Rue Garrett is a normal red-blooded American male, in spite of his success. And that like the rest
of us, his head doesn't always dictate his heart or
body's responses.''

Damon's tones became more serious as he continued. ''You, Jamey, in case you hadn't noticed, are a
very pretty woman, and intelligent to go with it. That
can be a rather lethal combination when it's leveled at
some mere man,'' he added, the teasing note creeping
back into his voice. ''But if I'm reading you right,
you're one of those independent Yankee ladies who
has a real thing about making her own way in life.'' The

last was spoken with a meaningful glance in Mac's direction, despite the light way the remark had been delivered. Mac had once again retreated into uncharacteristic reticence, and Damon hadn't missed his friend's reaction. This time, however, Mac seemed to be quietly absorbing the flow of language around him, rather than stewing in anger.

"Perhaps you're right, Damon," Jamey responded, choosing to focus on his final statement as a means of changing the subject entirely, of getting Rue Garrett out of the conversation once and for all. "I don't think independence is limited to Yankee ladies, but it is important to me to stand on my own two feet before I start walking all over some man's feet."

For a moment Jamey felt dismay. What she was saying could only be making Mac feel worse, if his expression was an accurate mirror of his emotions. But he had to learn sometime just how strong her commitment to her career actually was. And now seemed as good a time as any to start, she thought as she finished what she had been thinking. "And I love my work. It would be awfully hard for me to give up the freedom to travel and take on whatever consulting assignments come my way in order to stay home and cook and keep house. I may want those things someday, and I *know* I want children, but I'm just not ready for it yet." The remembered planes and angles of Rue's face clouded her determination for an instant, and Jamey wondered just who she was working hardest to convince—Mac...or herself.

Mac looked pained as she said the words that confirmed what he had already suspected. Perceptively Meg intervened. "I think we're all overreacting to an event that should be cause for celebration, not argument, so why don't we simply change the subject?" It seemed as though she was beginning to feel she'd overstepped her bounds with her earlier furious response.

Her suggestion was greeted with agreement by all three of her companions, each relieved to drop the heat of the topic for their own private reasons. The arrival of the waiter with their dinners seemed to punctuate the decision.

The tantalizing aromas of perfectly prepared beef and seafood teased and tempted as Mac and Damon sliced into the juicy steaks they had ordered, and Jamey and Meg turned to the enticement of their own meals of Alaskan king crab. Succulent stuffed mushrooms complemented their dinners, as did the full-bodied spiciness of the Gewürztraminer Mac had chosen.

As they dined, conversation naturally turned to more comfortable topics. Mac and Damon reminisced about their college days and talked of the changes the intervening years had wrought in one another; Jamey and Meg were quiet through most of the meal, listening with indulgent affection to the two men. Jamey wanted to believe her own silence was the result of her tiring day, definitely not that it was contributed to in any way by her internal struggle to hold memories of that day at bay. Memories of the one aspect of her visit to Nashville that she'd mentioned to no one because it turned all her protestations to lies, lies she wanted to believe. But as she neared the end of her crab, her replete state only added to the feeling of weariness that allowed those very memories to gain the mental control they had been vying for all evening.

All she had to do to see Rue's face was to let her attention wander. But the image was wrong, showing her a smiling Rue instead of the angry one she had left at the door of his penthouse apartment.

Letting her mind drift into recollection of that final scene, she sighed. Rue was obviously unaccustomed to being turned down by any woman. He had tried at first to hide his displeasure when she had told him that she was committed to returning Steve to Tanasie Basin by six, and had offered to call and get clearance for them to stay. He had liked it even less when she had told him that it would be easier for her to obtain clearance than for him, but that she still couldn't stay, and had persisted in his efforts to persuade her. Finally she had felt forced to tell him that she was sorry, but she had already made plans for the evening. That was when he had sent Steve to put his guitar in the car, making it obvious that he was equally eager for the men in his band to leave too.

"With the superintendent?" he had asked snidely after they had gone, leaving him alone in the apartment with Jamey.

Surprised by the change in his attitude, she had answered simply, "Yes, with Mac," and had backed away in confusion as he advanced toward her with an angry glint in his gray-blue eyes.

"What's more important to you—a date or helping Steve?" he had asked insultingly.

"My commitments are important to me," she responded. "I've agreed to have dinner with friends, and I'm going to do just that. But even if it weren't for having made a promise, I couldn't stay," she continued, "and I *wouldn't* stay, not after a remark like your last one."

He had moved forward like some jungle cat stalking his prey until she was backed against the wall. Leaning forward, he placed one hand on either side of her, effectively trapping her.

"Hell, Jamey, I'm sorry. I didn't mean anything by that," he had growled as he gazed directly down into her frightened eyes. "In this business, a man spends a lot of time on the road. That means one night to a city and a lonely hotel room, and not meeting a lot of women who spark your interest. Most of the women we meet are hanging around because we've made a few hits, and they like to rub elbows—or whatever—with somebody they think is famous. If it weren't for the success of our music, they wouldn't be there. They'd be off chasing after some other group who had made a few hits. Can you understand what I'm saying?''

Looking down at her hands as she twisted them together, her blood racing at his nearness, she had merely shaken her head. Words had been impossible to come by. It had felt as though her heart had lodged in her throat and was choking off her air supply.

Pulling one hand away from the wall, he had lifted her chin until their eyes met again. "How can you say you don't understand? I know you felt the same thing this afternoon that I did. It was in your eyes every time I looked at you. God, Jamey, it was like being plugged into a socket, with little frissons of electricity constantly shooting through me." His expressive eyes had held hers captive, and she trembled now at the memory of what had followed.

"Jamey, what I'm saying is simply this—I'm intrigued by you, by whatever mixture of sugar and spice you're made of, and I want to spend some time getting to know you. Can you understand that?''

She had understood. Though she hated the admission, she had felt the same. And she had known that he was going to kiss her then, had even wanted him to. But knowledge and desire hadn't prepared her for the explosion of feeling she experienced.

As their lips met he had pulled her away from the wall and into his arms, gently teasing the corners of her mouth with his tongue until she had responded and let him deepen the kiss. And his kiss had lasted for what seemed minutes, leaving her weak, her legs unable to support her. She had never been so deeply affected by a kiss before, never before responded so totally, and it had frightened her.

As the kiss ended, leaving her clinging weakly to his strength, she had looked quickly down. With her forehead resting against his chest, she had felt the pounding of his heart as it matched the racing beat of her own, and listened quietly as he spoke in a soft voice. "Now do you understand? No, Miss Jamey Marsh, I won't let you off that easily. You may not stay here and have dinner with me tonight, but you'll see me tomorrow and the day after, and all the days I can manage until we go on the road again...for as long as being together pleases us both." Shifting his hands to her arms, he had pushed her slightly away from him. "Look at me Jamey."

Slowly lifting her head until she met his eyes with her own, she had struggled with her inner torment. No man had ever had this effect on her, and she didn't want this man getting through. It was too dangerous. Over and over she repeated to herself as she stared at him, *Remember Mother...remember Mother....* With a little negative shake of her head, she had looked quickly down again, unable to sustain her resolve while her gaze was locked with his.

"Damn it, Jamey!" He spat the words at her. "What's the matter with you?" Receiving no response, he pushed on angrily. "I won't take no for an answer. I'll be at your place at two tomorrow—and if you won't tell me where it is, I'll ask Steve. Do you think he's going to refuse an opportunity to learn more about music? Uh-uh, I've got you," he gloated. "You have Steve there and we'll discuss his options, but after that, it's going to be just you and me. Understand?"

His threat hit her with jackhammer force. Angry now, she pushed ineffectively at his chest and arms. "Do you think you can force your way into my life and just start telling me what to do? Who do you think you are?" The words came out in a furious torrent, her anger abetted by her inability to break free of his hold. "*I* run my life, and I decide *who* I'll see and *when* I'll see them. And I don't want to see *you*!" She gave up her struggle to evade his hold and stood glaring at him, breathing hard.

He answered quietly, the calm in his voice belied by the storm of emotion evident in his eyes. "That's too bad, Jamey. I just don't believe you, so you are going to see me—a lot."

He released his hold on her as Steve came through the door, and Jamey moved to safer ground. Her temper flared anew as she realized he was right about Steve, but there was nothing she could say that wouldn't alert the youth to the undercurrent of emotion that filled the room. She listened as Steve agreed to the meeting and supplied directions to her cabin. Traitorously her heart clamored that it was glad of Steve's unknowing defection, even as her mind warred indignantly with her jangled senses.

"Jamey?" Mac was looking at her with a puzzled frown on his face. "Where in the world have you been? This is the third time I've spoken to you, and you didn't even notice."

She returned to her luxurious surroundings, to her companions, with a bump. "Oh, I'm sorry, Mac. I'm just tired, I guess. It's been a long day, what with the budget and Steve's audition," she excused her absence with an apologetic smile. "I'm really sorry to be such a wet blanket," she offered, including them all in her effort to make amends. Jamey was surprised by how calmly she was able to respond, was grateful for the candlelight that masked the rush of color that stole over her cheeks. She was barely aware of her tightly clenched fists as she waited for someone, *anyone,* to say something in response to her inadequate apology.

"No, don't apologize," Damon intervened. "I'm really quite tired too, and I was just saying that Meg and I should be going. I have an early flight to Phoenix tomorrow," he explained.

"You mean you're only here for one night?" Jamey asked, his words adding guilt to her already confused state—guilt that she might truly be putting a damper on the only visit Mac would have with his friend for some time.

Damon smiled tolerantly at this evidence of just how far away her preoccupation had carried her. If she had been listening to their conversation at all, she would have known the answer. "Only one this trip," he confirmed, "but now that my baby sister is going to be living in the area, I'll be back." His explanation did a lot to relieve Jamey's contrition, but a glance at her escort revealed that he was still displeased, or uneasy, about something.

She found it impossible to shake the feeling that Mac was merely biding his time until they were alone. But biding his time for what? Surely he couldn't have guessed where her absent thoughts had taken her that evening. Surely by now he, at least, had forgotten Rue Garrett's existence.

Mac and Damon settled the bill while Jamey and Meg waited, then the foursome strolled idly out into the late-night air and toward their cars. As they walked, the men exchanged the sort of temporary farewell that only close friends can make, the kind that says without words that each carries with him the knowledge that the other will always be there when needed.

"And I want you to feel free to come on out to Tanasie Basin and start settling in," Mac said, slipping his arm casually about Meg's shoulders in a gesture almost like brotherly affection.

Meg smiled up at him. "Thanks. I expect I'll take you up on that. I'm eager to learn more about Tanasie Basin," she said, "and to swap tales with you about this brother of mine." Her earlier animosity had clearly died, Jamey thought, watching the twinkle that lit the other woman's eyes. She wondered fleetingly just what she had missed during the time when her thoughts had carried her back to Nashville.

Jamey and Mac stood in silence, waving when brother and sister drove away. Then they too entered their car and made their way out of the now sparsely populated parking lot.

Mac's silence as they drove toward Jamey's cabin was a continuing reminder of her feeling that he was biding his time. He hardly uttered a word on the long drive back, and Jamey could think of nothing to say to break the silence. Her thoughts were a confusion of what to do about Mac McCormack's increasingly possessive behavior, what to do about Jamey Marsh's unwanted interest in Rue Garrett.

At last, Mac pulled into her driveway and shut the engine off. Turning to her then, he asked, "What's the matter, Jamey?"

"Nothing. Really, Mac, I'm just tired," she evaded.

"I don't buy that, Jamey," he said softly, gently, more like the easygoing Mac she was accustomed to than he had seemed all evening. "You have more energy than most people I know, and you're not acting as though you're just tired. You seem distracted." He appeared reluctant to continue, and Jamey wished he wouldn't. She didn't want any more confrontations today. Her nerves had taken nearly all they could stand. But he did continue. "Did something happen today that I should know about?"

Yes! her heart screamed, but her mind took precedence. "No, Mac, nothing happened that you should know about," she said wearily. "Steve's audition went just as I told you it did. He was good, they liked his music, and they offered to buy his song."

Pangs of guilt hit her hard as Jamey realized that she was being unfair to this kindly man. He had nothing but her best interests at heart, and he could no more prevent his attraction to her than she could prevent her own attraction to Rue Garrett. She knew that. And she hated her lies. But she wasn't sure how you explained losing your heart to a man in a single afternoon, especially when the man who was asking was one who had been hoping that you would lose your heart to him. And she wasn't even sure she had lost her heart to Rue. She only knew that she was terribly attracted to him, and that despite her protests, she did want to see him again. And be kissed by him again. But how to tell Mac? Fair or not, she simply couldn't tell him that there was no hope of anything more than friendship between them in the same breath that she confessed the confusing pull she felt toward a man she'd met only that afternoon.

"Oh, Mac," she choked out, feeling closer to tears than she had in literally ages. "I've always known just what I was doing, where I was going, and now I feel so confused."

Reaching over, Mac ran a finger lightly down the softness of her cheek. "Come here," he said gently. Pulling her into the circle of his arms, he cradled her against his chest like a child. "What's got you so confused? Something to do with Rue Garrett?" he asked quietly.

"No!" The denial burst from her lips with surprising force, probably because she knew it wasn't true. Her confusion was thoroughly wrapped around her unwanted feelings for Rue Garrett. But Mac's solicitude had so nearly been her undoing, had so nearly wrung from her the yes that would have been the truth.

"Is it me?" he asked, his tones low.

"No...yes...I don't know..." Jamey almost wailed, unaware of the tensing of Mac's arms as he reacted to her half-expected response. It didn't occur to her then that Mac himself had precipitated the talk she'd been planning to have with him.

Haltingly, as though unsure of herself, Jamey tried to explain her devotion to her career. She tried to make him understand that she had no intention of ending up like her mother.

"I know that's not the answer you wanted to hear, Mac," she said solemnly, looking up at him, "but that's the way it is, and I don't want to go on letting you have false hopes. I've never been interested in *any* man before just because he was a man, and I don't want to be interested now—not in you, not in Rue Garrett...." She hadn't meant to bring his name back into things. "Not in anybody!" she added hastily. "I just want to go on with my career and be left alone, except for pleasant dates that end with casual kisses, like we've had for the past two months."

Mac had listened patiently. Her mention of Rue Garrett was revealing, but he didn't challenge her on it. "Jamey, you can't call all the shots in this world," he replied gently. "I know you feel like you can, or that you should be able to, but that's a lesson you'll learn as you grow older," he added, feeling at that moment the weight of every one of his thirty-nine years. "Some things simply happen, whether we want them to or not." He didn't bother to explain that comment before continuing wryly. "You know, this is the first time you've acknowledged my feelings for you. And you're right. I did have hopes for us. I guess I still do," he said questioningly, placing his fingers on Jamey's lips when she would have denied him his hope. "But maybe I've already used up more luck than one man can expect to have when it comes to the women in my life," he finished sadly.

"What do you mean, Mac?" she asked, willing now to let him have his say.

"Barbara," he answered simply. "I've never told you much about her. It still hurts too much when I think about her for me to be able to talk freely about her. I had twelve beautiful years with Barbara, and being married to her was wonderful. Thanks to her, my experience of marriage was that it's far preferable to the single life," he said prophetically, "and I don't plan to remain single forever." As though time had rolled back, Mac gazed out into the darkness and spoke again. "When Barbara died, I thought I would die too. But I didn't. I had little Emily to take care of, and that helped to keep me going. Emily still keeps me going, even though she's a young woman now and is spending this summer as a girls' camp counselor before leaving for college in September." He paused, his eyes returning to Jamey's face. "When I met you, it was like having the sunshine come back into my life. But that's because you're all the things Damon said—a lovely, intelligent, independent lady and more. You're also filled with love, Jamey, and all that love inside you is going to have to find a permanent home someday. If I can't be the man your love comes home to, I just hope the man who is will cherish it."

Deeply affected by Mac's words, Jamey reached up and kissed him, gently, on his lips. Mac returned the kiss, and they both knew it was a good-bye kiss, good-bye to Mac's hopes for a love relationship between them. But it was a greeting too, a hello to a deep and abiding friendship. It might take Mac awhile to relinquish all his hopes, but it was a beginning.

"Thank you, Mac," Jamey said softly. "I'm glad you told me about Barbara. I'm sorry you lost her, but glad you loved her so while you were together. She must have been a wonderful woman, to have had a man like you love her so much." To have gone on, to have suggested that there would be someone else for Mac, would have been crude, but Jamey was sure it would happen. She wasn't sure why the memory of Meg Carter smiling up at him as she accepted his invitation to come early to Tanasie Basin chose that moment to assert itself.

Holding her an arm's length away, Mac sighed and returned to a topic Jamey would just as soon he'd left alone. "But what of your meeting tomorrow, Jamey? I'm still worried about this Rue Garrett. I meant what I said earlier about performers. Some of them have such horrible reputations. Don't let him run roughshod over you, honey." The endearment slipped out, but they both ignored it, just as they ignored the implication that Rue might run over her in some way that had nothing to do with Steve's music. "Sure you don't want me to be here with you tomorrow?"

Smiling weakly as she sought to reassure him one last time, Jamey replied, "I'm sure, Mac. I'm a big girl, and all the real decisions are Steve's anyway. I'm only included because I've worked with him on this, and because I'm older...and wiser," she added, hoping it was true. It would have to be true if she wasn't to be proved the liar she felt at that moment.

"Okay," he agreed reluctantly, "but if you need me for anything, call. That's what I'm there for," he added, smiling sadly. "I want your promise on that."

"I promise. And, Mac, don't worry about me. Like Meg said, this whole thing should be cause for celebration, not argument or worry. And I really am just tired tonight," she tacked on, wanting to convince them both. "Everything will look better in the morning. That's what my mother always used to tell me, anyway." Smiling impishly now, she cocked her head to one side and added, "This has simply been a big day, that's all."

Jamey slid across the seat and opened the door. "I'll see you Sunday at church," she said as she closed the door and turned to walk up the path to the cabin. She didn't turn back to wave, so she missed the rueful shake of Mac's head that would have told her that he thought she still had a lot to learn about her own emotions. She might deny it, to herself as well as to him, but he still had an uneasy feeling that there was a lot more to her meeting with Rue Garrett than she had admitted.

Jamey moved quickly across the deck that ran the entire width of her tiny cabin, not pausing as she usually did to view the quiet nighttime beauty of the middle Tennessee countryside. Inside the cabin she leaned back against the door, listening to the sound of the engine as Mac drove away and trying to block out her emotions. She had never had a day like this one, she thought, and hoped she never would again.

She felt drained, but perversely, her body didn't feel tired at all now that she was home. She had grown to love her little cabin, with its open spaces, and looked on it as her sanctuary. It sat in a wooded spot on a five-acre parcel that had once been part of a working farm, with a creek forming the back boundary of the property. Now that Mac had gone, the only sounds were the restful sighing of the wind in the trees and the insects singing their night songs.

Jamey stared for a moment at the solid wood panels that ran throughout the cabin's interior, mesmerized by the swirling patterns of knots. Her eyes moved from the small, efficient kitchen and dining nook that ran, unhampered by wall or divider, into a living room of sorts. The cabin had been lovingly furnished by the Martins, the elderly couple who were her landlords and nearest neighbors and lived in what had been the original farmhouse, half a mile away. She glanced from sofa to solid wood coffee table to the overstuffed chair that graced a corner of the room, pleased by the comfortable, lived-in look of things. A small bath and medium-sized bedroom completed her home, and her sigh was audible as she thought longingly of the double bed Bonnie Martin had told her was the first bed she and Tom had shared as man and wife.

Not a good direction for your thoughts, she told herself

as she wearily surveyed the many plants that decorated the cabin, her own contribution to her comfortable little nest. But thoughts of Tom and Bonnie Martin persisted, and if she had to force her thoughts away from the evidence of the happy years the couple had spent together, she wouldn't willingly acknowledge it.

Sometimes she walked over on a Saturday and spent hours visiting with them, enjoying their tales of rearing their children on the farm and of watching their grandchildren as they had grown, playing in the fields and the cabin over the years. But she enjoyed their stories about the hard work of farming more than any others, she assured herself, remembering how often she had laughed with them over some anecdote about the old plowhorses or the many dogs that had shared the farm with them in the past. Jamey smiled now at the pleasant memories she was storing to take with her from Tennessee, and her own sudden eagerness to return to Oregon and her own two dogs. She denied to herself that her desire to go home had anything to do with Rue Garrett, with what she kept trying to convince herself was an unwarranted interest in the man. She focused instead on thoughts of her pets.

Perhaps she liked Tom and Bonnie's animal stories so well, Jamey thought, because she missed Digger and Charlie. If there was anything that bothered her about being away from Oregon for so long while she was completing this assignment, it was not having her dogs with her. She loved animals, and here she had to content herself with occasional visits to the stables that housed Tanasie Basin's trail horses. She had thought about getting a dog, but had decided that it would be too cruel to let it learn to love her, to depend on her, and then be unable to take it back to Oregon with her when she left.

Good Lord, she thought, *what am I doing standing here getting all maudlin about plants and animals and the Martins and this cabin when I should be getting ready for bed?* But sleep was still not an option her body was prepared to offer her at that moment.

Accepting her restlessness, Jamey moved away from the door at last and walked to the stove to put the kettle on. A cup of evening tea would help to make her drowsy. When the tea had steeped, she poured a cup and crossed to the overstuffed chair. Snuggling down into its cozy warmth, she let her mind and body relax.

As she sat, her legs curled under her, her thoughts returned to Rue Garrett. In the end she made no effort to prevent the thoughts. She had to make a plan. As much as she might wish that his kiss had not affected her so, the fact remained that it had. And she didn't know what she was going to do about it, she finally confessed to herself, except that she was determined not to become too seriously involved with any man at this time in her life. Her consulting jobs were just becoming frequent enough that institutions nationwide were beginning to hear of her and to consider her for contracts. She would be damned if she was going to let any man interfere with that!

And it was no good comparing her life to that of her sister. Samantha, three years older, seemed somehow to have escaped the effects of their parents' marital discord and to have won the best of both worlds. Not only was she happy in her career as a buyer for a chain of clothing stores, a career that had been briefly interrupted by the birth of her only child, she also gave every appearance of being crazily in love with her lawyer husband, even after seven years of marriage. But, living in Chicago as they did, time and distance had served to prevent Jamey from ever discussing with Samantha her own feelings about mixing career and marriage. It didn't matter anyway, she reminded herself, as she had no intention of trying to combine the two just yet. Her foolish thoughts were merely the product of her mental and physical exhaustion, Jamey assured herself.

Alone, away from the influence of Rue or Mac, or anyone who might try to shake her confidence in her ability to remain heart-whole, and cocooned in the warm safety of her little cabin, she let herself believe that she would be able to cope quite easily when Rue showed up tomorrow. Or later today, she thought, as she realized that it was now well after midnight.

Jamey stood and made her way slowly to the small bedroom, satisfied with the calm that washed over her as she undressed and slid at last between the sheets. Lying in bed, waiting for sleep to claim her, she concentrated on putting Rue Garrett from her mind. But her last waking thought was of the kiss they had shared, and her dreams that night were filled with his image.

Chapter Three

Humming happily as she tossed the dusting cloth to Steve and turned back to retrieve the cookies she had left baking in the oven, Jamey thought that she had been right. Everything did look better in the daylight! Since waking this morning, she had put a lot of thought into how she would deal with Rue Garrett if he should pursue yesterday's tactics, and was well pleased with her plan.

Mentally she reviewed it for the umpteenth time, never thinking to question why her plan should have required so much thought, or why it should still need reviewing hours after she had formulated it.

The plan itself was quite simple. She would be calm and friendly, she thought, and keep the focus of this meeting on Steve's music. But she would agree to go out with Rue if he asked her again. After all, what harm could there be in going out with a man you found attractive and exciting?

And there was a side benefit, Jamey rationalized. Going out with Rue should be proof to Mac that she had meant it when she said she had no intention of getting involved with any one man just now. She had gone out with other men just as she had with Mac, had enjoyed their kisses, but had always escaped heart-whole, and had managed in most cases to remain

friends with the man involved. She was sure she would
do so again, even if the men in question were Mac
McCormack and Rue Garrett. Basking in the confidence that her reactions of the day before had been
merely the result of being taken by surprise at her unexpected attraction to Rue, she discounted her response to his kiss, the restless tossing and turning of
the night as his image had filled her dreams.

Sliding the cookies onto the waiting plate, she nearly
tipped them onto the floor as she reacted to Steve's
excited shout, "He's here!"

Jamey spun around in time to see Rue emerging
from a brown and gold four-wheel-drive truck. Catching her breath with a gasp as her pulse began to beat a
rapid and unfamiliar tattoo in her chest, she felt her
hard-won confidence waver like a candle flame in a
breeze. But the flame didn't go out. She couldn't let it.

Seeking to calm her unsteady nerves, she turned
back to the counter and slid a second tray of cookies
into the oven before moving to the door to greet Rue.
At the door she watched, smiling shyly, as he moved
up the walk with a loose and graceful stride, his steps
eating up the distance between them.

"Hello, Jamey, have a good night?" he queried sar-
donically, as his long strides brought him face-to-face
with her on the deck. The hidden meaning in the question almost destroyed her already shaky composure,
but Jamey mentally squared her shoulders and responded calmly.

"Yes, I had a very pleasant evening. How about
you?" she asked as though the two of them were making ordinary small talk, greeting each other in the way
of casual acquaintances.

Dismissing her answer with a nod, he turned to greet
Steve, who had joined them at the door with a self-
conscious grin. "Hi, Steve," he smiled. "Ready to
learn something about the music business?"

Steve's grin became broader as he responded. "You bet, Mr. Garrett! I've been freaked out all day, waiting for time for this meeting," he added in the vernacular of his peers at Tanasie Basin.

Rue smiled. "Then how about if the two of you move away from the door and let me come in? Or are we having this get-together on the doorstep?" he asked teasingly, reminding them that their positions made an effective barrier against his entry.

As they both stepped back, embarrassed, Rue entered the cabin and glanced around, his gaze taking in the comfortable coziness of the room, the many plants that made it seem almost a continuation of the out-of-doors. His eyes sparkled with a pleased glint as he turned to look down at Jamey. "Nice," he said softly, his eyes catching hers. "You've turned this old place into a comfortable little home, haven't you?" he asked casually, almost musingly.

Jamey wondered at the odd question that was really more of a statement, but inordinately pleased that he approved of her home, hastened to explain. "I'm just renting it, but I added the plants to make it feel more like home. I'm only—"

"Jamey!" Steve's excited shout interrupted her explanation that she was only in Tennessee for a short time on a consulting contract. "What's that smoke coming from the oven?" he yelled, as they all turned to stare at the offending unit.

"Oh," she reacted, moving quickly across the room, "the rest of the cookies! I forgot them," she wailed, as she grabbed the oven door to yank it open, then jumped back with a yelp of pain as it burned her fingers.

"Jamey, you little fool!" Rue bit the words out as he pushed her out of his way, his other hand reaching for the potholder lying on the counter. He opened the oven door a fraction, checking for flames. Finding none, he opened the door fully and retrieved the now charred cookies, tossing them quickly into the sink and running a stream of cold water over the burnt mess.

Turning back, he snapped at her. "Let me see your hand, Jamey. Have you burned it badly?"

Shaking her head in rueful response, she extended her hand to let him see the blisters that were rising in response to the heat of the oven door. He pulled her to the sink and thrust her hand under the stream of cold water as he asked if she had any first-aid supplies, dispatching Steve to the bathroom for the kit as soon as he had received her answer. When Steve returned, Rue gently smoothed an ointment over her burned fingers and applied a light dressing. "That should take care of it," he said, gentle now. "But don't you know better than to grab a hot oven door with your bare hand, Jamey? The thing was smoking for a reason."

Moving away from him as he released her hand, not wanting him to recognize her trembling as anything more than a response to the pain in her now tender fingertips, Jamey answered penitently. "I know. I just acted before I thought. I'm not normally so careless," she confessed, then added in a saucy tone, "and I'm not hurt badly, so let's just forget it and get on with what we're here for."

Rue's eyes glinted with humor as she made the transition from hurt little girl to efficient businesswoman, and he thought that he had been right in his assessment that she was fiercely independent. "Sure," he agreed, assuming a casual attitude that Jamey wasn't sure she liked.

The three of them moved into the living room and sat down. Businesslike now, Rue quickly reviewed all Steve's options regarding the music he had written, from simply selling the song to an established performer like himself, to trying to find someone to back Steve in recording it. The latter, he explained, would be

very difficult until Steve had gained some experience
in performing for the public and begun to make a name
for himself.

An hour later they had exhausted all the questions
they could think of, but Steve had still made no definite decision as to what he wanted to do with "Sweet
Freedom." Calmly, as he bit into the last of the cookies
from the batch that hadn't burned, Rue told them it
would be best not to make a hasty decision, and Jamey
wondered at his patience. She had half expected him to
try to pressure Steve into selling him the rights to the
song so he could record it right away.

Turning to Jamey, Rue concluded, "Well, that's
about it. That should give you a lot to think about,
Steve," he added, glancing back at the youth, "and to
discuss with Jamey before you make up your mind.
When you've decided, I'll be glad to help you, no matter what your choice is," he assured them.

Standing and stretching his lean, muscular frame,
Rue suggested, "Why don't we drive up to Tanasie
Basin? I've never been up there, and I have to confess
to some curiosity about what it's like. You wouldn't
mind showing it to me, would you?" he asked, appealing to Steve.

Eagerly, Steve responded. "Heck, no! We have visitors all the time. And the guys will love it! They've all
been asking me if I could bring you up, but I didn't
know if you'd be interested."

Rue smiled at the boy's enthusiasm, but Jamey was
suspicious. How quickly he had dealt with getting Steve
back to Tanasie Basin, she thought as she remembered
what he had said the day before. "After that, it's going
to be just you and me," he had said, and Jamey's eyes
narrowed as she tried to gauge the sincerity of his request to learn what Steve's environment was like.

So intent was she on trying to analyze Rue's motives
that she nearly missed what he was saying, something

about Indians. "What was that?" she asked, jerking her attention back to the present.

Rue's grin as he repeated his words was just enough to have her wondering if he had somehow guessed what she had been thinking. The thought brought a pink glow to her cheeks.

"I was just explaining to Steve that the name Tennessee was actually derived from an old Cherokee word, *Tanasie*. The Cherokee tribe had a village in this area that was called Tanasie, and that's probably where they got the name for the institution," he told her, then went on to explain a little of the histories of the Cherokee, Chickamauga, and Chickasaw Indians as the earliest known inhabitants of what was now the state of Tennessee.

To say that Jamey was surprised by Rue's display of knowledge would have been putting it mildly, for he continued to entertain them with bits and pieces of Tennessee history during the drive to Tanasie Basin. And by the time they arrived, her nervousness about his intentions had been replaced by a growing respect for the handsome Tennessean.

As they entered the recreation room at Tanasie Basin, most of the activity that had been going on came to an abrupt halt as the residents crowded around the three of them. The air was filled with questions, everybody wanting to know at once what was going to happen with Steve's song.

Laughing at their youthful enthusiasm, Rue implored, "Slow down, guys! Steve's talent was only discovered yesterday, and he can't become a star overnight. But I'll tell you something," he added conspiratorially, "I think he just might do well in country music. Your friend has a lot of talent." Steve was beaming at the praise from this man who was fast becoming his idol.

Watching, Jamey thought that Rue could be good for

Steve. His world had been filled with the worst of male images, from his father to his uncles to most of his friends, and he could certainly do worse than to learn to pattern his behavior after Rue Garrett's. She just hoped that Rue's interest was sincere. Anything less could be a crushing blow for Steve.

Rue looked to Jamey for confirmation as Steve suggested that he join some of the guys in a game of pool. Nodding, she said, "Sure, it'll be fun. And I need to check on some things in my office, anyway," she added. "When you're ready, if I haven't come back up, Steve will show you the way to the school building."

Moving across the room, she glanced back to see that Rue's attention was now fully focused on the youths surrounding him. Perversely she felt piqued by his lack of concern and attention toward her, where before she had hoped for anything but that attention. She determined that she would stay in her office until he came to find her. *Maybe he's changed his mind,* she thought as she walked away, and winced at the little stab of pain that shot through her heart at the thought. It occurred to her that she hadn't intended her plan to work quite this well.

In her office Jamey was finding it difficult to concentrate on the papers before her. Looking up at the clock, she saw that it had been nearly an hour since she had left Rue playing pool with the guys, and she had accomplished nothing. She was no closer to a decision on her supply order than she had been when she started. The thought made her angry, and she shoved the papers back into their folder and turned to put the folder back into her file. Silently she cursed Rue Garrett for the confusion he had brought into her usually well-ordered life. What was it about him, she wondered, that could turn an efficient, adult woman into a silly, simpering, *scared* little girl?

"Hi." The file drawer slammed shut with a bang as

Jamey jumped in response to the quiet voice coming from the doorway of her office. Spinning around, she glowered at Rue, who was laughing at her reaction to his quiet greeting. "I decided you weren't coming back up, so Steve showed me the way down here," he went on before she could utter the angry words that hovered on her lips. "Are you always so jumpy? You told me to come down here if you weren't back before we finished," he reminded her teasingly.

Swallowing her unaccustomed anger, Jamey replied, "No, you just startled me. I'm not often interrupted when I'm here on a Saturday, and I'd forgotten you were here," she lied, trying to get back at him for his desertion of the past hour. "Are you ready to go?" she asked, turning to retrieve her shoulder bag.

"I'm in no hurry," he shrugged, moving into the office and making it seem suddenly too small. A noncommittal smile played around the corners of his lips. "I'd kind of like to know what it is you do here," he continued quietly, ignoring her anger of a moment before and the challenge of her lie about forgetting he was there.

Jamey was seething underneath at his nonchalant response to her provocation, but determined to remain just as cool as he was. She replaced her purse and turned resolutely to face him. Efficiently she explained all she had done since arriving at Tanasie Basin. She told him of the needs assessments, of testing all the residents to get some idea of the academic levels the teachers would be dealing with, developing a curriculum that would meet the needs of older teen-age boys who had a long history of school failure even though many of them were of at least average intelligence, and of interviewing and hiring the teaching staff who would begin work in two weeks. By the time she had finished her description, her anger was gone, lost to her own enthusiasm for the work she did.

As she had talked Rue had watched her closely, gauging her feelings for her work and asking pertinent questions when she came to something he didn't understand. Several times she had felt that he might be humoring her, and had looked for some sign that his interest was less than genuine. But she hadn't found any, so she had given him quite a complete description of her job. And now it was she who wanted to get away from Tanasie Basin, impatient, but unsure of what her impatience hinted at. All she was sure of was that this was a much more casual Rue Garrett than the one who had kissed her so thoroughly the day before. He seemed barely aware of her as a woman, as anything more than the catalyst in his involvement with Steve.

"Anything else you want to know about?" she asked off-handedly, matching her attitude to his.

"No, I can't think of anything right now," he answered, his eyes narrowing at the clipped tones of her voice. "Shall we go?" he suggested.

"Okay. I'm ready if you are," she responded, reaching for her purse once again as she moved toward the door. Jamey was conscious of her regret—regret that what was between them now seemed strictly professional.

BACK at the cabin Rue continued to confound her with his casual behavior. *You'd think yesterday was all a dream, a figment of my imagination,* she thought, and wished she could scream at him. Anything to relieve the tension that was building to flash point inside her! But she only answered his questions.

"How did you ever come to rent this place?" Rue asked quietly, his eyes alive with the same pleasure she had noticed earlier as he surveyed her home.

Jamey smiled nervously. "There really wasn't any trick to that. One of the staff members from Tanasie Basin had rented it before he and his wife decided to buy a home, and he mentioned it to me when he heard I was looking for a place. I made an appointment to see it, fell in love with both the cabin and the land, and the rest is history," she said softly.

Rue seemed inclined to say something more about the cabin as he leaned back in his chair, letting his eyes move slowly from object to object before gazing directly at Jamey. His piercing stare as his eyes held hers made her uncomfortable, and she was relieved when he spoke again—relieved, but surprised by the change of topic.

"Where does Steve fit into all this?" he asked suddenly, almost impatiently.

"I'm not sure what you mean," she answered, confused by both his question and his tone.

"Just that it seems unusual for a young career woman to have let herself become so involved with someone else's aspirations."

"I don't think that's unusual at all, Rue," Jamey responded quietly, still unsure of the direction his thoughts had taken. "Or maybe it is unusual. But then, Steve is an exceptional young man. As you've apparently noticed, he's very talented, but there's also a depth to him that seems to surprise even Steve at times," she added, a gentle smile tugging at her lips as she thought of her young friend's struggle to understand himself. "I don't know. Maybe he's like the younger brother I never had," she finished softly.

"Maybe," Rue agreed, his lips beginning to curve upward in a smile that matched hers. "You're certainly right about his talent, anyway."

Rue changed topics again. He asked her about her life before she had come to Tennessee, and his questions seemed to delve too deeply into her soul. But whenever she tried to question him about his life, he neatly turned the question aside without divulging much information. Thoroughly frustrated by the depth

of his questions and by his nonchalant evasions, Jamey
suggested that they go for a walk on the property.

"We can walk down to the back boundary, and I'll
show you the creek," she promised. Her thoughts
moved ahead to the tranquillity of the familiar spot, to
the sparkling meanderings of the crystalline stream.

"Good idea," Rue agreed, uncoiling his long frame
from the comfortable chair where she had sat the night
before trying to unravel the mysteries of her attraction
to him.

As they walked they slipped into an easy camaraderie,
and Jamey lost much of the tension that had been threatening to overcome her composure back in the cabin.
They had almost reached the stream when Rue caught
her hand, holding her back as he pointed out land-
marks. He showed her trees and told her what kinds
they were—hickory, red and white oaks, sycamore, and
tulip poplar; he pointed out wild flowers—dragonroot,
hop clover, yellow jasmine, and the beautiful iris,
which he told her was Tennessee's state flower. Standing with feet apart and shoulders back, exulting in the
pleasure of the moment, he taught her signs that told
where the little meadow creatures were likely to have
their homes, surprising her with his knowledge of nature and the nostalgic, almost wistful, note in his voice.
And when they turned to resume their walk toward the
creek, he retained his hold on her hand, and Jamey left
her small hand resting comfortably in his larger one.

Reaching the creek bank, Rue led her to a huge old
oak and they sat, leaning back in the shelter of its massive branches. Lost in pensive thought, they sat for a
while in silence until Jamey innocently questioned,
"What sort of flower is that?"

Had she had any idea, Jamey would not have asked
the question, but the flower was a particularly beautiful
one that seemed to grow in wild profusion in this hu-
mid southern climate. The flower extended from a

woody vine, the unusual blossoms like ten-pointed stars. Five of the points were a snowy white, with five more in an off-white hue, variegated with a lighter shade of violet, which rested above the purity of the snowy points in a turned overlay, creating the illusion of ten pointed petals. A vivid ring of violet hairlike rays encircled the yellowish heart of the blossom, leaving the impression of a protective tenderness.

Rue turned, leaning toward her to get a better view of the object of her curiosity. He could have told her much more than the name of the flower. He could have told her that though native Tennesseans referred to the plant as the maypop, it had actually been named by Roman Catholic priests for its imagined likeness to the passion of Christ's suffering, and to the crown of thorns He had worn on the cross.

Instead, he smiled enigmatically and answered softly, giving the blossom its true name. "The passion-flower...." His eyes, as his gaze caught and held hers, glinted with a hint of what the flower's name implied. It was as though the incident had tripped something in him, some thought that refused to be denied as he moved dangerously close to Jamey.

There was simply no adequate response she could have made to this quixotic man. He changed too quickly. One minute he was cool and impersonal, the next he was comfortably and casually informative and, before she could adjust to that added warmth, he was crowding her again in the same overpowering way he had the day before. She didn't know which man she wanted him to be, which Rue Garrett to respond to.

"W-well," she stammered, struggling to make sense of his erratic behavior, trying to bring her own hammering pulse back under control. Where did she go from here? What could she say to him? "What do you think Steve will decide to do?" she asked in a rush, opting for the safety of an entirely different topic. That her question was hopelessly out of context, she knew. But it was impossible for her to be rational with Rue staring into her eyes as though he could read her every thought, moving steadily closer as though her words no longer had meaning.

"You're quite a girl, aren't you, Jamey?" he asked in a soft, but somewhat biting tone. "All tough and professional on the outside, marshmallow soft on the inside. What happened to make you want to hide the real you?"

Alarmed by this newest change in him, this hint of anger following his sudden switch from casual to personal, Jamey leaned away from him. "I don't know what you're talking about! I'm j-just me," she responded jerkily.

"You know what I'm talking about. Yesterday you responded to me like a woman once I'd broken down the wall you surround yourself with, but today the wall is right back in place. You're like a scared teen-ager, wondering when I'm going to pounce on you and not sure which is worse—your fear that I will or your fear that I won't," he retorted. "Well, I hate to disappoint a lady," he drawled lazily as he finally made the move that would close the gap between them.

The movement of his lips as he muttered innuendos about Jamey's protective barriers, so like those of the passionflower, held her spellbound for a moment. His lips were inviting, she thought, so inviting....

Something snapped in Jamey's brain and she rose quickly, intent only on escaping Rue's overwhelming attraction. But as she turned hastily to move away from the danger he represented, much like one of the little rabbits he had been telling her about earlier might have done, her foot caught on a root of the old oak and she stumbled and fell headlong into the creek. Surfacing, she sat in the now muddy water, soaked to the skin and covered head-to-toe with bits of leaves and grass and mud. The heat of her irrational fear had drowned. Angrily she spluttered, "You idiot...."

Rue's look of tender intent had turned quickly to one of surprise. His surprise now turned to a roar of laughter, increasing Jamey's anger and frustration, and she flung a handful of mud in his direction. Deftly stepping aside, he watched as it plopped harmlessly onto the creek bank, then turned to raise his eyebrows at her in challenge.

"God, Jamey, you should see yourself...the mermaid of Muddy Creek," he roared, almost doubling over with his laughter. "See what happens when you try to get away from me?" he taunted.

"Get away from you, my foot," Jamey muttered, not caring whether he heard her or not. She rose, deceptively slowly, then charged toward him, intent on making him every bit as wet and muddy as she was.

He held her away easily, laughing at her struggle. But her strength was no match for his, and she finally gave up in frustration. Still laughing, he offered, "You can wear my shirt back to the cabin. It's long enough to be a dress on you."

"No, that's okay!" She rejected his offer quickly, color suffusing her cheeks at the thought of changing clothes in this secluded spot with only Rue for company. "My clothes are already soaked," she excused nervously, looking down at the garments that were now plastered to her slender body, "and there's no sense in getting your shirt all wet and muddy too," she added, forgetting that only a moment before that had been exactly what she wanted.

Serious now, he chided her as he stepped back to unbutton his shirt. "You may already be soaked, but it's getting late and the air has cooled considerably. I'm not willing to risk your getting sick from this little jaunt."

Looking up as the last button came loose, he caught

her frown as she chewed at her tender lower lip and added tersely, "And I'm not planning on watching you undress, if that's what has you so worried...though it's an intriguing idea," he tacked on in an undertone. "Go over behind the oak tree and change," he ordered, his authoritarian tone making it clear that he expected her to move, and fast.

Accepting the wisdom of his words and his shirt at the same time, Jamey moved rapidly to the tree. "Turn around," she begged.

With a laugh, Rue turned, and Jamey hastily stripped off her soaked clothes, wrapping them in a bundle after she had put his shirt on and buttoned every button, from just under her chin to the tail that hung almost to her knees.

He was chuckling again as she emerged from behind the tree. "See? You're almost as well covered now as you were before you fell into the creek," he teased as he turned back and let his eyes rove tantalizingly over the length of her sparsely clad body. "Let's get you back to the cabin," he urged, reacting to Jamey's shivering form. But her shivers were as much a response to his wandering eyes as to the cool evening air.

Catching her around the waist and turning her for the walk back to the cabin, Rue spared no concern for the fact that he was now shirtless. But Jamey was well aware of his half-naked body and couldn't seem to help the furtive glances she cast at his masculine, hair-roughened chest. She had stumbled twice when Rue stopped, asking her what was wrong.

Color flooded her cheeks and she was grateful for the darkness that surrounded them as she answered breathlessly, "Nothing. I'm just a little chilly." Tilting her chin upward, she added, "And you're walking faster—"

But she got no further. Catching her breath, she stared into his eyes, mesmerized, as he turned her into his arms and his strong mouth descended and laid claim to her soft and trembling lips.

A low moan escaped her as she gave up her day-long resistance and yielded to his attraction. Lacing her fingers in his curling hair, she pulled his head lower and returned the kiss fully, feeling only the heat of the blood racing through her veins as she experienced the stirrings of desire for the first time in her life.

Rue's hands moved sensually down the length of her spine to the gently rounded contours of her hips as he drew her ever closer to the warmth of his own body, and she shuddered. The kiss became one of many as his mouth discovered her cheek and earlobe, finally sliding down the slender column of her throat as he blazed a trail of fire wherever his lips touched.

"Jamey," he whispered, "I've wanted to hold you all day, to get you in my arms and love you," he added ardently. But his words, so tenderly spoken, broke the spell of enchantment that had held her mindless in his arms.

Frightened now of the unfamiliar sensations as her body clamored for fulfillment, she pulled slightly away from him and whispered shakily, "No, Rue, this is wrong. We hardly know each other, and—"

"What does time have to do with us?" he asked quietly, interrupting in an intense, but gentle voice. "I want you like I've wanted no other woman, and have since I first saw you ... you with your flashing eyes and raven hair," he added, the delicate tracing of his fingertips on her arms still playing havoc with her newly awakened senses.

But the thought of other women in his arms shattered her innocent acceptance of his caresses and she stepped back, breaking contact with him. She felt chilled to the very core of her being as her emotions fought a fierce battle over the idea that Rue was far from innocent. Mac was right, she thought. And the only wise course of action was for her to get out—*fast*! Get out before his experience had her toppling the barriers of twenty-six years of cherished values and beliefs! It occurred to her, though only briefly, that this was practically the first thought she had spared for Mac all day—and that the thought was so parental in nature that the man in him surely wouldn't thank her for it.

"Jamey?" Rue spoke her name quizzically, reading the pain in her eyes before she had time to mask it.

Hurt, humiliated by her own behavior, she spun on her heel and began walking briskly in the direction of the cabin. Assessing her reaction quickly, Rue caught up with her and stopped her with a viselike grip.

"Jamey, what am I going to do with you?" he asked in a low voice, speaking to the back of her head. "Warm and loving one minute, cold and scared the next. Are you really such an innocent that you didn't know what this was all about? What was that look you gave me back there before I kissed you?"

After a moment of silence, while she stood rigidly in his grip, he went on. "Please don't be afraid of me, Jamey. I'd never willingly do anything to hurt you."

Still stinging from her shame at responding so wantonly to his caresses, and the pain of realization that his expertise at lovemaking had come from his experiences with other women, she kept her back to him. Flinging up her head, she retorted, "What makes you think you have the power to hurt me? We shared a few kisses in the moonlight, that's all," she threw out, nearly choking on the words. "I'm just not willing to let it go any further."

Breaking his hold, she continued toward the cabin. He matched his long stride to her shorter one, and they returned in angry silence.

At the door of the cabin Rue finally broke the silence. "Look, Jamey, I don't know what kind of game you think I'm playing, but I assure you, this is no game," he spat out angrily. Turning to leave, he added, "I'll pick you up at ten in the morning."

"No!" she shouted at his retreating form. "I go to church on Sunday mornings, and—"

"I know," he threw back, pausing in his stride. "The guys at Tanasie Basin told me. I'm going with you." Turning back, he added mysteriously, "I have a feeling those guys know a lot more about the staff members than you folks think they do." His statement was a curious one, but she had no time to ask what he meant.

"No!" she shouted again. "I don't want you to go with me," she called frantically, "and I won't be here when you get here!"

Rue didn't pause this time. He simply flung back at her in a threatening tone, "You better be!" as he lifted a lightweight jacket from the seat of the truck and shrugged into it before swinging his long frame into the vehicle and flicking the engine into life.

"Damn, damn, damn...." Jamey swore as she turned and let herself into the cabin, flinging her bundle of muddy clothes into a heap on the kitchen floor. Her mind was a beehive of activity.

Stalking to the bathroom, she tore at the buttons of Rue's shirt, venting her anger on the garment as she jerkily removed it and hurled it into a corner of the tiny room. Hastily she showered away all traces of her muddy experience at the creek, but her inflamed thoughts were not so easily erased.

"Damn," she muttered again as she stepped out of the shower and caught sight of Rue's shirt lying tauntingly on the floor where she had thrown it, a muddy reminder of the man she'd most like to forget. She knew what the shirt meant. Now she would be forced to see him at least one more time in order to return the blasted thing to him.

Furious, but not sure whether she was most angry with Rue Garrett or herself, she launched into a full-scale war against dirt. Slinging Rue's muddy shirt into the washer with her own clothes, she slammed her burned fingers against the side of the machine. It was her first awareness that somewhere, maybe at the creek, she had lost the bandage Rue had placed so gently on her burn. She ignored the loss, almost glad for the distraction of her pain as she spun the appliance into action and moved on to other areas. She whipped around the tiny cabin, cleaning where there was no need, desperate in her drive to release her pent-up emotions. If she had slowed down long enough to analyze her fury, the intensity of her feelings toward Rue Garrett would have scared her out of her wits.

Chapter Four

Jamey had never stood a man up before. She had never had reason to, but that was precisely what she intended doing this morning. And if Rue Garrett was foolish enough to ignore her refusal to see him today, then that was his problem, she thought. Her anger had abated, but her determination was almost a tangible force.

Slipping the light blue silk dress over her head, she watched in the mirror as the flowing material fell down around her and molded itself gently to her slender curves. The dress was one of her favorites, and her decision to wear it today had been quite deliberate. The ice-blue hue of the material coupled with the graceful cut of the garment to lend her an air of cool, remote sophistication that never failed to bolster her self-confidence. And Jamey needed all the confidence she could muster this morning in order to walk out the door and leave Rue Garrett standing high and dry.

Satisfied that her appearance could leave no one in doubt that she was capable of dealing with life quite aptly, Jamey quickly brushed her freshly washed hair into shining waves, checked her light makeup for the final time, and grabbed her purse as she hurried out the door. She practically flew down the path to her waiting car, looking for all the world as though some demon was hot on her heels.

With desperation lending speed to her movements, Jamey glanced down the country road in both directions before pulling out. She had been half afraid that Rue would show up early, having realized her intent to leave without him, and she heaved a sigh of relief now at how easily she had escaped him. There was no sign of his brown and gold truck as she flicked a nervous glance at her rearview mirror.

The closer she came to the little country church she attended every Sunday, the calmer she felt and the broader she grinned at her thoughts of Rue Garrett's anger if he should actually show up at the cabin and find her gone. By the time she arrived at the church, Jamey's nervousness had yielded to an almost jaunty pleasure in her successful flight.

She was smiling cheerfully as she walked into the church, though the smile slipped a little as she made her way toward the pew she had shared with Mac so often over the past months. She had no idea how he might react now that time would have allowed their conversation of Friday night to sink in.

"Good morning," she greeted him softly, sliding in beside him.

Mac turned, a surprised smile lighting up his features. "Well, good morning. I wasn't sure you'd be here today," he said, a hint of strain marking his words. "But not only are you here, you're early," he continued, a teasing note entering his voice as he followed that comment with a remark about her usual habit of arriving just on time and slipping into the church without a minute to spare.

"An overabundance of energy," Jamey smilingly excused, more willing to let the conversation slide into gentle teasing than to follow up on that brief hint of tension she had detected. She wondered just what he thought might have kept her away today, suspected his thoughts centered on Rue Garrett. But if he was curious about yesterday's meeting, he'd have to do the asking, she decided. "I've been up since eight this morning."

"Well, that's a switch," he taunted pleasantly, following her lead. He was well aware of the pleasure she took in sleeping late on Sunday mornings. Jamey made no secret of the fact that her Sunday mornings were precious to her, one luxurious opportunity to lie in bed until the last possible moment, for she was always up early and going full out on the other six days of the week.

"I know," she grinned, but made no comment as to why this Sunday had been unusual.

As other members of the small congregation entered and found their usual places in the little church, Jamey and Mac smilingly answered each hello and took part in the small talk that was habit among the local folk. These people were accustomed to seeing Jamey and Mac seated together in church, and more than once had hinted that they wouldn't be surprised by an engagement announcement. Neither of them had ever disabused anyone of the notion—Mac, because he had hoped it would happen; Jamey, because she didn't want to stimulate any more gossip about her relationship with Mac than was already circulating. She and Mac were both relative newcomers to the small community, though Mac was a Tennessean born and bred, and as she would be leaving soon, she saw no reason to discuss her private life with her temporary neighbors.

For that reason, if for none other, she was glad that Rue wasn't with her today. All she needed was that added bit of speculation, she thought, to have these people suspecting her of stringing two men along when, in fact, she wasn't really involved with even one man. She glanced back at Mac as she reassured herself of her independence, noticing for the first time how truly handsome he was, and surprising herself with the observation. She had simply never thought about it before. But he wasn't as handsome as Rue, she told herself, didn't have the rugged charm Rue had. She quelled that line of thought immediately. What did she care what either of them looked like?

The pastor entered through the double doors at the rear of the small sanctuary, greeting individuals informally as he made his way to the raised pulpit at the front of the room, and Jamey focused her attention on his progress. The congregation became quiet as he reached the platform, facing forward to listen to Reverend Brown. A low murmur in the back of the room, unusual in a time when quiet reigned, was Jamey's only warning that something out of the ordinary was marking this Sunday as different.

She turned to look over her shoulder, wondering what the disturbance was, and found herself staring wide-eyed at the stunningly handsome man who wore the gray pin-striped suit as comfortably as the only other clothes she had ever seen him in—jeans and casual shirts. Rue strode calmly down the aisle, the tan of his face standing out in stark relief against the creamy whiteness of the collar that complemented the darkness of his vest and jacket. He stopped beside the pew where Jamey and Mac were seated, his lips lifting in a smile that never quite reached his eyes, and she had no choice but to move over and allow him room to join them—not unless she wanted to make a scene and really start tongues wagging. The implications of the murmurs still rippling through the small congregation were lost on her as Jamey wondered nervously how Rue had found her. She was torn between a tingling fear and a surging pride that the vital masculinity of the man now seated to her right was focused solely on her.

"Well, good morning, Rue!" Reverend Brown's voice boomed from the pulpit. "It's been quite awhile since we last saw you."

"Yes, sir," Rue returned respectfully, turning his piercing scrutiny away from Jamey. "I'm afraid being on the road keeps me from getting back as often as I'd like."

"Well, it's mighty good to have you back with us today, son. Welcome home," the Reverend concluded as he bowed his head, indicating that the service was about to begin with the traditional prayer.

Jamey's eyes were wide with shock as the meaning of the exchange sank in, and with a last frantic glance at the man she had tried to avoid, she bowed her head and closed her eyes tight. Rue was known to these people. No, not just known, *well* known, she thought as her mind wrestled with this whole new set of problems.

What supplications Reverend Brown offered in his prayer, or the topic of the day's sermon, Jamey couldn't have said. She was so busy trying to digest this surprising turn of events that she was only marginally aware that life was proceeding, for the moment, without her conscious participation. For her, the church contained only three people—she and Mac and Rue Garrett.

She registered the antagonistic glances passing over her head between Rue and Mac. *Oh, Lord,* she prayed, *please don't let these two get into a confrontation here!* Her eyes skittered first to Mac, then to Rue, and her indrawn breath was loud in her ears as her glance caught the full force of cold gray-blue eyes as they hinted at the retribution she would pay for her puny efforts at evading him. Fear sent her mind reeling with thoughts of further escape plans.

When the service came to an end and everyone began filing toward the doors and out into the bright sunshine of the August day, Jamey made a last bid for freedom. She knew it was cowardly, but she hadn't really wanted to deal with either of these men. She certainly didn't want to cope with both of them ... together! She tried to slip around Rue to make a hasty exit, but was effectively thwarted in her intent by Reverend Brown's mellow voice.

"Jamey," he called, beaming at her as he made his way to where she and Rue and Mac formed a stop-action line of three. "Are you responsible for bringing this prodigal son home to us?"

She smiled weakly and made a small movement with her hand, but found no words to answer him. Rue slipped his arm around her waist and answered for her. "She sure is! If you'd let me know you had someone as pretty as Jamey in your congregation, Reverend, I'd have been back long before now," he teased as he smiled down at her.

Teasing he might be, but Jamey could feel the tension in the arm that encircled her waist. She felt it as certainly as she sensed the strain that marked Mac's reaction to Rue's proprietorial words and conduct. Only then did she realize that, though there could be no doubt that Mac knew exactly who Rue was, there was every possibility that Rue had no idea who Mac was. She glanced from one to the other of the two men, dismayed by the implied challenge in their eyes as each took the other's measure.

"Oh, I'm sorry," Jamey exclaimed, unwillingly filling the breach left by what she hoped only she would know had been her own panic-filled oversight. "Rue, this is Mac McCormack, our superintendent at Tanasie Basin," she added breathlessly. She felt no need to go further with the introduction. Reverend Brown had made Rue's identity quite clear more than an hour earlier.

"Pleased to meet you, Mr. Garrett," Mac said almost warily. There was no ring of sincerity in the hollow greeting.

"Glad to meet you," Rue responded as he took the initiative and extended his hand to the other man. "Jamey and Steve have told me a great deal about you."

Somehow, the words sounded less complimentary than they should have, and Jamey was almost mesmerized by the sight of two large hands clasping in an acknowledgment neither of the men seemed pleased to make. The sound of Reverend Brown clearing his throat called attention away from the grudging act.

"Jamey has spent part of her time this summer working with Steve Carlson, one of the boys from Tanasie Basin. The lad has a fair amount of musical talent, and through her efforts Mr. Garrett has taken an interest in the boy," Mac said quickly, as though explaining away the strained atmosphere that surrounded them.

"How fascinating," Reverend Brown remarked politely, his raised eyebrows as he surveyed the three of them speaking clearly of his doubt that Rue Garrett was merely interested in this lad with musical talent that Mac spoke of.

His gaze rested on Jamey for only a second before he lifted his eyes to question Rue and Mac about Steve, but it was enough to remind her that Rue's arm was still wrapped lightly around her waist. It was enough to make her nearly squirm with embarrassment as Rue too intercepted the pastor's glance and smiled with him, as though sharing some explicitly male secret.

The three men talked briefly of Steve and his music as Jamey listened distractedly. She wondered how she could gracefully escape Rue's arm, wondered if Mac was aware that he kept addressing Rue as Mr. Garrett, granting him the respect that he seemed to command as naturally as though he had been born to power. The thought brought her no pleasure. It only added to her fears as she remembered her efforts to stand him up, the threat implied by his angry gaze as he had seated himself beside her in the church, and the probable meaning behind the look he had shared with Reverend Brown.

Fear caused the pace of her pulse to accelerate, and her discomfort brought with it a new determination. That no one seemed able to defy Rue and get away with it only added a dimension of anger. The feeling strengthened her resolve to get away from him, and she eased out of his loosely placed hold and turned toward where her car was parked.

"Excuse me a moment, gentlemen." Jamey heard Rue's words as she speeded her steps and knew with a sinking feeling that, for the moment at least, there was no escape for her. She also knew that his words had left Mac no option but to stay where he was.

Rue caught up with her easily and walked with her in silence, smiling. Jamey was relieved that he was smiling. Perhaps her fears had been groundless.

At the door of the car, which she locked out of habit because it was policy that all Tanasie Basin staff lock their cars while on campus, Rue held out his hand for her keys, indicating that he would open the door for her. She passed him her keys without a word, surprised that he was not only allowing her to leave, but actually helping her. He unlocked and opened the door, his hand at her elbow as he helped her into the car.

Jamey shied away from the contact and held out her own hand, expecting him to return her keys. The cold glimmer in his eyes stunned her as he pocketed her keys and turned on his heel. He strode away, tossing back a terse "Be back in a few minutes." His harsh words assured her that he was by no means through with her. His smile had disappeared.

Jamey felt stupid. She should have known, she berated herself, should have guessed that Rue Garrett would never allow himself to be so perfunctorily dismissed. As irritated with herself for her own stupidity as she was with Rue for his high-handedness, she sat in tense silence, watching as he rejoined Mac and Reverend Brown and other members of the congregation who had gathered around and were greeting him as an old friend.

"Good afternoon, Jamey" came the soft voice from outside the car. As she turned to acknowledge the greeting, Jamey's frown became a smile as she saw that the owner of the gentle voice was Mrs. Townsend, a diminutive lady of uncertain age, probably somewhere in her seventies. She was a great favorite of Jamey's, always smiling and cheerful and full of kind words for everybody.

"Hello, Mrs. Townsend," she returned as she opened her car door and got out again, her anger dampened. "How are you today?"

"Oh, pleased," the old lady answered, "just so pleased to see young Rue Garrett back here today. It's been so long, and I know his grandparents have missed him," she went on, unraveling a little of the mystery for Jamey. "It's just too bad that they couldn't make it to church today, but, if I know Rue, he'll be stopping by to say hello to them. Always was a good boy, that one."

"Oh, do you know him well, Mrs. Townsend?" Jamey asked, intent now on gleaning as much information as she could from this unexpected source. The thought of Rue as a small boy was an intriguing one that brought a smile to her lips.

"Yes, heavens," Mrs. Townsend offered cheerfully, "watched him grow up, did my Robert and me. He'd come out for a visit with his parents, and what a little rascal he was—always into something! Why, I can still remember Bonnie's tales of the scrapes he'd get himself into, playing with his brothers over at the cabin and down by the creek." She stopped suddenly, peering at Jamey through crystal-clear eyes that spoke of the happy years she had spent here, the twinkle in her eyes growing as she measured the confusion that caused Jamey's eyes to widen. "Why, Jamey, didn't you know that Tom and Bonnie Martin are his grand-parents?'' she quizzed, naming Jamey's landlord and his wife. ''And that he grew up playing in your little cabin?''

She laughed, a merry tinkle, at the surprise on Jamey's face. ''No, I can see you didn't. You must not know him well yourself yet, or you would have known that. How he loved that cabin when he was a little boy!''

They both turned to find the object of their conversation, and Jamey tensed as she picked him out, alone in earnest conversation with Mac. The thought that he was now trying to play some very adult games at the little cabin and down by the creek had entered her mind, but was driven out as her concern grew to enormous proportions. What could he be saying to Mac? She barely heard Mrs. Townsend's parting words, which had something to do with feeling badly for Mac and expecting that she would be getting to know Rue Garrett *very* well if his behavior that morning was anything to judge by.

As Rue broke away from Mac and headed back toward her, the two men apparently parting on less than friendly terms, Jamey scrambled back into her car. It might offer little protection from him, but she would have taken any help she could get at that moment! She watched helplessly as Mac too took a step in her direction, then changed his mind and strode briskly toward his own car.

''Don't ever try to do that to me again, Jamey!'' Rue ground the words out as he came to a halt by the driver's side window. ''Otherwise, I'll quit trying to understand whatever it is that makes you so afraid of me, and prove to you once and for all just what's going on between us.'' The threat left her speechless, and she stared at him warily as he ordered, ''Now drive back to the cabin. I'll follow you and pick you up there. And

don't try any more tricks today, or so help me, I'll
make you regret it!" Leaning through the window to
slip the key into the ignition, he laughed scornfully as
Jamey hastily shifted as far away from him as the small
car would allow. Without another word, he turned and
was gone.

She was shaking so hard she could barely get the car
into gear to send it forward as Rue pulled up behind her
in the blue Mercedes she had parked beside that afternoon in Nashville. The irrational thought that watching
for his brown and gold truck this morning had done her
no good skipped through her mind and flew out the
window as she glanced in her rearview mirror. Jamey
caught Rue's grin as her car jerked into movement, and
anger rose anew that he was enjoying her discomfort.
But even her anger wasn't enough to make her test the
limits of his patience any further. Something in the
tone of his voice had made her believe that he meant
every word of his threat, and she was taking no
chances. During the short drive back to the cabin, she
focused all her attention on operating the car, too
shaken to even *want* to think of what form Rue's retribution might take.

"I'll just go and change into something more casual," she called nervously as she jumped from her car
and practically ran toward the cabin.

"No," he ordered from his own car, halting her
movement. "I like you just the way you are, and we
have somewhere to go. Get in," he finished, swinging
the door on the passenger side open.

Seated in the low-slung Mercedes, Jamey still felt
threatened by Rue, but not so threatened that she
couldn't appreciate the luxury of the vehicle they were
riding in. The black leather upholstery was rich to her
touch, the dash panel like something out of a sleek air-
liner. "Nice car," she said softly, hoping to appease his
anger. "What did you do with the truck?"

"Left it at home," he bit out, not appeased. "Why did you leave before I got here this morning?" he asked, swiveling her a glance that said he intended to have an answer.

Nervously she looked away from him, her eyes registering but not really seeing the countryside as they passed swiftly by. "Because I don't like to be ordered around...and because you're moving too fast for me," she responded honestly.

"Okay, I can accept that," he said reasonably, recognizing the depth of honesty in her simple reply. "But I can't, and *won't,* accept your not being there when I tell you I'll be over!" he added, the anger returning to his voice as he remembered the surprise that had turned so quickly to anger and then grudging admiration when he had realized that she had actually defied him, had stood him up. It was unlikely, he thought, that he would ever admit that grudging admiration to her.

Jamey had taken enough. No man had ever treated her so firmly or spoken to her so sharply. No man had ever been given the chance, though there were those who had tried, but she didn't think about that. Just as angry now as Rue, she retorted, "Then listen to me! I told you no! Did you think I was kidding?" she asked, her cryptic tones matching his.

"Yeah, I guess I did. And you should have been! Good God, Jamey, I'm not trying to tie you up and haul you away. I just want to spend some time with you."

"Then let me help choose the time, Rue," she pleaded, her anger quickly diminishing as she accepted his reasonable argument. About to ask what he would have done if she had already made plans to spend the afternoon with Mac, she stopped cold at the memory of seeing the two of them in earnest conversation, at the realization that she had been so concerned about Rue's reaction to her behavior that she'd forgotten all about the other man. "What did you say to Mac at the church?" she asked suspiciously, long dark lashes falling over brown eyes that suddenly flared in confusion.

He laughed at her change of mood. "We just had a man-to-man talk, nothing for you to worry about," he tossed out as he maneuvered the car into a long, familiar driveway. Stating the obvious, he changed the subject. "We're having dinner with my grandparents. I saw you talking with Mrs. Townsend, so I don't imagine you're still in the dark about my ties to this area."

"No," she answered quietly, forgetting for the moment that his response to her question had been far from satisfactory. "But why didn't you tell me yesterday? I thought it seemed kind of odd that you should know so much about the property and that you were so interested in the cabin, but it never occurred to me that it was because you had lived here."

"Oh, I didn't live here, just spent a lot of time visiting." Glancing over at her, he confessed, "But I wanted to live here. What kid wouldn't choose this over the city?" he asked wistfully, his arm making a sweeping arc as he indicated the lush expanse of land around them. "I'd still choose it, and one day soon I'll make that preference a reality."

Jamey had to agree with his sentiments, and for the first time since he had walked into the church that morning, began to feel at ease in his presence. She pressed for the answer to his secrecy. "Why didn't you tell me?"

Rue's eyes were warm as he shifted his attention to her face, his gaze feasting on the soft beauty of doe-brown eyes and slightly parted lips. "My only reason for not telling you was that I wanted to delay the added pressure of your knowing that you were already somewhat involved with my family. I simply didn't think you were ready for that knowledge yet," he affirmed solemnly.

Jamey's gaze dropped quickly away from Rue's, her mind rejecting the warmth reaching out to her through his gently spoken words. She was spared the need to respond as the farmhouse came into view before them.

Tom and Bonnie Martin rose from their positions in the two rocking chairs that graced the porch of the old farmhouse as Rue brought the car to a stop. Hand-in-hand, they descended the steps as Rue rounded the car, calling a greeting to them as he opened Jamey's door.

The rightness of the white-haired couple, the sheer permanency represented by their age and by the two-storied homestead that provided the backdrop for the joys and sorrows of the years they had gladly given one another, temporarily dazzled Jamey. She stepped from the car, bewildered by the mental picture of another elderly couple—she and Rue—greeting progeny removed by time, but firmly tied by blood and love.

"Howdy, son! It sure is good to see you!" Tom Martin beamed, clapping his grandson on the shoulder and grasping his hand in a firm handshake. "And with our little Jamey," he added, turning to include her in his greeting with an affectionate smile. His welcome interrupted her mental foray into the uncharted territory of love and the endless commitment it demanded.

Bonnie Martin was close behind her husband, waiting her turn to say hello to her grandson. Rue turned and swept her off her feet in a hug as he twirled her around. "How's my girl?" he teased, kissing her cheek.

"Happy to see her young man," she bantered back, but the tears dampening the corners of her eyes were evidence of deep emotion as she clung to him. He swung her to the ground and she clasped Jamey's hand with a little squeeze. "And with a young woman of his own!" she bubbled, beaming at Jamey.

"Well, didn't I tell the both of you that we should be

getting young Rue out here to meet Jamey?'' Tom
Martin quizzed, shooting them both an I-told-you-so
look. "But you wouldn't have it! No, you said to me,
just leave things alone, Tom. The Lord takes care of
those things, you told me," he sermonized. "Well, I
guess you were right, but it sure could've happened a
lot sooner if you two had listened to me," he grumbled
in an undertone.

"Now, no matter, Tom. You were right, as usual,"
Bonnie interrupted, consoling him. "We can't stand
here in the yard all day," she said to all of them, "so
let's go up on the porch and have a little natter before
dinnertime. I want to know everything you've been doing since you were last out to see us, Rue," she
ordered, taking note of Rue's amused expression at the
consternation written on Jamey's face.

Jamey remembered well the numerous times Tom
Martin had suggested introducing her to his grandson.
She also remembered her laughing rejection of the idea
as she had pleaded that she was far too busy to let herself become involved with any man. At the time, Tom
Martin had snorted indignantly at her response, in-
forming her that she would soon change her tune if she
met *his* grandson.

The older couple resumed their places in the rocking
chairs, leaving Jamey and Rue to sit together in the
porch swing that hung from the sturdy rafters. Casually
placing his arm around her shoulders as he set the
swing into motion, Rue launched into conversation
with his grandparents. Jamey squirmed a bit at the intimate gesture, which was sure to leave his grandparents
with the wrong impression of their relationship, she
thought. It was beginning to look as though everyone
was getting in on this act, trying his hand at matchmaking. First Reverend Brown with his prodigal son comment, then Mrs. Townsend's parting prophecy, and
now Rue's grandparents, who just happened to be her

landlords and nearest neighbors. And Mac! Even Mac had contributed to this mess, she thought, by giving in to whatever Rue had said to him earlier. She was in no mood to be fair, to admit that Rue had possessed the winning hand in that confrontation simply by dent of having believed he had a date with her.

How convenient for him, she thought caustically. But remembering that Rue still had no idea that she would be leaving in a few weeks—and she had no intention of telling him yet—she smiled a private smile and focused her attention on the talk flowing around her.

Rue was telling tales of being on the road, and of the things that happened in the recording studio. Listening, Jamey was surprised at his ability to laugh at himself and his experiences, and at how easily he could make her laugh. This was a whole new side to Rue Garrett, a side that showed her that though he hoped to have some influence on the world through the medium of his music, he refused to take himself too seriously. He enjoyed life, took great pleasure in the simple living of it. And in so doing, he brought as much joy to the few who knew him well as he gave to the many who knew him only through his music.

"We were just swinging into the final number of our Atlanta concert," he was saying, referring to Mississippi River's most recent road trip, "when Randy's son came toddling right out on the stage and, in his determination to get to his dad, went through the drums instead of around them." Rue wiped a mirthful tear from under his eye before continuing. "Sue—that's Randy's wife," he explained to Jamey, "saw what was happening and tried to call Tad back, but it only scared him and when he jumped, so did his dad's drums. And the whole world came crashing down...or at least it sounded like it had," he said, bursting into gales of laughter again at the memory. "Randy reached for Tad, and both of them ended up in the middle of a heap of clanging percussion equipment, with Tad screaming to beat the band—right in the middle of that stage in that huge auditorium!''

Tom Martin, laughing so hard he was nearly crying, slapped his knee and squawked. ''What'd you do, son?''

''What could I do?'' Rue asked, a sheepish grin stealing over his ruggedly handsome face as his laughter died down. ''Just made some off-the-wall comment about the quality show the fans were getting for their money, introduced Tad as a budding star, then returned him to his mortified mother while Randy and the rest of the guys set the drums back up so we could finish the show. We did a couple of extra numbers that night,'' he finished.

Talk turned then to various members of Rue's group and their families, and Jamey realized that Tom and Bonnie knew them all well and felt genuine affection for them. She, of course, had met the men who played in the band, though she hadn't met any of the support staff, but thought that she wouldn't even recognize any of the men she had met if they were to walk right up to her. She had been too absorbed by the perplexing feelings Rue had awakened in her on that day of Steve's audition. But listening, she was beginning to feel as though she knew them all very well.

Jamey was thoroughly relaxed by the time Bonnie Martin suggested having dinner, and she stood to go with her to the kitchen as naturally as though she had done it a thousand times before. As they moved through the screen door into a hallway that ran the length of the house, the men remained to continue their talk without their womenfolk.

''I'm so glad you and Rue finally did get to meet, Jamey,'' Bonnie started in as soon as they were out of earshot of the men. ''You just seem to be ideally suited to each other,'' she went on, ''and if the way Rue treats you and looks at you is any indication, he thinks so too," she added smugly.

"Mrs. Martin," Jamey said gently, not wanting to hurt the older woman's feelings, "Rue and I are just friends. We met because he's interested in a young man I'm working with at Tanasie Basin, the one I brought over to meet you a couple of weeks ago, and that's really the extent of it. Please don't go trying to do any match-making," she implored. "Your grandson is a fine person, and I'd hate to lose his friendship," she finished, thinking that her words were rather an understatement of her feelings for Rue. She had already known that there was a compelling physical attraction between them, but this visit with his grandparents had shown her a deeper side to his personality that had shaken her to the core. It would be so easy to fall in love with him if she would only let herself, she thought, but still she clung to the belief that career and love couldn't mix successfully.

"Well, we'll see," Bonnie Martin declared knowingly as she carried a plate heaped with fried catfish to the table that stood in the center of the large, high-ceilinged dining room. "Both of you are fine young people," she affirmed with a pat on Jamey's hand, pausing as she passed her on the return trip to the kitchen. The table was loaded with catfish, hushpuppies, fresh corn and collard greens from the garden, and a pitcher of iced tea when they called the men in to eat.

Jamey was sure she had never laughed so much in her life as she did during that Sunday afternoon dinner. Rue and his grandfather told one story after another, each trying to top the last one the other had told, until they were all spending more time laughing than eating. But surprisingly, there was little of the delicious meal left by the time they moved away from the table.

It had been Jamey's first taste of catfish and hush-puppies, and she had loved them, especially the hushpuppies, which were small, round fritters of deep-fried cornmeal. Her enthusiasm over the meal had prompted one last story from Tom, a tale about the one that *didn't* get away at the annual Catfish Derby on the Tennessee River at Savannah. Just how tall that tale was Jamey could only guess, rooting her sure thought that he was somehow having her on in the glimpse she caught of Bonnie's knowing smile and Rue's shout of laughter as his grandpa measured off a length from the tip of his nose to his fingertips. When he went on to explain, straight-faced, that catfish were so-named because of the catlike sounds they made when they were pulled from the water, Rue could stand it no longer.

"I've never seen a catfish that size at *this* house, Grandpa!" Rue's gibe made it sound as though Tom Martin's statements could be fact. Jamey gazed wide-eyed from Rue to his grandfather, trying hard to imagine a four-foot-long catfish. And making mewing sounds, on top of that! She had never heard of any fish, other than porpoises, that could make actual noises. It was the twinkle in Bonnie Martin's eyes, matched by her twitching lips as she struggled to hold back her laughter at Jamey's round-eyed wonder, that finally gave his game away.

"Catfish rarely get that big, Jamey," Rue laughed. "The kind we catch around here are channel cats, and a few do get quite large, but most are relatively small compared to that description. They're scaleless fish with whiskerlike feelers called barbels near their mouths, and they certainly don't mew like cats! They're called catfish because of their whiskers."

Bonnie Martin laughingly informed Jamey that she would have to get used to the teasing banter that went on whenever Rue and his grandfather got together. "They never let up," she told her.

Jamey joined in the laughter at her gullible near-acceptance of the tale, stating firmly that she was sure she never wanted to eat *any* fish that could talk to her. Her statement brought another hoot of laughter from her companions.

The rest of the evening passed quickly, spent in relaxed conversation, until it was ten o'clock and time for Rue and Jamey to leave, he told them regretfully. But he promised he would be back to see them again soon. "After all, it follows that if I can't stay away from Jamey, I certainly won't be able to avoid coming over here to swap stories with this old codger," he gibed, chuckling at Jamey's blush, and the blustering swagger his grandfather gave as he challenged him to a tall-tale contest any time the young whippersnapper thought he was up to it.

"Oh, I do like your grandparents, Rue," Jamey said with a smile as they drove away.

"I'm glad," he returned. "They like you too. In fact, I'd say they were intent on doing a little matchmaking, wouldn't you?" he asked, transferring his gaze from the road to her face. His eyes seemed darker in the moonlight and he watched her closely as he added, "Not that they need to. I think we're doing just fine on our own."

"Rue, will you quit that?" Jamey implored, her tone treating his remarks as light banter. "I told your grandmother how we met, and the truth about our relationship, which I'm sure she'll tell your grandfather. So now that that's out of the way, you can just quit deviling me!"

"Ahhh, my pretty," he drawled, twirling an imaginary mustache, "but you don't know what I had to say to my grandpa while you womenfolk were in the kitchen... or what advice he gave me," he added in mock-mystery as he turned into the drive to Jamey's cabin.

Laughing, Jamey pretended to be the victim in his melodrama. "Oh, Mr. Villain, please tell me," she beseeched in her best Little Nell imitation, "for I shan't be able to sleep a wink till I've found the solution to my dilemma!"

"Never, my beauty!" he roared. "You'll not escape my plans for you!" he went on fiendishly, turning toward her with his eyebrows drawn down threateningly.

His expression was so mock-menacing, and so uncharacteristic of Rue, that Jamey burst into peels of riotous laughter. Her mirth was infectious, and his fierce visage became a wide grin as he joined in her laughter.

They laughed at their little production all the way into the cabin, where Jamey put on a pot of coffee before moving across the room to seat herself beside him on the couch. Somehow, the time they had spent together had changed their relationship. Jamey trusted him now, and sitting near him felt natural and right. How could she not be comfortable with someone who made her laugh so easily?

Rue turned to look into her eyes, and Jamey thought he was going to pull her into his arms. She was almost leaning toward him in an attitude of submission when he moved away from her and stood up, leaving her alone on the couch. Disappointment washed over her as she realized how badly she had wanted him to hold her, to kiss her and make her forget for a moment that their professional worlds were poles apart.

"Jamey, I have to go away tomorrow."

His words hit her hard, stunned her. They were so unexpected, coming on the heels of her thoughts about their careers. She opened her mouth to speak, but no words came out.

"The band is scheduled to appear in a country music special that's being filmed in Las Vegas, and I'm one of the hosts for the show," he explained. "We're supposed to finish and fly back to Nashville by next Friday, and I'd like to see you then," he said softly from his position several feet away from her. "Okay?"

Speech returned. "Okay," she agreed quietly, her

gaze locked with his. "If you like, I'll cook dinner for us here." Rue nodded his acceptance.

Jamey felt as though she had been doused with cold water, and a little shiver shook her. That his job was one that frequently took him off to new and exciting places she had known, but she hadn't expected to be confronted with it quite this soon. Not when they were just becoming comfortable with each other.

It made it clearer than ever to her that they had met at the wrong time in both of their lives, for her career demanded that she travel quite a bit too. She forced a smile to her lips, trying to hide the tiny tremors that threatened to give away her distress, as she moved to the kitchen and poured two cups of coffee. They talked in lowered voices as they drank, neither confessing what was really in their minds, and Rue stood up to leave as he finished his coffee.

"I better get on the road if I'm going to get enough rest tonight to be ready for a day of travel tomorrow," he said, and Jamey walked with him to the door. Leaning down to press a gentle kiss against her lips, a kiss that held no hint of the passion they had shared before, he whispered that he would be at the cabin about seven the following Friday night. Then he was out the door and gone.

Jamey slumped dejectedly into the overstuffed chair as she listened to the sound of his car driving away. Her fingertips lightly caressed the lips that had so recently felt the touch of his. Pain seared through her at the thought of not seeing him for five full days...and nights. And then another pain made a bid for her attention—the thought that she had given her heart too quickly, too quickly on two counts. She had known Rue Garrett for only three days, surely not enough time to justify the powerful feelings that raged within her; certainly not long enough to justify her questioning of the worth of her carefully plotted career goals.

Chapter Five

"They say absence makes the heart grow fonder, Jamey," Mac teased sarcastically. His half-bitter words dragged her back from yet another mental review of all that had passed between her and Rue since their first meeting such a few short days ago. Sardonic amusement flickered over the familiar features of his face as he eyed her lunch tray, and Jamey looked down with dismay at the odd assortment of foods she had loaded onto it.

Absence was the operative word, she thought peevishly. Rue had so disrupted her customary composure that even the most ordinary of tasks became troublesome. But she didn't know who "they" were to make such sweeping dictates about how she, or anyone else, for that matter, was supposed to feel. The omniscient "they." The thought went unvoiced as she made a conscious effort to expel the image of Rue that had plagued her since his departure two nights before. It didn't seem possible that today was only Tuesday, or that Tuesday could ever have seemed so far from Friday, going either forward or backward in time.

Jamey added a carton of milk to her tray and turned to make her way across the dining hall to one of the small round tables that littered the large room, coolly returning Mac's unpleasant banter. "They also say that absence makes the heart grow fonder...for someone else." Jamey could have bitten her tongue out for her carelessly spoken words as she watched Mac's eyes light up with renewed hope. That little error was further proof of how poorly she was coping, she thought. Damn! She wasn't coping at all, merely bungling clumsily along.

"In this case, for some*thing* else," she amended hastily. "I don't know how many times I have to repeat that my career comes ahead of everything else at this point in my life," she added, making sure that her point was understood.

Jamey walked away, annoyed at the exchange with Mac and at herself for allowing Rue to have such a devastating impact on her life. *Careers are not made in heaven, they're individually determined and pursued,* she reminded herself grimly. She had heard those words so often as she was growing up. Her mother had printed them indelibly in her conscience.

And now? Now thoughts of a handsome, virile man impinged, making it nearly impossible for her to focus on anything other than the thought that she would see him again in three days. Her distraction was showing in her work, and in her responses to those around her, especially Mac.

Mac's attitude toward her when she had arrived at Tanasie Basin for work the day before had surprised her. His behavior could only have been described as marginally antagonistic. In public, there had been the usual polite queries as to how her weekend had gone; in private, he had probed deeper, his questions making it apparent that his opinion of Rue Garrett hadn't changed one whit, unless it was for the worse. She could still hear the words he had snapped at her.

"Look, Jamey," he had growled brusquely, "I've already tried to warn you once, but you apparently didn't listen. The man is dangerous, and he's only going to hurt you if you let him get any closer."

Confused by the intensity of Mac's warning, Jamey had forgotten her usual reserve for a moment. "How can you know that, Mac? I'm not some foolish little schoolgirl who gets hurt by every passing Lothario!"

"I'm sure you're not," he had responded smartly, "but you're the one who chose the word Lothario. I want you to remember that later, when you're hurting, because it's a far better description of Rue Garrett than I could have come up with on such short notice."

Mac's words had dredged up the fears she had tried to hide from herself. The memory of the two men immersed in contentious conversation had sprung instantly to life, directing her response.

"What exactly are you talking about, Mac?" Jamey had asked quietly, her heart pounding painfully in her chest. "Did Rue say something to you yesterday that I should hear?"

"Obviously not," Mac had snapped, "since you didn't hear any of our *private* conversation." The stress he had placed on the privacy of his conversation with Rue had made it clear that he considered it to be none of her business.

Jamey had been amazed by the acid quality of his rebuff, by the obvious lack of trust and fellow-feeling Mac projected toward Rue. And from that inauspicious beginning to the week, they had descended to today's clash.

She looked up as Mac approached the table, confusion mirrored in her eyes as he seated himself beside her. She honestly hadn't expected him to react this way, especially after she had so carefully explained to him her career goals and her reasons for avoiding romantic entanglements. But she had overlooked ego, and Mac's had apparently been stung badly by what he seemed to view as her defection to the enemy camp.

"Look, Jamey, what you're feeling is nothing new," Mac said tiredly, no more satisfied with their previous encounter than she had been. "This old disease has been going around for centuries, and it attacks almost everybody at some time or another, but you're making a serious mistake if you think Rue Garrett is interested in anything more than a good time."

Jamey didn't respond. She tensed and kept her eyes fixed firmly on the tray of food in front of her, embarrassed that the subject was being pursued where other staff members might overhear. What she really wanted to do was to yell at him, yell that it didn't make an ounce of difference what Rue Garrett or anybody else was interested in! But it did. What Rue was interested in definitely made a difference. And Mac's vehemence that she was making a mistake, coupled with his refusal to tell her anything of their conversation at the church, frightened her terribly.

Ignoring her stiffened posture, Mac continued. "What you feel for Rue Garrett is strong, that much I'm sure of, and you aren't going to exorcise that particular devil by pleading that your career comes first—either to yourself or to him. Take a look—"

"Stop it!" Jamey hissed the words at him.

Mac was taken aback by the intensity of emotion that flared in her eyes, making them darker than ever. But he was no fool. He backed away from the topic, though irritation at her sharp words was rapidly taking over where any kinder feelings left off. He had been going to tell her to take a look at the evidence that proved the truth of what he had been saying—the evidence of her own preoccupation, as well as that of the widespread knowledge that few entertainers had stable love lives— and to invite her to dinner. He turned back to his meal instead, his thoughts returning to the conversation he had shared with Rue Garrett.

The man was straightforward, he admitted to himself, honest and intent in his direct approach. When they had talked on Sunday, Rue had quickly shown himself to be a man who believed in plain speaking. He had made it clear that his plans for that day included Jamey, and that Mac's interference wouldn't be appreciated. Mac had recognized the determination of a man who had decided what he wanted—at least temporarily, he told himself smugly—and that he would have it. But he still didn't trust the man. Didn't trust him and didn't like him.

"Jamey?" Mac's tone was filled with concern as he tried again to draw her out, to press his point home. "You don't have to put yourself through this, you know. He can't force his attentions on you."

Again she was yanked back from thoughts of Rue, thoughts that bore no resemblance to what Mac suggested. The man had no right to dominate her mind, she thought irrationally. Anger shortened her tone as she looked up and snapped, "Right! And then what happens to Steve when I tell him to get lost?" she asked caustically.

Irritation flared in Mac's eyes at her terse response. "I'll see you in my office as soon as you finish your lunch," he ordered, the words that had been in his mind lost to her insubordination.

Jamey had regretted her sharpness of tone immediately, as well as her use of the one excuse she had promised herself she'd never rely on. But she remained undaunted in her belief that Mac had no right to interfere in her private life. It didn't matter that his concern was genuine, that only a few days earlier he had still hoped she might be interested in him. She had never granted him right or reason to believe any such thing, she assured herself.

"For professional or personal reasons?" she asked in a tone that she hoped sounded more like her normal, calm voice.

"Professional," Mac retorted, not giving an inch. His administrative capabilities were evident in his demeanor, and Jamey reluctantly acknowledged his right to call her on the carpet for her behavior as he stood and left the dining hall without a backward glance. He had given an order. It would be followed.

Jamey pushed the food around on her plate for another five minutes before admitting to herself that she wasn't hungry, wasn't going to eat. She had eaten little since Rue left.

Damn him! There he was back again, Jamey thought, as she pushed away from the table and headed resolutely for Mac's office. Might as well get this over with and try to force herself back into concentrating on her job.

Jamey tapped at Mac's office door and entered at his barked order to come in. Never one to avoid admitting her mistakes, she apologized immediately. "I'm sorry, Mac. I know I haven't been myself these past two days, and that what I said a few minutes ago was inexcusable, but I want you to know that this is where it ends. That's a promise," she added, and meant it. One way or another, she *would* exorcise Rue Garrett from her mind.

Mac's eyes softened at her quickly voiced apology. She made it impossible for him to stay angry with her for very long. "No, you haven't, have you, Jamey? But then, neither have I," he proclaimed softly. "Anyway...apology accepted," he said, smiling, though he didn't see how she could possibly live up to her promise. "How are you coming along with the contract agreement?" he asked, his words abetting her efforts to center her attention on work-related matters.

Reluctant to admit to him that she had made little headway on the document, she evaded his question by establishing a deadline for the project. "It's coming along fairly well. I'll have it on your desk by tomorrow afternoon."

They both knew that under normal circumstances, she would have completed the contract that spelled out the division of responsibilities between institution and school staff by the end of the day. But circumstances weren't normal, so concessions were silently made.

Jamey smiled, grateful that he had left Rue out of the conversation for once. "I should get back to work now. There's a lot yet to be done." She knew that her apology hadn't really cleared the air between them, but she simply wasn't up to giving him an explanation of her feelings. She wanted them to go away.

"Right," Mac responded. But as she left his office he reflected on the words he had left unspoken. The war between Jamey and Rue was on, and he knew it, just as he now knew that he could have little impact on its outcome. The battle lines had been drawn, and his only satisfaction was that he was no longer certain that Rue Garrett would have such an easy time winning. Some of the battles, maybe...probably! But the whole war? Jamey was a very determined young woman. That Rue was also strong-minded and determined he acknowledged, but the pain of the skirmishes and battles was far from over. It would be an interesting clash of wit and will, a clash he fervently hoped the singer would lose.

Back in her office, Jamey worked painstakingly at completing the contract she and Mac had discussed. She was surprisingly successful at forcing thoughts of Rue from her mind as she bent to her task. By the end of the day she was pleased to note that she had made substantial progress on the project.

She was toying with the idea of staying late and finishing the contract when someone knocked on her office door. She glanced quickly over her draft of the section relating to the provision and maintenance of appropriate school facilities before inviting the caller to enter, using the moment also to quell her irritation at being interrupted just when her work was going along smoothly.

"Hi," Meg said pleasantly as she opened the door and peeked her head through at Jamey's bidding. "Planning on working late tonight?"

"Well, I hadn't originally planned to, but. ..." Jamey left the sentence open-ended, allowing the mass of paperwork scattered across her desk to speak for itself. "Anyway, hi, yourself," she continued, leaning back in her chair with a relaxed smile. "What brings you here today?" she asked, suddenly aware that she was genuinely pleased to see Meg, didn't resent the interruption at all.

"I thought I'd take Mac up on his suggestion that I start getting settled in," Meg responded with a little laugh, "so I've spent the last hour grilling him about the ins and outs of life at Tanasie Basin ... and passing along the message that Damon is alive and well in Phoenix. But back to your plans, Jamey. All work and no play?" she teased, grinning. "There's one sure thing about paperwork. What you don't get done today will still be there tomorrow. And Mac thought it might be fun for the three of us to drive into Nashville for dinner and to sample a bit of the nightlife," she added in a compelling tone.

"No, I'd really rather not go, Meg," Jamey answered quickly. She wasn't encouraging Mac any further, she thought. Nor was she going to subject herself to more of his diatribe against Rue. She'd already decided that the wisest thing she could do was forget him. And listening to Mac's maligning comments, when they only made her blood boil with the desire to rush to his defense, wouldn't help at all. "I'm awfully tired," she added, realizing that she'd given Meg no reason for her hasty refusal. "But you and Mac go ahead," she suggested. "It sounds like fun."

Meg had grown strangely quiet as Jamey responded to the invitation, and Jamey wondered what the other woman was thinking.

"I'll have to see what Mac says," Meg answered softly, slipping a bright red curl behind her ear as she spoke. "Are you sure you won't change your mind, Jamey? Mac's going to be disappointed."

"I'm sure." Jamey's tone was firm. She couldn't be certain, but the way Meg was looking at her, it almost seemed she was seeking the answer to some question she was reluctant to voice. She also seemed oddly satisfied by Jamey's refusal—not in any insulting way, but satisfied all the same.

The look was there for only an instant before Meg changed the subject. "What's happening between Steve and Rue Garrett?" she asked.

Again Jamey answered quickly. "Not much at this point. Steve knows now what his options are," she said, enumerating them briefly, "so it's a simple matter of his making a decision. We really don't know much more now than we knew Friday night," she added. "And speaking of Friday night," she continued, using her comment to avoid any further conversation that might involve Rue, "tell me more about Damon's 'alive and well' status."

Her ploy worked. Meg launched into a repeat of Damon's description of Arizona's incredibly dry heat and terrain that was starkly beautiful in its own barren way.

"Mmm, I know," Jamey agreed consideringly. "I was in Phoenix last summer, and I remember how surprised I was to find the heat almost comfortable and the countryside amazingly appealing in its barrenness. What I remember most vividly, though, are the incredible sunsets, with a red glow outlining naked hills." She closed her eyes as though she would see again the scene she described.

"You know," Meg said softly, "you and Damon almost make me jealous of all the travel your work involves. I haven't traveled much yet, haven't really had much of an urge to go to faraway places, but both of

you make it sound so interesting that I'm tempted."
Meg was quiet for a moment before adding, "But I'm
really more of a homebody, I guess, and if I had a job
that kept me on the move, I'd see even less of Damon
than I do now."

The soft sincerity of Meg's words tugged at Jamey's
heart and she opened her eyes to gaze intently at her
new friend. "You and Damon are really very close,
aren't you?"

"Very," Meg confirmed. "He's always been protective of me. Still is," she added with a wry smile, "even
when I'm not sure I want his protection. But that's
probably because our dad died when Damon was four-
teen, leaving him to become the 'man of the family' at
an awfully early age. Damon handled the responsibility
well, though," she went on. "He managed to take care
of Mother and to help her get me through my gawky
teen years without too many problems. And now that
he's away from Tennessee so much of the time, we
really miss him, but we're awfully proud of him."

Jamey smiled. "I can see that every time you mention him. Your love for him shines through, and I'm a
little envious of that, I think," she confessed, surprised
by the twinge of envy she was experiencing. "I don't
think I've ever felt as close to anyone—not even my
sister—as you seem to feel with Damon."

"You will someday," Meg answered softly. "Someday soon, maybe."

Jamey's low laugh was intended to break the intensity of the moment, a moment that thoughts of Rue
had made suddenly uncomfortable. "I think I might
enjoy that," she said lightly.

When Meg finally left her office, after one last repeat
of Mac's invitation and one more refusal, Jamey
turned back to the contract. But her mind kept straying
to thoughts of a long, hot shower, to the temptation of
spending a relaxing evening...alone. She realized then

that her excuse to Meg had been true. She really was
tired. The emotional turmoil of the past few days had
taken its physical toll, had weakened her defenses, and
she needed time alone to renew her perspective and rid
herself of her infatuation with Rue Garrett. Jamey
straightened her desk, leaving the folder of papers she
had been working on in priority position for her attention tomorrow morning, then left the building.

At home, the tiny cabin with all its familiar comforts
provided reassurance. Jamey lingered in the shower,
letting the warmth of the rejuvenating spray of water
ease away her tension before slipping into a pair of terry
cloth shorts and matching T-shirt.

Halfway through her dinner preparations, the silence
grew loud in her ears. She moved across the room to
turn the radio on, then opted instead for recorded music. Jamey deliberately avoided any music that would
remind her of Rue, skipping over the selection of country music cassettes that she had listened to so much of
late to let her eyes rove the classical music segment of
her tape library.

Tchaikovsky. She removed the cassette from its case
and slipped it into the tape deck, reveling in her freedom as the strains of music filled the cabin and lifted
her spirits, giving her a renewed sense of purpose. She
moved gracefully to the tempo of the music, swaying
gently as she shredded lettuce for a shrimp salad.

Dinner completed, she selected a book and settled
down to read, lounging full-length on the couch. She
was bent on avoiding thoughts of Rue, resolute in her
determination to set her memories aside. He had dominated her thoughts enough these past few days, and she
meant to put an end to it.

The novel was a good one, a well-written account of
the conflict between a husband and wife who had separated and were contemplating divorce, and the impact
of their actions and reactions on their only child. Dis-

tracted by the desire to rewrite the words before her, to have the couple settle their differences and mend their broken relationship, she was stunned to discover that the characters in the book had been superimposed in her mind's eye with the physical traits of Rue and herself, the child a precious blending of the two of them. Their pain became hers, and she recoiled from the agony of the scene she had conjured up. But surely the picture was accurate, and any liaison between her and Rue could only result in a similar plight.

No amount of effort could alter the very real images that now stood between Jamey and the neatly printed pages. She welcomed the intrusion of the telephone ringing her away from her uncomfortable thoughts.

"Hello." Jamey's voice was low, husky, a product of the hurtful fantasy that had captured her imagination.

"Jamey, are you all right?" Rue's voice shot anxiously across the wires to her. From more than two thousand miles away, he registered her pain and sought to ease the hurt, unaware that he was the root of it.

"What? Oh, oh, yes, I'm fine," she lied, her voice still not fully under control, her preoccupation apparent in her stammered reply.

"You don't sound fine. What's going on?" His words were clipped, quickly spoken.

Jamey struggled to still the hammering pulse that had accelerated at the sound of his voice. Thoughts reeled through her mind as she fought for composure. "N-nothing. I was just taking a nap when you called, and I'm not completely awake yet," she fabricated.

Rue hesitated, but accepted her explanation. He didn't know her well enough yet to realize that Jamey rarely took naps. She had no need to. She had always slept like a baby at night, waking the next morning with more than enough energy to carry her through a busy day and evening.

"Were you dreaming of me?"

His voice had dropped to a low, seductive pitch that robbed her of the will to resist the image of his lean, hard lines. Her heartbeats increased again as his features swam before her eyes, and she sagged against the wall, needing its support. *Thank God he's not here,* she thought.

Jamey was caught between fantasy and reality, and the grim fantasy that revolved around the novel she had been reading offered the only straw she could grasp. There could be nothing between her and Rue. Such a love could only be destructive for both of them.

Laughing softly at her lack of response, Rue picked up the threads of the loosely knit conversation. "You must have been in a deep sleep, Jamey. You're still not with me. I'll let you get back to your nap as long as you promise to dream of me, but I wanted to let you know that things are going according to schedule here and that I'll definitely see you by seven Friday night."

"Okay," she answered numbly, relieved that he had so readily accepted her small deception.

His voice was gentle as he ended the brief call. "I'll be dreaming of you.... I miss you, Jamey." The line went dead before Jamey could say anything in response to his tender words.

She replaced the receiver slowly, turning to gaze blankly at the darkness beyond the window. Dear Lord, what was going on? How had she got into this predicament and, more importantly, how was she going to get out of it?

There seemed to be no rational answer to the question as Jamey paced restlessly back across the small room, her book forgotten. She sank into the comfort of the overstuffed chair, aware that it had been the scene of so much soul-searching of late, but still seeking revelation as she picked idly at the tan Herculon upholstery. She was caught in a whirling vortex of thought that niggled at her relentlessly.

It was time to face facts. Rue Garrett had rarely been

out of her thoughts since she had met him, and certainly not since he had left her Sunday night. She was obsessed with him! And he showed no sign that he might back off and give her time to come to grips with her obsession. If this continued, she thought, she would be lost.

Her thoughts were a jumbled mixture of Rue, her career, her mother, and, on the edges of it all, images of a small face that bore an astonishing resemblance to both Jamey Marsh and Rue Garrett. No! She rejected the images. She wasn't ready for that yet!

Out of her confusion, one thought grabbed at her attention. Rue was still unaware that she was on a temporary contract. Rationalizing away the feelings of guilt and cowardice at the plan that was rapidly developing in her mind, she resolved that he wouldn't find out. And that she would work all the hours necessary in order to leave Tennessee before it was too late for her to salvage anything of her already bleeding heart. If she redoubled her efforts, she could probably complete the requirements of her contract with Tanasie Basin within four weeks, instead of the more reasonable pace she had set for herself when she had planned to return to Oregon in six weeks time.

JAMEY was disgusted, and more tired than ever. Despite her determination and the fact that she had never suffered from insomnia in her life, she had slept poorly these last two nights, tossing and turning as she had sought to put thoughts of Rue and his reaction to her impending departure out of her mind. But like a caldron with contents not quite ready to boil, her watchfulness over her thoughts had merely delayed her success at preventing them. And even when exhaustion had at last rendered her unconscious, she had awakened several times during the night, jolted out of sleep by the tenor of her dreams.

However tired she might be, though, she was still

intent on carrying out her plan. On Wednesday morning, hours before the deadline she had set, she had presented Mac with the completed contract agreement. The agreement had been approved, signed, and was now history as far as Jamey was concerned.

Job descriptions for each teacher were in place, as well as guidelines for evaluation of their performance. Textbooks and supplies had begun to arrive and had been organized quickly and efficiently by Meg, who appeared to have taken Mac's invitation to get an early start on settling in at Tanasie Basin very seriously. Jamey had been grateful for her help. It had freed her to focus on other tasks, tasks that were bringing her steadily closer to her goal.

Mac had been startled by her increased output at work, and had reminded her that there was no need for such haste. There was still more than a week to go before school began.

She had explained her dogged will to complete these technical tasks with the rationalization that she wanted the next week free for a review of all the policies and procedures that would assure the smooth operation of the school. Her statement had gained appeal as she had indicated the additional desire to set aside more time for working with Steve.

In truth, there was little left that she could do for Steve, other than to offer her continued support and encouragement. He was working on a new song, secure in the knowledge that Rue Garrett was willing to give him time to think through everything they had discussed before committing himself. He had also developed an irritating urge to tease Jamey about Rue, eager to test her attraction to his idol, and Jamey was fed up with the effort of laughing off his innuendos.

For a moment Jamey's concentration slipped again away from her work. A youthful face mocked her, an impish grin implying that her denials had been recognized as less than true.

"Come on, Jamey," Steve taunted in her mind's eye. "I bet you're just as ready for Mr. Garrett to come back from Las Vegas as I am. Aren't you?" His words had held a hint of suggestion, suggestion that had nothing to do with music and everything to do with a teenager's idealized notions about romance.

Jamey swallowed hard at the memory, just as she had at the time Steve had made his statements. "Mr. Garrett's return really doesn't affect me one way or the other, Steve," she had responded, conscious of her increased agitation as the youth's expression had revealed his disbelief. "All either of us is interested in at this point is helping you with your music," she had vowed...and tried to believe. She *knew* Steve hadn't believed.

Jamey was also aware that Mac hadn't fully believed her reasoning, but had chosen the path of least resistance in letting her have her own way. She wasn't aware that he had decided there was little he could do about it if she wanted to work herself into a coma. He was certain that somehow Rue Garrett was at the base of her sudden spurt of activity. Perhaps, he thought, this was simply Jamey's way of dealing with her uncertainty. It had never occurred to him that she was plotting a hasty retreat from Tennessee and Tanasie Basin and, most of all, from Rue Garrett.

IT WAS late Thursday afternoon when the first news reports made their way back across the nation from Las Vegas. There had been a major fire in the hotel and casino where the performers and film crew for the upcoming country music special, "Children of the Land," were staying. There was as yet no firm count of the dead and injured, though it was known that at least seven people had lost their lives in the blaze that had swept quickly through the open corridors and gambling areas of the luxurious resort.

Mercifully Jamey was working in her office, alone and unaware of the tragedy. Mac heard the report first from his secretary, who had burst into his office with tears streaming down her face as she stammered out what she had heard on the radio. It had taken him a full five minutes to calm the girl enough to get out of her that she had heard no news of Rue Garrett or any of the members of his band, but that her tears were purely a reaction to the knowledge that Rue was staying at the hotel and that *something* was going on between him and Jamey. Rumors had been running rampant through Tanasie Basin State School, though those who were talking had been careful not to do so when either Mac or Jamey were around to hear.

Mac listened to the news report himself, wanting to have as much information as was available before alerting Jamey. He took in the stunned tremor that shook the voice of the newsman on the scene. There was still no indication as to the whereabouts of Rue Garrett, but in an updated report it was announced that the other five members of Mississippi River had been located and had sustained no injuries. They had been standing in the lobby when the officials had begun to evacuate the building, and Rue had been standing with them, idly discussing some of the events of the day's filming. But none of them had seen him since they had left the building and regrouped in the drive that swept up to the front of the massive complex.

Mac quietly unplugged the radio and switched it over to battery power, the enmity he had felt toward Rue dulled by a feeling of guilt. But guilty or not of maligning the man out of jealousy and masculine pride, Jamey had to know, he told himself, and it would be better if she had someone with her to offer support when she heard the news. He issued instructions to his secretary, then left the administration building to cross the field to the school.

"Sit down, Jamey," Mac said gently as he entered her office and interrupted as she leafed through a file drawer.

Her eyes flew to his, the quiet order instantly seizing her attention, then widened with surprise as she took in the taut expression that pulled his pleasant features into a grim mask. Something was dreadfully wrong! That much was obvious, but Jamey couldn't imagine what it could be. She had never seen Mac so shaken.

"What is it, Mac? Has something happened to Emily?" Her voice was thick with concern as she grasped quickly at the only possible source she could conceive of that might cause him so much pain. Any number of accidents could happen at summer camp, no matter how many precautions were taken.

"No. Emily's fine, Jamey. Sit down." He repeated his previous order more firmly this time.

Jamey sank slowly into her office chair, fear beginning to creep into her mind as she noticed for the first time the radio tucked under his arm. Her gaze rested on the small beige box as he placed it on her desk without turning it on.

"There's been a fire, Jamey...at the hotel where Rue and the band are staying in Las Vegas."

Her heart leaped into her throat and she sat deathly still, staring at Mac, as the color drained from her face. Too calmly she questioned, "Are you trying to tell me that he's—"

"He's okay, Jamey!" Mac interrupted before she could voice his own fear. "I know he's okay! They've already located the other members of the band, and the reports indicate that Rue was with them when they left the building." He paused.

"Has anybody seen him, talked to him?" Her words came out in a harsh, rasping sound that grated on even her own ears.

"No, not yet, not since he left the building with the others," Mac answered gently. His hand moved to his forehead, the gesture implying weariness, yet his voice was firm with conviction as he continued. "But they will! It's not unusual for people to get separated, to get lost in the crowd in the midst of a tragedy like this." But, he silently questioned his own assurances, wasn't it unusual to lose track of a man as well known as Rue Garrett?

"Tragedy? What do you mean, tragedy?" Jamey clutched at the word as though it were a death knell. She reached for the radio, knocking it off her desk in her horror-induced clumsiness.

Mac caught it, replacing it on the desk as he repeated what he knew. "There are at least seven known dead, Jamey, but Rue is *not* one of them! We would know if he were!" He pressed the button, turning the radio on to let her hear the news for herself.

Jamey stood and paced the small office, her arms wrapped around herself as though she were trying to prevent some vile cold wind from robbing her of her own life. She wished she were alone. Mac's concern was understood, but she couldn't push the thought of his animosity toward Rue out of her mind, and all she really wanted was solitude. She shut him out as she acknowledged to herself the strength of her feelings for Rue, the depth of her pain.

The announcer's voice droned on with other news of the day. Jamey barely registered the words as she sought to insulate her abraded emotions, then snapped to attention as the phrase "late announcement from Las Vegas" penetrated her consciousness.

"There is still no word as to the whereabouts of one of the performers and one of the producers who were staying at this plush Las Vegas resort while filming a country music special that is scheduled to be aired in October of this year.'' The male voice calmly continued. ''The missing men are Rue Garrett, leader of the popular Mississippi River, and Mike Pettinger, a producer of the show. There have been no reports on Mr. Pettinger's location, but a number of eyewitnesses have reported seeing Rue Garrett. The most recent report indicates that Mr. Garrett left the building with other members of his band, but was later seen returning into the burning building.

''Emergency personnel are still working on the scene, searching for victims and treating survivors. There are seven known dead, while scores have been transported to local hospitals for treatment. We will continue to update this tragic event for you throughout the evening.''

Jamey turned away, the pain like a raw wound. Why had he gone back into the building? She shuddered as she faced the possibility of never receiving his smile again, nor seeing his gray-blue eyes alight with warmth and humor, of never again hearing his voice—not even to answer her pitiful ''Why?'' in search of explanation for her loss.

''Come on, Jamey. I'll take you home,'' Mac said softly.

''No, Mac. I'm okay.'' She stiffened away from him in rejection as he reached out to console her. There was no consolation.

Mac's arms fell helplessly to his sides as he remembered the pain of losing Barbara, the need to be alone at first to cope with his frustration and anger over his inability to save her. It had only been later, after he had worked those feelings through, that he had been able to accept the support offered by friends. Jamey had the same need. He needed no further proof that her feelings for Rue Garrett went far beyond mere physical attraction.

"All right," Mac acquiesced gracefully. "I'll walk you to your car and follow to make sure you get home okay." He lifted her purse and passed it to her as they turned and walked in silence from her office.

Jamey's movements as she started her car and pulled out of the parking lot were automatic. Her only conscious action was to press the button that brought the car's radio to life. She had to know....

Cruelly the gentle melody of "Rolling Water" wafted through the air. Rue's voice sang clear and strong. The disc jockey repeated the extraordinary news that Rue Garrett had not yet been located and was feared dead. The car swerved a bit as Jamey reacted to the first hint that those in authority now doubted that Rue had survived.

Mac's radio was also on, and he swore at the inhumanity inherent in man's preoccupation with tragedy and death. But he held firm to his conviction that Jamey would come through this with body and soul intact. She was a survivor.

Jamey was too numb to think in terms of her own survival as she entered the cabin. Her wounds were too new, memories of Rue too strong as they sprang at her from objects he had first seen and touched less than a week ago, from objects he'd known all his life. She fingered the leaves of a plant as though contact with another living thing might somehow help.

Nothing seemed real as she moved about the room, unconsciously touching, before finally coming to stop in front of the television. She would see him again, but she wasn't sure she wanted to—not in news clips that confirmed his death while he moved in living animation on the screen. She turned it on.

The phone rang at almost the same instant as her fingers left the button. Jamey came close to letting it ring, unanswered, as a picture of Rue flashed onto the television. But the thought that it might be Mac, who would almost certainly come over to assure himself that she was all right if she didn't answer, settled her choice.

She spoke abstractedly into the receiver, a portion of her mind still clinging to the brief glimpse of Rue she had caught as she turned to answer the phone. Now, why had they shown that picture? He had looked like a dirty little boy, grime smeared across his face, his shirt ragged and dirt covered.

"Jamey Marsh speaking," she answered formally, as though she were taking a call in her office.

"Jamey, this is Rue!" The deep timbre of the voice was painfully familiar. She swiveled back to look at the screen, clutching the receiver in shocked disbelief.

"Jamey!" The voice was urgent with demand.

"It c-can't be! You're dead...or on TV...." Her words trailed off, her head snapping back and forth from television to telephone, uncertain which to respond to first. The telephone won.

His laugh was deep, throaty, vibrant with life. "No, I'm very much alive! And very glad to be that way! If I'm on TV, it's a canned interview."

Jamey detected the strain that crept into his voice as he ended his proclamation. "Oh, Rue, what happened? They said you went back in, that you had probably died in the fire! Why?"

Rue knew instinctively what she was asking. What could be so important that he had risked his life for it?

"Need, Jamey...the craving to sustain life," he stated firmly. "I knew that some of the film crew were still working, and that unless someone went back in right then to get them, they would be trapped. I *had* to do it!"

As surely as his words were a statement of fact, a clear declaration of his love for life, they were also a plea for her understanding. Rue had known his risk, but had acted quickly to do what had to be done. He was seeking her forgiveness for risking what was growing between them. Without words, she gave it.

"Rue...." His name was merely a breath as Jamey struggled through the timeless void that melded terror and relief. "Thank God you're okay," she choked out as tears at last began to flow from her eyes. "Can you tell me what happened?"

"There's not much more to tell," he answered softly. "I didn't have much trouble getting back to where the film crew was working, but by the time we—Mike Pettinger and I—had rounded up the seven crew members and wet down some towels to hold over our noses, the entire hallway was a wall of flame." The ragged edges of his voice as he spoke belied his calm description. "A couple of the crew were disoriented by the thick smoke and took a wrong turn behind us—a dead end—so Mike moved back with them to keep everybody together while I retraced the path I'd taken to get in to them."

Jamey's sob as she imagined the horror of trying to move through a burning building to safety was buried by Rue's consoling words. But her mind filled with chilling images of men and women battling death, of some winning and some losing.

"The smoke was our biggest problem, actually," he went on, minimizing the dangers they had faced. "It got so thick so quickly that we had to spend most of our time crawling, trying to stay low where the air was a little clearer. But obviously we made it," he said lightly.

"Yes." The word felt inadequate, but it was all Jamey could manage at that moment. The lightness of Rue's tone, the too simple accounting of what he had been through, weren't enough to erase the reality that he and death had brushed closely against one another only a short time earlier. She gripped the receiver tightly, as though by holding it close she could somehow touch the man whose voice she'd feared she might never hear again.

Slowly, as Rue talked of wrapping things up in Las Vegas, Jamey's tension drained away. Relief became almost tangible, very nearly another living entity, as the shimmering, salty tears that slid silently down her cheeks became tears of joy as well as sorrow. Tears of joy that Rue and his colleagues had survived, and for her own release from the agonies of the last long hours; tears of sorrow for the seven or more who had lost their lives, for those who had loved them and were now left with only their memories.

Conversation became softer, more intimate. They spoke in muted tones, as though there was a need to shut out some unwanted listener. And though it didn't occur to Rue at the time, Jamey revealed far more of her feelings toward him in what she didn't say than in her delighted response to the news that he and the band still planned to return to Nashville the next day.

Chapter Six

Jamey stepped from the shower and reached for the large lime-green towel that hung from the wooden bar. She felt squeaky clean, and the water that still clung in tiny droplets to her slender body left her feeling deliciously cool for the first time in hours. The day had been blisteringly hot—hotter than normal for even the late-August Tennessee climate—and the humidity had reached a percentage level almost as high in number as the temperature that had climbed well beyond the ninety-five-degree mark on the thermometer. At least the temperature was beginning to drop, she thought gratefully as she patted at her glistening skin and wrapped the towel sarong-style around herself, tucking in the loose end to hold it in place.

She padded into her bedroom, where she let the towel fall away from her, enjoying the soothing feeling of the gentle breeze that stirred the air and blew softly across her bare, damp skin. The sensation was surprisingly sensual, and Jamey moved to stand before the full-length mirror that hung on the wall opposite the double bed.

She assessed the slim lines of her body and the small firm breasts that were reflected back at her. She had never really studied her body before, had never given it much thought beyond accepting that the whole of her appearance was generally pleasing to the male eye. She turned slightly, eyes and fingers seeking the small brown mole that dotted her hip just above the line where tan gave way to paler flesh. Suddenly it seemed important to her that the curves and valleys of her body be not merely pleasing, but compelling.

Pink tinged her cheeks as the wondering thought of whether Rue would think her body beautiful entered her mind, forcing her to acknowledge that she was looking forward to his touch. She was eager to know the feel of him as he took her in his arms and kissed her, his lips gently persuading. And he would be with her in little more than three hours time! Pink became crimson as she struggled to alter the path her wayward thoughts had taken.

"Stop it," she mouthed at the image in the mirror, the stranger who seemed to have invaded her body and mind. Brown eyes twinkled back at her with more than a hint of recalcitrant mischief. Jamey was no longer thinking of her need to hold Rue at bay, to keep him at a safe emotional distance. Yesterday's terrifying events had temporarily changed that.

A gentle smile tugged at the corners of Jamey's lips as she relived the moments they had spent on the phone and the pride she had felt later as she learned by watching the late news the full story of his reentry into the burning building. Rue had been less than honest with her in his account of his actions. He hadn't lied exactly; he simply hadn't told her the whole story. Jamey had felt no surprise at the discovery that he had left out some of the more gruesome parts, but had listened intently as those he had gone back in to save had filled in the blanks.

The fact of the matter was that there were at least eight people who owed their lives to Rue Garrett. He had risked his own life in order to alert them to the danger they were in, and had been very lucky to have led them all to safety, guided only by instinct and the strength of his will to survive. Chills rippled over her body as Jamey faced again the knowledge of all that Rue had risked. She turned from the mirror and moved gracefully to the small glass-topped dressing table.

Jamey lifted her comb and ran it restlessly through the lightly tangled mass of raven strands made darker by their dampness. The events of the past twenty-four hours were vivid in her memory. They tugged at her as relentlessly as she tugged at the tiny snarls in her hair, drawing her time and again away from the present. Her mind slid back in time to contemplate the happenings of her day.

The morning had been comparatively easy to get through. She had arrived at Tanasie Basin at her usual time, but had stayed there only half the day, taking the afternoon off with Mac's blessing. Really, she thought, she might as well have taken the entire day off, for all the work she had accomplished that morning. Most of her time had been spent fielding questions and responding to the elated congratulations of her colleagues. They had acted as though she had done something wonderful herself, implying a far stronger relationship than actually existed between Jamey and Rue. But she had been too happy to dampen their spirits, or her own, by correcting them.

Most important had been the time she had spent with Steve. He had run his young fingers through his summer-lightened blond hair countless times, his eyes bright blue with tears that didn't fall, but that he didn't try to hide.

"Oh, God! I thought I was going to die," Steve had said at one point, his slight teen-age frame taut with recollection. "And it wasn't the music, Jamey," he had said over and over, as though amazed by his own capacity to hurt for others, to feel beyond his own wants and needs. "It was Mr. Garrett...and you," he added, his eyes holding hers boldly, challenging her to deny how badly her own fear had hurt, "and his grandparents. I even thought how they must be feeling. They're nice people," he had said sincerely, naively, with all the seventeen-year-old innocence of discovery at finding that age need not be a barrier to friendship.

"I know," Jamey had answered, her response encompassing all his words. She had feared that her own simple words were inadequate, but somehow they hadn't been. Steve had known she was agreeing with everything, denying nothing. He had reached out shyly for her hand, squeezing her fingers in shared comfort.

She had left Tanasie Basin shortly after lunch, blissfully unaware of the trying afternoon that awaited her. In response to Rue's request she had driven to his grandparents' home. They had been tormented by the news reports of the previous day, nearly inconsolable in their grief even when he had called to assure them that the reports of his death were inaccurate, and he had asked Jamey to spend some time with them to offer added reassurance. She had gladly complied with his request, for Tom and Bonnie Martin had become very dear to her.

Expecting to be confronted with a continued fear that mingled with the tension of relief, Jamey had turned into the long driveway at greater than normal speed. She darted down the private roadway, only to end up slamming on her brakes and skidding to a stop as she stared in dismay at the line of cars parked in front of the house. A quick glance at the porch had confirmed that there were not merely the two she had expected to find, but a crowd gathered there, a crowd that filled the large porch and spilled over into the yard. Her hand had moved back to the gearshift, ready to slip the transmission into reverse. But it was too late.

"Jamey!" Bonnie Martin had moved quickly down the steps, hurrying toward her as she had reluctantly emerged from her car.

The older woman had embraced her warmly. No words were necessary as Jamey returned the greeting, clasping Rue's grandmother in a silent act of empathy. It was a womanly act, an expression of their deepest maternal instincts, and they had smiled at one another knowingly through eyes that shimmered with unshed tears. Each had suffered the agonies of potential loss, and they were only now beginning to accept that providence had smiled on them in sparing Rue's life. The crowd of well-wishers had no longer seemed to matter as Jamey walked arm-in-arm with Bonnie Martin toward the porch.

The next few minutes were a whirl of introductions, she remembered, and many of the names and faces remained blurs in Jamey's memory even now. But one fact had come quickly, emphatically, to her attention. Most of the people she had met that afternoon were related to Rue. There had been aunts, uncles, cousins, but those she remembered clearly were his parents and brothers. She also thought she had it straight in her mind which wife went with which brother, which children to each couple. Rue's family was a close group, and their coming together at this time had been a natural celebration of life itself.

Scraps of conversation came back to her as she leaned forward, cupping her chin in her palm and letting her elbow rest on the small dressing table.

She had been introduced to everyone on the porch, names and faces running together as she had tried to keep track, smiling politely and answering their greetings. Then she had been whisked inside, where Bonnie had presented her to a tall, lovely woman whose auburn hair curled to frame a classically beautiful face, a face that had aged well. Startlingly blue eyes had gazed at her with interest, and the woman's mouth had curved upward in an encouraging smile.

"Jamey, I'd like you to meet Gwen Garrett. Gwen is

our only daughter, and the mother of these two rascals...."

Jamey had followed the direction of Bonnie's smile to find two towering, handsome men eyeing her. "Russ Junior, named after his father, and Tom, named after his grandfather," Bonnie had continued proudly. "They're Rue's brothers. I'm sure their wives are around here somewhere...." Her voice trailed off as she scanned the crowd, but failed to spot the faces she sought. "Oh, well...later. Boys, this is Jamey Marsh, Rue's girl."

Jamey had opened her mouth to make a teasing remark about Bonnie's references to these two huge men as rascals and boys, but she closed it quickly as red flags of color stole over her cheeks. The old-fashioned term, "Rue's girl," implied more than she was willing to allow, and she had stammered her reply. "I'm p-pleased to meet you. But I'm n-not really—"

"Lord, Rue was telling the truth!" Russ Garrett had interrupted her denial, laughing heartily. "She really does blush!" The words explained his remark as he turned to grin at his brother. "I never would have believed him if I hadn't seen it for myself."

Gwen Garrett intervened before anything more could be said, scowling in mock severity at her eldest son. "Now, you just leave Jamey alone, Russ," she had ordered as she gently eased Jamey away from the two men with a request that she walk with her for a moment. Jamey allowed herself to be led outside, out the back door into ankle-deep grass, and they had slipped quietly away.

"Those boys are as bad as their father and grandfather," Gwen sighed.

Jamey said nothing. Her relief at escaping the innuendos of the two men whose faces were stamped with features similar to those that sprang unbidden from her memory had been too great.

Gwen had turned to her as they strolled at a leisurely pace in the shade of a row of yellow poplars. "I'm so glad to finally meet you, Jamey," she had said softly, "though I could've wished for our meeting to come about under different circumstances." She had indicated the crowd milling about in the distance with a rueful shrug of her shoulders. "Taken all together, we can be a pretty overwhelming lot, and I expect you're feeling rather floored at meeting so many of us at one time."

What an understatement! Jamey thought. Even in her wildest imaginings, she wouldn't have expected anything like that. It had seemed that half the population of Tennessee was there. And that most of them were Martins or Garretts!

Gwen had continued talking. "But Rue has told us so much about you that we feel we know you already. We're delighted that you two have found each other," she had gone on, as though Jamey and Rue were an established couple.

Jamey had quickly forgotten her fevered thoughts about the size of Rue's family as her mind had turned to struggle with the idea that Rue had told his family about her. When? Heavens, she had only known the man a week! She had tried to push the thought aside as she hastily set about correcting the erroneous impression Gwen Garrett had obviously formed.

"Thank you, Mrs. Garrett. I'm delighted too, but not for the reason you seem to think. You see, Rue and I are simply two people who enjoy each other's company, brought together by a mutual interest in the musical talents of a third party." The stilted words sounded ridiculous, and Jamey had nearly groaned aloud at the stiff formality of her little speech.

The need to return the warmth being offered to her had prompted a tumbling rush of words. Jamey had gone on to explain about Steve and his music, about how she had become involved in trying to help Steve, and how her involvement had led to her meeting with Rue. But she had said nothing that revealed the intense physical longing that pulled her, like a puppet dangling on strings, toward the other woman's son.

Gwen hadn't interrupted to tell her that she already knew most of what Jamey was saying. Instead, she had watched and listened, her observations bringing her into agreement with her youngest son. Jamey was indeed an independent young woman, as he had said, but she was also rather confused. Gwen's clear blue eyes had hidden more knowledge, both confirmed and intuitive, than Jamey, in her inexperience, could have credited. But if she had been aware of Gwen's thoughts, her discomfort would have been amplified far beyond the mild feeling of unease that had weighted her own thoughts and words.

A smile had lifted the corners of Gwen Garrett's lips as the old phrase "The lady doth protest too much" sprang to her mind. She had recognized that Jamey was, on top of everything else, a very frightened young woman—scared stiff of her growing feelings toward Rue.

Rue had been reluctant to introduce Jamey to his family until he had known her longer, and his mother now knew why. He was concerned that the implications of such a meeting would frighten her away. And he had been right, Gwen thought, though fate seemed to have wrested that decision from his control. Jamey had been dumped squarely into the middle of not just his immediate family, but almost the entire troop of Garretts and Martins.

Gwen had stayed close to Jamey for the remainder of her visit, determined to provide a buffer between Jamey and her exuberant family. She had been intent on protecting whatever fragile ties existed to link the lovely girl to her son.

"Jamey, this is Rue's father—Russ Senior," Gwen had said as she stopped Jamey beside a tall, slender man whose eyes sparkled with humor.

"Hello." Jamey had looked up to meet those smiling gray eyes with her own. The introduction really hadn't been necessary, except as a social convention. "It's easy to see that you're Rue's father. He's very like you, isn't he?" she had asked, a dimple showing beside her mouth as she placed her hand in his.

"Well, thank you," Russ Garrett had said jovially, enfolding her small hand in both of his. "I'll take that as a supreme compliment, coming as it does from . . . one of Rue's fans," he had finished teasingly after an almost imperceptible pause.

Jamey had been charmed. Here at last was someone who wasn't determined to pair her off romantically with Rue Garrett!

"One of his biggest fans at the moment, as it happens," she had teased back, unaware that Russ Garrett had caught the warning glint in his wife's eye and steered clear of any bantering remarks about Jamey's relationship with his son. "Rue is a very special person," she had added sincerely, her thoughts a kaleidoscopic sequence of changing events, from Rue's involvement with Steve and herself to his heroic actions in yesterday's fire.

"That he is," Russ Garrett had returned with undisguised pride.

Jamey had felt she could have spent the rest of the afternoon in the comfortable presence of Rue's parents, but her need to be alone had taken precedence as others joined them. She simply couldn't cope with their teasing assumptions about Rue.

"I really have to be going," Jamey had said as soon as she felt she could gracefully make her exit.

Gwen had walked with her to her car, had laughingly

rejected Jamey's hesitant offer to postpone her plans to see Rue.

"No, dear, Rue would be furious with us if we interfered with your plans! In fact, he's probably going to be pretty miffed when this motley crew shows up to meet him at the airport," she had laughed softly. "He's not one for overt gestures. For all his success, he's still just plain old Rue Garrett, and we love him for it."

The soothing tones had evoked again the memory of Rue's face, and Jamey had been touched by the maternal love that shone from Gwen Garrett's eyes. She had been moved by the gentle pressure as her fingers were lightly squeezed in a gesture of compassion.

Jamey hadn't recognized Gwen's protective actions as anything more than the warmth of the southern hospitality that she had learned to enjoy during her brief time here. Nor had she recognized Gwen's relief at her departure. She had been too relieved herself at finally getting away. She was consumed with the need to put distance between herself and the implications of the open acceptance Rue's family had shown her. Jamey had wanted time—time to think!

Time! The thought brought her up short. What time was it? Jamey's eyes flicked to the clock on the stand beside her bed. It was nearly five.

"Oh, no!" she groaned aloud. There was just enough time left to get everything ready. The cabin was tidy, thank goodness, for she still had to begin preparing their meal and settle the matter of what she would wear.

She wanted to look her best when Rue arrived, to look perfect for him. That thought was now uppermost in her mind as she swung open the closet doors and rummaged through her wardrobe.

Jamey gently removed a pale yellow dress from its hanger and held it against herself as she turned toward the mirror. The pale color accentuated her deepening

tan, the soft cut of the dress highlighting her feminin-
ity. The dress was sleeveless, exposing delicate arms,
and the scooped neckline hinted at the soft womanhood it covered. The skirt was full, swirling and teasing
as she moved. Pleased, she slipped the dress back onto
its hanger and hung it carefully on the closet door.

But what to wear between now and the time she
would don the pale yellow dress? It was so hot, she
thought as she wiped away the beads of moisture already collecting on her forehead. She discarded the idea
of jeans, grinning mischievously at a mental picture of
herself zipping around the cabin in the all-together.
Then her eyes fell on the shirt Rue had loaned her for
the walk back to the cabin after she had fallen into the
creek. Its loose-fitting comfort would be perfect for the
task of working over a hot stove, for holding memories
of Rue close to her as she worked.

Jamey quickly slipped into a pair of lacy briefs, setting the matching bra aside to be put on later. She
pulled Rue's shirt on, laughing softly at the memories
evoked by the simple action. The shirt really was long
enough to be almost a dress on her, as Rue had commented. Hugging it to herself, she drew pleasure from
the feel of the material that engulfed her slender
curves, from the thought that this same material had
hugged itself to the contours of Rue's larger, male
frame. Jamey all but danced from her bedroom to begin the final preparations for the evening she would
share with Rue.

Two hours had never seemed so vast a span of time,
Jamey thought. She wanted Rue with her now. But
there was a way to have a part of him with her.

Sliding the cassette into the tape deck, Jamey listened for a moment to the sounds of "Rolling Water"
before moving to the kitchen. She sang as she worked,
her voice blending harmoniously with Rue's rich, deep
tones.

By five thirty the two Cornish game hens had been nestled side-by-side in the oven for nearly half an hour, baking under a glaze of melted honey and butter. She checked to see that the Pinot Chardonnay she had chosen to go with their meal was already chilled to the proper temperature, then turned to slice the fresh broccoli into smaller pieces. Her movements as she worked were evidence of her mood. Jamey was happy. Rue would be here in only an hour and a half.

The timer on the stove called for Jamey's attention, the steady buzzing sound bringing her back again to baste the small birds. Leaning forward, she set the timer for another half hour—time for the final basting that would see the birds through to golden-brown perfection—before opening the oven door and bending down to brush them lightly with the honey and butter mixture. Still bending, she licked at the sticky sweetness that clung to her fingers.

"Now, this is the kind of homecoming I like." The deep, masculine voice came from directly behind her. The words were lazy, heavy with meaning.

With her fingers still resting lightly on her lips, Jamey spun around to find Rue lounging casually in the open doorway. He was leaning there as though he had been enjoying the view for some time, taking in the tanned expanse of legs revealed to him by her previous position. The brown corduroy jacket that matched the slacks that clung to his long, powerful legs hung over his shoulder, held easily by one hooked finger, and Jamey's first impulse was to move into his arms, to press herself against the texture of the darker brown material of the shirt that covered his broad chest. She resisted the urge, forcing her eyes to travel the short distance upward to Rue's face. His gray-blue eyes seemed darker than she remembered, more vivid. They sparkled with emotion. Unable to sustain the intensity of his gaze, Jamey shifted her eyes quickly to the clock hanging over the refrigerator.

"I know. I'm early," he said softly, reading her last transparent thought. "I had to get away from that gang at the airport," Rue growled, "had to see you. And I didn't want to give you time to get all prettied up...not when I was just going to make a mess of all your hard work."

His words called her attention again to her scanty attire. She looked down at his shirt, her cheeks crimson as she realized how he must be reading the situation. Here she stood, cooking *his* dinner, listening to *his* music, and wearing *his* shirt. And precious little else, she thought wildly. Only the lacy scrap of her bikini panties.

"The heat," she said lamely, her words barely more than a whisper as she searched the floor for a hole to swallow her up.

Rue pushed himself lightly from the doorway and moved into the room, dropping his jacket over the back of a chair. Indecision gleamed in Jamey's eyes as his movement caught her attention, and she looked up to find him advancing toward her with a slow, steady tread. He was savoring every second of this humiliating encounter.

This wasn't the way she had planned it! She had wanted to be wearing the feminine yellow dress when he arrived, to look cool and self-possessed and desirable, to look as good to Rue's eyes as he did to hers.

Jamey would never have believed that her state of undress was far more appealing to him than any dress she might have worn. Rue liked the look of her in his shirt, liked the thought that it made her seem like his woman. And he liked the tousled disarray of her hair, the way the raven tresses curled about her small face, giving her the appearance of being part angel and part imp. He wanted the feel of her against him, the taste of her on his lips. He stopped only steps away from her.

"Come here, woman." Rue's voice was thick with desire, his eyes inviting her to make the final commitment.

Jamey bolted! She made a beeline for her bedroom, intent on at least covering herself. The situation was fraught with dangers she could only half imagine, and she desperately needed the security of being fully clothed.

Rue followed slowly, sure of himself, but Jamey missed the sound of his footsteps in her single-minded haste. Her first warning that he had entered the room behind her came when his arms slid beguilingly around her, his fingers moving to the buttons of his shirt to help her as she worked to release them. She tensed in reaction. Had he misread her dash to the bedroom?

"Here, turn around," he commanded seductively. "I can't do this with your back to me."

Rue's hands were gentle as they lighted on her shoulders, turning her to face him in one smooth movement. His eyes searched hers, and the moment to push him away was lost as Jamey let herself be drawn into his arms, her eyes still locked with his. Apparently, he *had* misread her intent, but Jamey was no longer sure she cared. Her heart was skipping beats in its effort to keep up with her fevered senses.

Rue lowered his head slowly, his eyes devouring the sight of her as he took in her dazed expression, the trembling of softly parted lips. He halted his slow advance long enough to lift gentle fingers to her lips, tracing the outline of their fullness like a blind man who learns of his world only by touch. His hunger for this woman was far more than merely sexual, and he knew it.

The touch of his fingers on her lips was like fine-grained sandpaper, his fingertips callused from their frequent pressure against steel guitar strings. They felt good, so good, and her tongue touched them lightly, responding to the sexual tension of the moment in a way she barely understood. Jamey was all feeling and reaction, her response to him instinctive.

The moist touch of tongue to flesh released Rue from his gentle exploration, and he moaned her name as the arm around her waist tightened, pulling her closer yet to the full length of him. The callused fingers moved from her lips to her cheek, tenderly caressing, as he closed his eyes and let his mouth descend at last to hers. His hand slid down the length of her arm, then around to her back where his fingers laced together, his arms forming an unbroken circle that bound them together.

Jamey felt the need in him as she responded with explorations of her own. Both arms lifted to slide around his lean waist, then moved upward toward his broad shoulders in a tactile search of the muscles of his back.

Tongues met, tangled, tasted, and went back for more as their intensity heightened, all reason yielding to the passion rising between them. Lips still clinging hungrily, Rue slid his hands up and around her waist, his movements sure as they led him unerringly toward his goal. His fingers worked slowly, sensually, at the buttons that still held the shirt closed around her. He freed them one by one, then slid the shirt gently down her arms, letting it fall unnoticed to the floor.

Jamey was lost. There was nothing virginal in her lack of modesty—or in her response as she arched against his male contours. She was too far gone to retreat, too far gone to even *think* of stopping him as his hands came up and palmed her small breasts. The sensation of callused fingers gently probing increased the heated feeling rising in her veins, and her voice was husky with a yearning she had never known before as she groaned his name. Her hands moved up as though they had a will of their own, seeking to release the buttons that stood between her and having the full warmth of his hard flesh pressed against her tender skin. She fumbled at the fastenings, her inexperience showing, and Rue's larger hands came up to help her.

"Let me," he said softly, his words no more than a whisper. Brown eyes lifted languidly, trustingly, to meet the promise reflected in the depths of gray-blue eyes that studied her intently.

"You're so beautiful...." His resonant tones were filled with longing as he let his eyes rove the length of her nearly naked body. Her body gave him pleasure, and she was glad. Jamey's lips curved into a tender smile.

The last button was released, and Rue gathered her to him again. Her fingers curled into the mass of coppery hair that covered his chest as she lifted her face to him for yet another drugging kiss. Jamey wanted this moment to go on forever. Rue was with her, he wanted her in his arms, and she wanted to be there. The significance of sacredly held values faded into oblivion, years of training and planning for her career temporarily forgotten, as she gave herself up to the age-old call for bonding with one chosen mate.

As he lifted her in his arms and took the few steps that brought him to the edge of the bed, Jamey leaned her head against his chest and heard the thunder of his heartbeats. The sound thrilled her, gave her a sense of primitive power that tightened the curling sensation in the pit of her stomach. So this was what all the excitement was about, she thought dreamily. As short a time as a week ago, she would have laughed if anyone had tried to tell her that she would crave the touch of *any* man. But crave this man's touch she did!

Rue lowered her gently to the bed and stretched himself beside her, his lips taking over where his hands had left off. He caressed each taut nipple in turn, and fire licked along her veins as Jamey reacted to his sensual touch. A low moan sounded deep in her throat, and Rue laughed softly, pleasurably, at the mutual seeking of two hungry bodies. His lips returned to hers, his mind fighting to reject the strident buzzing sound that came from somewhere inside the cabin.

For a moment Jamey imagined herself at home in Oregon, the insistent buzzing an interruption by some impatient caller with finger pressed firmly to the doorbell. Slowly reality surfaced from the hazy recesses of her brain, and she shook her head slightly to clear away her confusion.

"The birds," she whispered. "Rue, I've got to see about the birds." She struggled against him in an effort to shift his weight from hers.

"What are you talking about?" he growled.

Rue moved to push her down again, but the moment was lost for her. Reality returned with a vengeance. Two quite small birds had saved her from making a complete fool of herself, from giving up everything in her mindless surrender to the man who leaned across her.

"Our dinner...." Jamey renewed her struggles, one arm pushing at Rue, the other moving upward in a futile attempt to cover her bare breasts.

Realization dawned as he understood the two words she had spoken. "Leave it," he moaned, his eyes holding hers as his hand lightly caressed her shoulder. "My hunger right now isn't for food...and neither is yours."

"N-no, Rue." Jamey's words were spoken as firmly as her shaken senses would allow. She became still, fearful that her continued struggles would only incite him further. "I c-can't...I don't want our dinner to be ruined." She had to find a way to convince him, to get him to release her before she yielded again to the need and desire that still raged within her. The caressing motion of his hand was pulling her down into a foaming sea that churned and roiled against the shores of her sanity.

With a heavy sigh Rue rolled away from her. Jamey stayed beside him for a moment, trying to slow her ragged breathing. He turned back, his look questioning, and Jamey rose hastily to put distance between them before he could reach out for her again. He watched through eyes filled with pain as she hurriedly pushed her arms back into the sleeves of his shirt, fumbling over the buttons in her haste to cover her near nudity. Jamey didn't understand his pain.

She practically ran from the room, her only thought that she had to get away from him for a while, had to give her overheated emotions time to cool. She raced into the kitchen, leaving him on her bed, and threw herself into her dinner preparations. How was she going to face him when he came out here? she wondered miserably. Blinding tears filled her eyes, almost causing her to drop the pot of broccoli as she placed it over the burner.

Jamey kept her back to Rue as he emerged from the bedroom some minutes later, pretending an impossible fascination with the game hens as she basted them for the final time before sliding them back into the oven.

Rue's voice was calm as he spoke. "I'm going for a walk, Jamey. I'll be back in a little while." With her back to him, she missed the hurt that lingered in eyes that were still darkened with passion.

"All right," she mumbled, her gaze riveted on the broccoli as it began to tumble in the boiling water. She refused to look at him. How could she face him after what she had just done? "Dinner will be ready in half an hour." Her voice trembled as she spoke.

Jamey listened to the sound of Rue's footsteps as he walked away from the cabin. Tears began to course slowly down her cheeks at the thought that he must hate her now, must think her a little tease. He had no way of knowing all that was going on in her mind, she thought. There was no way he could understand how badly she had wanted to surrender to him, to admit her love for him. Nor would he be able to understand her inability to relinquish either her values or the years of careful planning and training that had prepared her for her career as an educational consultant. Jamey's sobs increased as she struggled with the opposing urges warring within her.

The broccoli blurred before her eyes as Jamey accepted what she had just admitted to herself. She was in love. She hadn't let herself fall in love. It had simply stormed into her life and taken hold of her, taken over before she had time to throw up the barriers to keep it out. And, foolishly, she had fallen in love with Rue Garrett, a man who moved in circles where values were discarded as casually as old clothes, a man whose success in his own career would never allow him to understand the importance of her career to her. He simply wouldn't see either—her values or her career—as being of any consequence.

"Oh, God! What am I going to do?" The plaintive cry was softly voiced, as only a cry from the depths of the soul can be.

Jamey moved about the small kitchen, her actions automatic as she made cheese sauce, put the wild rice on to cook, and heated the wheat rolls that completed the meal. Her mind was busy with thoughts of Rue and her career, of Tennessee and Oregon. Both were separated by a great—and it seemed to Jamey, unbridgeable—distance.

She turned to set the table, her sobs diminishing through sheer force of will. If this was love, she hated it! It was one more thing her mother had been right about. It hurt, and it robbed you of the power to think rationally.

The ringing of the phone startled Jamey, pulling her away from the task of setting the table, pulling her away from the sudden knowledge that she had allowed her reaction to the dangers Rue had faced in yesterday's fire to dim her intent. She caught it on the second ring and stretched the cord to its limits as she carried the receiver with her to the kitchen to resume her chore.

"Hello." Jamey's voice was still a bit ragged, and she was uncomfortable holding the phone to her ear by the pressure exerted between shoulder and chin.

"Jamey, this is Mother, honey. Do you have a cold?" The question was typical, filled with motherly concern.

"No, Mom, I'm just trying to do two things at once, as usual," she answered, trying to infuse her voice with its customary brightness. Her discomfort was amplified a thousand times over by hearing the voice on the other end of the line, and she clutched at the phone, dinner forgotten. It seemed as though just thinking of her mother had telepathically transformed itself into this call, and the timing couldn't have been worse. "Is anything wrong?"

"Well, no. Nothing's wrong, dear. I just have a message for you from Paul. Your father and I are going out of town for the weekend, and Paul didn't feel this could wait, so I thought I had better call you tonight," she explained. There was barely a pause for breath as her mother launched into the meat of her message. "Paul says he's been contacted with offers of two more consulting jobs for you. They're both local jobs, and the timelines don't nterfere with anything else you have scheduled, so he wanted to know as soon as possible whether or not you wanted to accept them."

Jamey listened in silence, grateful that her mother's explanation precluded any need for her to speak. Paul Cameron had been something of a mentor to Jamey. It was he who had suggested that she enter the field of educational consulting, having recognized her potential talents in that area when she had taught in the school where he was principal. He helped her now by allowing her to give his office number as a phone contact when she was away on out-of-town jobs. He was a good friend, and he wouldn't have had this message relayed to her unless he deemed it necessary and important. Jamey's heart thudded painfully.

Deanna Marsh's voice drove on, excitedly, about the specific dates of the contracts, the job sites, and the nature of the work to be done. She was accustomed to acting as a go-between for Jamey and Paul and filled in the needed information efficiently. Jamey caught her breath on what was nearly a sob, her decision made with surprising speed.

"Okay, Mom. Tell Paul I'll accept both of them." She paused, her eyes scanning the calendar on the wall. "And unless something unforeseen comes up here, I'll be flying home on September fifteenth," she named a Saturday only three weeks away. Her mother heard the slight wobble in Jamey's voice, but said nothing about it. She put it down to the fact that Jamey was trying to do two things at once, as she had said.

"Isn't that quite a bit sooner than you had expected?" The words held a note of surprised pleasure.

"Yes, two weeks sooner. Things here are falling into place more rapidly than I had thought they would," she lied. They were, but only because Jamey had redoubled her efforts in the past week. "And I'm looking forward to a break between jobs." That much, at least, was true. She would need a break in order to pull herself together after leaving Tennessee, after leaving Rue.

"Oh, Jamey, I'm so proud of you! You're doing so well in your career, and it's still difficult for me to put into words just how good that makes me feel."

Jamey scowled bitterly at the phone. *If only you knew what I'm sacrificing for this,* she thought. "Thanks, Mom. You know I enjoy it."

The steady tread of footsteps advancing across the deck announced Rue's return, and Jamey prayed for a way to end the conversation quickly. She wanted no contact of any sort between Rue and her mother, not even the minimal contact of having him stand in the room listening while they talked.

Rue stopped in the doorway, watching angrily, his eyes raking over the length of her. Jamey looked down, realizing with dismay that the rage in his contemptuous glance was caused by her attire. She was still wearing his shirt—over only her lacy panties.

"Mom, I really have to go." Jamey interrupted the flow of speech from the other end of the line. There was a pause before she spoke again. "I *know* we usually talk longer, but I'm in the middle of cooking dinner," she said, remembering her mission, "and it's going to be ruined if I don't get off the phone and see to it." Another pause cut through Jamey's rapid words. "Okay, I know. Give the word to...Paul." The hesitation had been nearly imperceptible, but the softened tones as Jamey said the man's name had caught Rue's attention, making her effort to remain calm apparent to him as he stood glaring at her. "I love you too. I'll call soon. Bye, Mom."

Jamey moved across the room and placed the receiver in its cradle, then turned back to face Rue. It was the hardest thing she had ever had to do.

Chapter Seven

"Go get dressed, Jamey!" Rue snapped the words at her. He was furiously angry, and his mood was reflected in every formidable line of his body. He shoved away from the doorjamb, his movements ominously stiff as he loomed nearer. Restrained violence held his jawline rigid as he stared at her through eyes that had become cold, narrowed slits.

Jamey looked down again, shying away from the chilling menace in his eyes. She felt ashamed, and more than a little afraid of him in his present mood. He had every right to be angry with her, she acknowledged, angry that she had failed to change from his shirt into something more suitable while he walked off the strain of their unfinished lovemaking. Color drained from Jamey's cheeks at her remembered response to him, a response that had exposed a sexual appetite she hadn't even known she possessed, and at the realization of how he must be interpreting her neglect. He probably saw it as an open invitation to continue what they had started.

Weakly she sought to explain. "I'm sorry, Rue.... Mother called...." Contrition filled her voice as she lifted a trembling hand slightly toward the phone.

"I heard." He cut her words off in a tone still filled with anger. "Just shut up and go get some clothes on before I take up where we left off before," he threatened.

Rue's heated words confirmed her fears. They galvanized Jamey into action. She spun around and rushed from the room, eager now to get away from Rue and the threat of his burgeoning wrath, anxious to make her escape from the love she had confessed for him in the deepest recesses of her soul.

She wouldn't be able to turn back if he pulled her to him again, would not even *want* to turn back, Jamey thought as she faced the irrevocably painful consequences of the decision Paul's message had forced. Not even if Rue's only motivation was the desire to hurt her. And he was angry enough to harbor that intent if she pushed her luck any further!

Jamey had never given any thought to what Rue might be like if he ever got truly angry. But she acknowledged to herself now that if she had thought his reaction to her refusal to have dinner with him on the first day she had met him, or his reaction when she had tried to stand him up by leaving for church without him, had been formidable displays of anger, they were nothing compared to the emotion that gripped him tonight. She shuddered to think of the risk she had so absentmindedly taken, the risk of being the recipient of whatever punishment he might mete out in an anger that was obviously far greater than on either of those occasions. It didn't occur to her that the one-sided scrap of conversation he had overheard had caused the feeling to mushroom. And all because of her halting reference to another man—Paul.

Jamey quietly closed her bedroom door, her hands shaking as she sought added protection from the dangerous presence in the living room of the tiny cabin. Leaning limply against the door, she looked with regret at the lovely yellow dress hanging in front of the closet, waiting to mold itself to the lissome contours of her body.

"You could've prevented this," she whispered at the garment as though it had life, as though it could understand her trembling protest. A light breeze stirred, causing the delicate material to billow and sway, beckoning her to cross the room. It seemed an auspicious omen, a promise that things could only improve. They could certainly get no worse, she thought despondently.

A touch of hope mingled with the fear she felt as Jamey moved away from the door and lifted the yellow dress from where it hung, slipping it gently from its hanger. She would wear it anyway, even though it could not now set the mood she had so optimistically planned earlier that afternoon. The best she could hope for was that, fully clothed, she would be less vulnerable to any attack Rue might mount—verbal or physical. And maybe, she prayed, the feminine delicacy of the dress would gentle his anger. Cold shivers of fear ran through her at the thought of how Rue might respond if he should discover her plan to deceive him, to leave telling him of her departure until the last possible minute.

Jamey took great pains to see that her appearance was as near perfect as she could make it. She removed Rue's shirt and folded it neatly, then donned the lacy bra she had so casually laid aside earlier. She eased the dress over her head, letting it fall freely into place before smoothing the folds of the skirt and turning to her mirror to salvage what she could of the tear-ravaged wanness of her face.

Her cheeks were pale, streaked with the traces of the tears she had shed. But she wasn't about to leave the safety of her bedroom, not even to try to wash away the damage the glass revealed. She settled instead for a light cleaning with a moist towelette. It was better than nothing, she thought as she applied a light coat of foundation to her skin, relieved to see that it was effective in covering most of the misery that showed there. Nothing could be done to hide the redness of her eyes, though. Only time would erase the hurt that lingered in the fathoms of their brown depths.

Jamey lifted her brush and ran it through her long black hair. It fell around her shoulders and down her back in soft waves, framing her elfin features with Madonna-like grace. She sighed, then drew a bolstering breath. She was ready to meet him, to beard the lion in *her* den.

Jamey listened. No sound came from the living room. The cabin was so quiet that she might have been the only one there. The tempo of her pulse increased at the thought that perhaps she was. Perhaps Rue did hate her now and had gone without so much as a word of farewell. Taking another deep breath to steady the fluttering fear that assailed her, Jamey opened the door and walked slowly toward the living room, in dread of the emptiness she might find there.t

Her eyes searched the small room, flitting painfully from the couch to the chair, the light in them dying as she registered the vacant space. Slowly she turned toward the tiny kitchen, her heart feeling like a heavy weight in her breast. She would have to deal alone with what should have been a romantic meal for two.

But he was there! He leaned lightly against the counter, the size of him dwarfing the small cooking area.

"You look lovely." Rue's eyes smiled at her, but his lips did not.

Jamey's heart took a dangerous leap. "Thank you," she said softly, a tremulous smile filled with questions hovering on the fragile curve of her lips.

"Are you ready for dinner?" A tiny grin lifted the corners of Rue's mouth and began to spread over the harsh planes of his face, taking life from the glint that lit his eyes.

"Yes," she answered breathlessly, the radical change in him robbing her lungs of their will to take in and expel air in the normal way. "I'll just get everything ready—"

"Too late," he interrupted. Rue's words directed her attention to the table, neatly laid with service for two, to the plates of food lying in readiness for their meal. She hadn't even noticed, hadn't registered the empty expanse of the counter she had left littered with the items that now dotted the round oak table.

Jamey turned, then swiveled her head back, looking over her shoulder and up at him from an awkward position. This was the result of his anger? Rue answered the utter amazement reflected in her expression with a mocking lift of his eyebrows.

"Don't break your neck!" He laughed openly at her. "I'm not totally incapable of fending for myself, you know. I've done it for a long time. And all your efforts would have gone for naught if I hadn't rescued our dinner," he added, reminding her of her hasty retreat from his anger.

"Oh." Jamey's mind reached for a suitable reply, one that would cover the confusion and embarrassment his teasing words dredged up, but nothing came. She stared into his eyes, biting gently at the fullness of her lower lip.

Rue left her no time to dwell on the problem as he dropped a tiny kiss on the tip of her nose, then propelled her gently forward, his hand resting lightly on the small of her back. He pulled Jamey's chair out and seated her before continuing around to his own place, amused by the pink blush that had spread over her cheeks. He had recognized her confusion, but could never have guessed at the wealth of emotion churning away at her behind the worried look.

Rue's conversation during the meal was general, a careful avoidance of any topic that would remind her of his gaffe of this afternoon, when he had so nearly rushed her into something she obviously wasn't ready for. She was the picture of innocence in the pale yellow dress, and that very innocence stilled what remained of his anger, quieting his inner demand to know who Paul was. After all, the man was at a distinct disadvantage. He was far away, hopefully a fading memory, whereas Rue was here...and now. And Jamey was not indifferent to him, of that he was sure. Confidently he used his considerable skill with words to draw her thoughts away from what had gone before, until Jamey was once more relaxed and natural in her responses to him.

"You're a good cook, Jamey," Rue said, and she laughed spontaneously. He sounded so surprised, as though it wasn't possible for a woman to be adept both in and out of the home.

"Did you think I wouldn't be?" she asked teasingly.

"Didn't think about it," he answered in tones that matched hers, "but I'm glad to find you are. It's a healthy skill for a woman to have," he added, emphasizing "woman" to let her know he had recognized her light reference to chauvinism.

"Oh, Rue," Jamey laughed, comfortable with the calm that settled over her as he played his word games. It didn't occur to her that he was deliberately leading the conversation down safe paths.

"No, really. It is!" he continued, beginning to sound very much like a real chauvinist. "But it's a healthy skill for a man to have too," he added, his wide smile bursting the bubble of her suspicion. "I'll have to show you sometime just how well I've developed my own culinary prowess."

"You're on," she shot back at him. "But don't tell me you learned these fantastic skills at your mother's knee."

"As a matter of fact, I didn't," he said consideringly. "I learned at my daddy's knee," Rue teased, laughing at her surprise. "At least, some of it. Admittedly, Mom added quite a bit of expertise on the kitchen end of things, but Dad does a mean barbecue, and all three of us boys were required to learn to handle both indoor and outdoor cooking. We resisted like crazy at the time," he confessed, "but I expect Russ and Tom are just as glad now as I am that our folks insisted on preparing us for bachelor living. TV dinners get old in a hurry."

Jamey could well imagine Gwen Garrett, calm and cool and serene, as she demanded that her all-male household learn to cope with domestic chores. She could also picture the grumbling resistance three teenage boys would have mounted. Her thoughts of Rue's family reminded her of the afternoon she had just spent with them, and she knew a sudden, very explainable discomfort.

"What did you think of my family?" Rue asked as though he could read her mind. But he wasn't a mind reader. Her thoughts had been easy to discern. They were written all over her face. "Quite an exuberant group, aren't they?" he prompted, his easy manner already easing the tension that had begun to knot her insides.

"Quite," she agreed softly, "but nice."

"I don't know if I was surprised to see them all at the airport or not," Rue went on quickly, before she could destroy the tranquil foundation he'd laid for their conversation. "But I surely was embarrassed. Lord! They looked like a horde of civilians come to welcome their war hero home." The pride in his voice as he lightly disparaged his family's en masse greeting at the airport made his depth of feeling for them apparent, and Jamey laughed with him at his description of deplaning, only to find himself wishing he were far away.

Anywhere but in the middle of Nashville's airport with his family making a scene simply by being there in such numbers.

Jamey's fractured spirits had needed the respite he provided, needed the tranquil breathing space in order to regroup from the devastating discovery that she was in love with him. So much had happened in such a short space of time that she didn't even think to question him about how his family had come to know so much about her. She was too busy trying to cope with the fact that, with each new glimpse into the gentle nature of this man, her love grew until she thought her heart would surely swell and burst with the sheer wonder of it.

As they finished their dinner, Rue was describing the complex process of taking an idea for a song from its embryonic beginning in a songwriter's mind to its logical end as a recording. They left the table, still discussing the subject as they shared the chores of cleaning the dishes and tidying the kitchen. And when Rue offered to take her to a recording studio, to show her firsthand what he had been describing, Jamey eagerly accepted.

"Now, come here, Jamey," Rue said as he draped the drying towel on its peg and reached for her hand. "I want to show you something."

Rue led an acquiescent Jamey onto the deck, where he pushed her gently into a wooden chair. "Wait right here," he ordered softly.

Jamey waited, watching as he moved lithely to his truck, then strode back across the intervening space carrying a guitar case. Her eyes were luminous with the love she felt for him as he took the chair beside hers and began to open the case.

"Rue," she started quietly.

"No, don't say a word," he commanded gently, laying a callused finger across her lips. "Just listen."

Rue played, but the song was one Jamey had never

heard before. It was more a love song than anything else, she thought, a love song to life. She closed her eyes and listened intently to lyrics that blended so perfectly with the music that they evoked a feeling of utter peace, of simply being glad to be alive. It was a perfect denouement to the fire he had survived.

"Like it?" he asked in a muted tone as the final chord faded into the night song of insects.

Bemused, Jamey could only gaze at him for a moment after opening her eyes. "It's beautiful, Rue," she said at last. Her words came out soft, awed. "Did you write it after the fire?"

"No," he denied, "before. It's an expression of the way I've been feeling lately," he added tenderly, his eyes never leaving her face.

Jamey hoped he meant he'd been feeling that way since their meeting, but she couldn't be sure. And she dared not ask, she thought. To ask would be to give away her own discovery of the love that was growing inside her.

Rue leaned across the small opening that separated their chairs and placed his lips gently on Jamey's. His free hand came up to caress her cheek as he whispered against her mouth, "Just the way I've been feeling lately." His kiss was feather-soft and lasted for only a second before he pulled back, lifting his guitar to play again.

The songs he played now were more familiar. Some were songs Mississippi River had made famous; others had been performed by a variety of singers. But never so beautifully, Jamey knew, as they were done in that solo performance. Rue sang only for her. Her heart sang only for him.

At length, Rue set his guitar aside and reached for her hand. They sat for long minutes in silence, a silence Jamey was reluctant to break with words, lest they damage the meaning of the small moment in time—a moment made more precious by the newness of her love.

When Rue at last broke the silence, it was to tell her of all the places he wanted her to see. Time passed quickly, with Rue naming off spot after scenic spot that he wanted to show her—The Hermitage, the stately home of President Andrew Jackson that was located about twelve miles east of downtown Nashville; the sprawling Opryland Park on the outskirts of the city; the Country Music Hall of Fame, where memorabilia of days gone by reminded all who went there of the city's musical heritage; and the Parthenon, the world's only full-scale reproduction of the ancient temple at Athens. Jamey was fascinated by his descriptions and forgot for a while that whatever they shared over the coming three weeks would be all that they would ever share—until he rose to leave her.

Rue didn't question the sadness that filled her eyes as Jamey walked with him to the steps. He was taking no chances on putting a foot wrong and upsetting the delicate balance that had been restored between them. It was enough that, for some reason, Jamey had acquiesced to all his plans, agreeing to see him as often as he wished.

He would have had trouble believing that her sadness and her acceptances were wrapped in a cloak of guilt, as much as in her desire to spend every possible moment of the next three weeks with him. Jamey had convinced herself that it was the best way—no, the *only* way!—to keep Rue unaware of her true purpose.

Their parting kiss was a chaste facsimile of the passion they had known earlier. Explosive emotions that ran wildly just beneath the surface of the tender kiss were held tightly in check, but brought back a flooding rush of painful thought. Only three weeks, three short weeks, until the date she had told her mother to expect her.

Jamey squeezed her eyes tight, forcing back the tears

that threatened to betray her terrible secret. *Surely,* she thought as her arms tensed fractionally around Rue's lean waist, *not even Mother could begrudge me this short time with the man I love.* But how would she ever explain the reasons for her departure to Rue when the time came?

Rue put her gently from him and gazed into her eyes for a moment before speaking, looked at her as though he were searching for something. "You get more warning this time, Jamey," he said at last, and she tensed. Suddenly she didn't want to hear what he had to say. A shiver of premonition feathered down her spine.

"Warning about what?" she asked softly. But she knew. Oh, she knew.

"I checked our calendar before we left for Las Vegas," he answered, confirming her fear, "and our next road trip begins September fifth. We'll be gone twenty-four days."

Jamey felt cheated, cheated out of what little time she had left with him. And the feeling almost, but not quite, outweighed her agonizing relief as she realized he wouldn't, be around to either witness her departure or try to prevent it. The chaos of her thoughts held her silent.

Rue misread her silence. He knew she cared, but maybe she didn't care enough. He moved toward the truck with a soft "Good night." Though Jamey couldn't know it, his fingers actually trembled as he worked the key into the ignition. He wanted her so badly. And not only physically. Rue wanted all of her—heart, soul, mind...and body.

Jamey stood for interminable minutes, listening as the sounds of the powerful vehicle faded into the sounds of nature singing its own quiet song, a song that mocked in its permanence. Even the insects would be here, would share this land with Rue, far longer than she would. "Three weeks..." she whispered, the words themselves an agony, coming out on a shuddering breath that hung in the night air. Three weeks that had suddenly been slashed to less than two.

Determinedly Jamey pulled her shaken emotions together to face what had to be, to somehow get through the coming eleven days without revealing her secret to Rue. Her decision had been made. She would snatch these days of love from her life and worry about counting the cost of her actions later. Jamey had no doubt that her memories of these days would add greatly to that cost, but she was willing to pay. No one had forced her to commit herself to the two new consulting contracts. No one had forced her to commit the foolish act of falling in love with Rue Garrett. And certainly no one other than Jamey Marsh could be held accountable for the grim intent of turning her back on Rue and the love she felt for him.

THE next days were both a pleasure and a pain for Jamey. She threw herself full-strength into her efforts at Tanasie Basin during the working hours that seemed longer than they ever had before, and spent each evening, short though they seemed, with Rue. He showed her parts of the Nashville area that Jamey had feared she would have to forgo now that she had moved her departure date up by two weeks. And they grew closer to each other in ways that only made that impending departure much harder to face.

Jamey came to hate her deception of Rue, each day a renewed struggle against her growing desire to change the plans that would rip them apart. The combination of hard work, the mingled joy and sorrow of moments spent with Rue, and the constant battle for control of her own thoughts and emotions had drained her. But staying so busy helped. It left her little time—only the long, lonely hours of tossing in her bed, trying to sleep— to truly contemplate the harsh reality of her plan.

There was no repeat of the intense physical passion that had so nearly evolved into total surrender on the day of Rue's return from Las Vegas. Rue treated Jamey like a delicate Dresden doll, his caresses tender and gentle, wooing her in the courtly fashion of the old South. There were times when she wished he would sweep away her right to hold fast to her decision, would pull her into his arms and let his emotions carry them both away on a tide of sweet possession. But those were weaker moments. And Rue was unaware of her decision, anyway.

Jamey took one day off from her rushed work schedule during the time before Rue's departure on the road trip. On that day she went with him to the recording studio where he and the band taped their music. She stared unblinkingly at the elaborate equipment being used by the group who were taping that day, was stunned by the sheer complexity involved in the process of cutting a record. She and Steve had used good equipment for the tape they had made to send to Mississippi River, but the machinery laid out before her made the smaller ones at Tanasie Basin seem like toys. Jamey laughed aloud at how ridiculous that tape must have seemed to Rue.

"Why did you even listen to it?" Jamey smiled shyly up at him as she asked the question.

Rue laughed as he tweaked her nose. "Curiosity!" he assured her. "I was absolutely floored that anyone would have the audacity to do such a thing. I expected to get a good laugh out of some idiot's amateurish efforts, and got the surprise of my life," he added, remembering how his interest had grown each time he had replayed the segment of tape where Steve played and sang "Sweet Freedom."

"Fate, you reckon?" he queried teasingly as his eyes smiled into hers.

"Fate," Jamey agreed quietly, a rush of pain causing

her heart to pound. The meaning she attached to the word was radically different from his. Jamey's definition hurt. Rue's gave him pleasure as he tugged at her hand, pulling her behind him into the soundproof silence of the control room.

The days since his return from Las Vegas had been happy ones for Rue, and this one held a special magic all its own as he shared his love of music with Jamey. He squeezed her hand, willing her to understand as he talked.

"Songs sort of grow by themselves, Jamey," Rue explained. "You get an idea, and then the idea takes off on you—sometimes when you're sitting down writing it, and sometimes when you're working on it with the group." His eyes held a faraway look, as though he were locked in a time warp between the present and some idea that had suddenly filled his consciousness, clamoring to be released. The look he gave her was warm as he smiled enigmatically, pulling his attention back to the studio. "But it takes all this and more before it's ready to be released to the public." Rue's hand made a sweeping arc, indicating the intricate layout of the sound control room and the spacious expanse of the studio room that spread before them on the other side of the thick glass wall.

Jamey wondered fleetingly what he had been thinking, but the look was gone. Rue had schooled his features to reveal nothing more than his pleasure in the moment they were sharing. She turned her head, her eyes following the path dictated by his words.

The studio room was designed to be as soft and absorbent of sound waves as possible, he told her. "Otherwise the music comes out sounding thin and tinny." The carpets were thick, plush, and the room was incredibly large. Its size allowed space for the musicians to spread out so that the individual microphones that picked up the notes from each instrument wouldn't record any bleed-through sounds from the other instruments being played in the room.

The sound control room was dominated by an enormous console with myriad sliding controls. Rue clarified the intricacies of the twenty-four-track recording system, lightly touching the board as he indicated the twenty-four rows of knobs, one for each of the tracks.

"These knobs control the sound effects being created by the musicians, and the dials above them show the strength of the sound coming in on each track," Rue continued, displaying a knowledge that extended beyond the talents that were instantly apparent whenever he picked up a guitar.

He went on to explain that songs were usually recorded in stages, taping first the instrumentation, then overdubbing the vocals after everyone was satisfied with the results of the instrumental track. "And once it's recorded, the tape is ready for mixing and mastering. Mixing is simply adjusting the sound on each track until the right blend is reached, and mastering is using the finished product from the studio—the master tape—to cut the master disc that's used to stamp out the records that end up in stores," he finished.

As they left the studio Jamey glanced up teasingly. "You make it all sound so easy."

Rue laughed. She had wanted him to laugh. The sound was her own special music, and she stored it in her memory.

"Right," he bantered back, "just as easy as your work sounds to me!" Rue slid his arm about her waist and, bending down, pressed a quick kiss to Jamey's lips.

"Hey, you two! No hanky-panky in the halls! This is a place of serious business." An incredibly deep voice that literally oozed with a southern drawl interrupted the moment, the tones filled with amusement as though he had made a great joke.

Rue looked up, a wide smile spreading across his

mobile features. It was hard to tell whether he was grinning at Jamey's obvious embarrassment or at the pleasure of seeing the other man as he extended his hand.
"Hi, John."

"Rue," the man acknowledged, clasping his out-
stretched hand. "Who's this pretty little honey?" he
asked, laughing richly at Jamey's deepening color as he
turned piercing eyes on her.

Rue introduced them, then proceeded to talk briefly,
easily, with the man about their latest album releases.
Jamey stood and stared, dumbfounded.

When the man moved down the hallway, Jamey
turned her head, craning her neck as she watched him
disappear into the sound control room. "Rue, that was
Johnny Cash!" she whispered, uncaring of the awe revealed by her quietly excited words and sparkling eyes.

"Yeah," he chuckled, "it was...and still is."

"But you know him!" Jamey's statement might
have been a question.

Rue's tones were respectful as he responded to her
implied puzzlement. "Jamey, John Cash is one of the
finest men who ever walked this earth. He's given me a
lot of help along the way, and I'm proud to call him
friend."

Suddenly Jamey felt very much out of her league.
Rue was so casual, so easygoing, that he made it easy
for her to forget who he was. But who he was loomed
between them now, eclipsing the fragile web of doubt
that tempted Jamey so beguilingly, urging her to stay.
Rue was a rising star, and Jamey withdrew, afraid of
being burned beyond recognition by the heat of his
magnetism.

Maybe spending so much time alone with Rue
hadn't been such a good idea after all, she thought. She
was already in way over her head, and though her escape was well planned, Jamey realized that her path to
freedom was no longer clear before her. Flames spi-

raled, blocking the way in every direction her mind turned. She could almost imagine that the danger she was in rivaled that of Rue's experience in the hotel in Las Vegas. The thought chilled her.

Jamey swallowed hard as she looked away from Rue's questioning glance, grasping and discarding idea after idea for somehow spending less time alone with him between now and the day he would leave. In her panic she could think of nothing to suggest that wouldn't instantly raise his suspicions.

"Jamey?" Rue touched her shoulder gently, confused by her sudden withdrawal.

She eased away from the contact, forcing a smile as she forced another lie. "I'm okay. I was just thinking about Johnny Cash being your friend," she said quietly as she turned and led the way out onto the sun-washed street.

Rue walked beside her easily, shortening his stride to match hers, smiling to himself at her stunned reaction to having met John. He was unaware of the frantic thoughts that spun on and on in her head as he ushered her into his car.

Jamey wasn't sure how she would endure the rest of the afternoon and evening. She had begun the day with such eager anticipation, looking forward to touring the studio with Rue, then going on to Opryland. She'd been excited about the thought of seeing not only the environment where Rue's work really began its journey toward the fans he sought to reach, but also of wandering hand-in-hand with him past Opryland's stages, some of which he had performed on in the past and others he might perform on in the future. Now she was afraid her visit to the 120-acre musical entertainment theme park would be little more than a struggle to behave normally, to keep Rue from recognizing her fear as she searched for some alternative that would force them into the company of others.

A wry smile, a grimace really, moved across Jamey's expressive features as they entered the park and were immediately swallowed up into the throng of tourists who had come to enjoy Opryland's offerings. The Nashville visitor's guide Rue had bought her told her that the park hosted about two million visitors each year, visitors who had come to sample the entertainment provided by more than a dozen musical shows, more than twenty rides that thrilled and amused in varying degrees, and by the artistry of craftsmen who displayed their wares and their talents throughout the grounds.

If anything, she felt more alone with him than ever in the anonymity the crowd forced on them. Oh, she noticed the curious stares of passersby as they eyed Rue, wondering why he looked so familiar and whether or not they dared draw his attention away from the girl at his side by asking his name. But it wasn't the sort of crowd she had in mind. Jamey longed for familiar faces, familiar voices, people who could make her feel more at ease simply by being there, by sharing Rue's attentions with her.

"A penny for your thoughts," Rue offered, a slight frown marring his features.

"They wouldn't be worth it," Jamey said as lightly as she could manage. "I was just wondering what we should do first," she fibbed, lifting her guidebook so he could see the page she had turned to. She had to snap out of it, she thought, forcing a smile to cover the worriedly thoughtful look she knew she'd been wearing.

"That's easy. The Opry," he said firmly, an answering smile replacing his frown as he reached out to close the book and take her free hand in his own. Jamey gave him her hand willingly, grateful that he had believed her so readily and that his frown was gone. She didn't want to see his frown in memory when time and distance had come inextricably between them.

As they walked toward the massive structure that was now home for the Grand Ole Opry, Rue told her something of its history, and Jamey tried to listen. But her mind still wandered, still sought a solution to her problem.

"The Opry was originally aired from the fifth floor of the National Life building in downtown Nashville, but grew in popularity so rapidly that it was soon moved to Studio C, an acoustically designed auditorium that held all of five hundred fans." Rue shook his head at the number that, by today's standards, was minuscule. "After that became too small, it was moved first to the Hillsboro Theater, then to an old tabernacle in eastern Nashville, and later to the War Memorial Auditorium." Absorbed now in his subject, Rue continued, unaware that he still held only part of Jamey's attention. "In 1943 the Opry moved to Ryman Auditorium, which seated three thousand. I'll take you there sometime," he added, smiling down at her and accepting her hasty nod in reply. "It's a fascinating old place. It was built as a religious tabernacle in 1891 by Tom Ryman, who was a riverboat captain, but became the stage for the Opry from 1943 to 1974, when this was completed," he said, indicating the sophisticated theater that loomed ahead of them. But even as his eyes moved from Jamey's face to the modern building he led her toward, his mind still walked the hallowed grounds of Ryman Auditorium. "You know, sometimes when I'm in Ryman, I'd swear I can feel the presence of the greats who've played the Opry," he said softly, his words an odd mixture of reverence and respect.

Jamey wondered if his thoughts included Johnny Cash at that moment. Hers did. And they started it all over again, the uneasy feeling that had begun to slip away from her as she too became absorbed in Rue's thoughts and words.

Rue shook his head, clearing away the mists of time that had carried him to an era long since past. His smile was tender as he led Jamey into what he told her was the largest broadcast studio in the world, and easily the most sophisticated theater in America. He still held her hand, and the movement of his thumb against her palm caused a tingling throughout her body. Her reaction to the sensual caress, and her efforts to hide her desire to turn into his arms, provided a new distraction.

Jamey worked to focus her attention solely on his words as he led her around the auditorium, pointing out the church pews, like those at Ryman, but carpeted now for comfort, that seated well over four thousand fans. And at last, as he showed her the stage where the most talented of America's country music stars appeared before the familiar red barn backdrop, she succeeded in shaking the thoughts that had plagued her, if not in suppressing her desire to feel the gentle pressure of Rue's arms slide around her and his lips come down to claim hers. She imagined him on the stage, bathed in the beam of spotlights as the most modern of audio equipment carried his music to millions of listeners—to those who filled the auditorium and to those who listened to the radio broadcast of the Grand Ole Opry show.

When they left the Grand Ole Opry House, Jamey walked contentedly at Rue's side throughout the picturesque park, enjoying the variety of themed musical shows, and laughing with him as they sampled some of Opryland's rides. Later, as she nestled peacefully into the comfortable seat of the Mercedes on the drive home, she forgot everything other than her own sweet pleasure in moments spent with Rue.

The ride seemed short, too short, as they rolled along in a silence that felt soft and warm, like snuggling into a downy comforter on a cold winter night. Rue's hands at the wheel were sure, and Jamey had to resist the urge she felt to reach out and touch him each time he shifted gears, the backs of his fingers lightly brushing against her cotton-clad thigh.

"Home again," he said softly as he brought the car to a stop in the drive.

"Yes," Jamey whispered, watching as he deftly flicked the key, silencing the powerful engine. Watching as he turned toward her for only an instant, then turned back to open his door and step out.

Rue offered his hand to help her from the car, then slid his arm around her shoulders as they walked slowly onto the deck. At the door he turned her gently into his arms. He held her, simply held her, for a moment, his cheek resting against the top of her head as his arms tightened around her.

"See you tomorrow night?" he asked finally, quietly, lifting his head and drawing back from her to let his eyes meet hers. "Around seven?"

Jamey nodded. A lump rose in her throat as she gazed into his eyes, as she responded to the gentle pressure that pulled her toward him. The lump dissolved as his lips met hers. She slid her own arms around Rue's waist, clinging to the strong male feel of him, and her thoughts floated free as she reveled in the sensations of love and longing his kiss evoked.

"Jamey," Rue whispered as his lips left hers, "I—" He stopped, and she opened her eyes to gaze questioningly at him.

"What?" she asked softly when he remained silent.

His hands moved to her arms, set her away from him. "I'll see you tomorrow night...at seven," he said firmly. One hand came up to brush lightly across her cheek, to tuck a wayward strand of raven hair behind her ear before he turned and moved quickly toward his car.

For the moment Jamey's thoughts were focused on

the words Rue had left unsaid. She wondered what he had started to say, what he'd thought that had prompted him to leave her so abruptly. She lifted her hand, waved in answer to his own wave of farewell, then turned to go inside, her mind still filled with questions.

But later, alone again after Rue had kissed her so tenderly and put her from him so firmly as he left to return to Nashville, her thoughts returned to the unsolved puzzle of what could be done to keep her from sinking any further into the abyss of her love for him. Her mind sought unsuccessfully for some alternative, something to suggest that would involve more than just the two of them.

She was still wrestling with the problem when she arrived at Tanasie Basin for work the next morning, but pushed it away at the sight of Mac waiting for her in her office. A solution would have to be found later, she thought as she smilingly answered Mac's cheerful greeting.

Jamey's smile of greeting grew into a radiant beam as Mac explained his presence. He casually, unwittingly, answered the question that had seemed to be without answer by suggesting a camping trip for the long Labor Day weekend.

Mac wanted to take a group of perhaps eight boys on the trip, to travel by horseback to one of the small lakes nestled on the acres of state land surrounding Tanasie Basin State School. He needed two adults besides himself and Meg in order to proceed with his plans. And he was inviting Jamey and Rue to fill those slots.

"It was Meg's idea, actually," Mac admitted when Jamey's look questioned the offer. The thought that a camping trip didn't sound like any plan her sometimes overcautious friend would suggest had occurred to her, but was quickly cast aside for more favorable thoughts of the growing influence Meg seemed to have with Mac. Meg still wasn't technically due to begin work at

Tanasie Basin until the following week, but she had already put in long hours. And many of those hours had been spent with Mac. Jamey liked the feeling she had that Mac was developing a close friendship with the lovely red-haired woman, a friendship that would add to the one he already shared with her brother.

"But are you sure, Mac?" she asked suddenly, thinking with a sinking feeling that she couldn't endure a weekend of hostility between Rue and Mac. Not even for the sake of solving her problem.

"I'm sure," he said, a wry smile crossing his face. "I don't think I've been exactly fair to Rue Garrett, Jamey," he apologized. "At least, Meg assures me I haven't. The man is far more than young Carlson's idol. He represents a world of phenomenal success—crime-free success—that provides a healthy example for all our residents," he added sincerely. "And you know the boys would be delighted to have him along." Mac's voice held appeal as he ended his request.

The olive branch had been extended and Jamey accepted it gratefully. She'd been uncomfortable with the enmity that had existed between two men she cared so much for, though she knew it couldn't really matter in the long run, for she would be leaving soon. Very soon, she reminded herself, and her heart started to pound at the thought.

Jamey was enthusiastic about the idea, agreeing readily with Mac's comment that the boys would be delighted to have Rue go with them as she strove to hide her sudden agitation. She had long since accepted that there was no way to avoid spending this last weekend with Rue, to avoid adding even more to the cost that she now feared she could never pay. She had also admitted to herself, quite honestly, that there was no way she would give up these last precious days of being with Rue. But being with him in a group, especially the group Mac proposed, should be far easier than coping with the now constant pain she felt when they were alone together.

Thoughts of the camping trip, of the lively group who was going, comforted her as she drove home after a productive day of work. They calmed her fears as she changed into light blue cotton slacks and a V-necked white top, and later fortified her belief that they *had* to go as she met Rue's resistance to the idea.

"Almost any other time, Jamey," Rue said firmly as he pulled her into the circle of his arms, "but not this last weekend before the road trip. I want to be alone with you, just the two of us," he whispered, nibbling at her ear.

Jamey's skin tingled where his lips made contact. "But I've already told Mac we'd go," she fibbed, alarmed by the way her body reacted to his touch over and over again. She wanted to melt against him, but she couldn't. Somehow, she had to convince him, she thought. "And the guys are really looking forward to your being there."

Rue leaned back, his eyes slightly narrowed as he watched her. Jamey brushed at an imaginary speck of lint on his shirt as she worked to maintain her composure. She was acutely aware that, though Rue didn't know it, this was their last weekend together. Period. But the ache that thought brought with it was cast aside in her need to protect her own fragile emotions.

"This means a lot to you, doesn't it?" Rue asked finally, still watching her closely.

Jamey only nodded.

"Even though it means giving up our last weekend alone before I leave on a twenty-four-day tour?" he questioned softly.

Jamey's eyes widened at the gentleness of his tone. She choked back the impulse to yield to his persuasions, the love she felt for him almost overpowering the wiser course of talking him into the trip.

"Going camping will be good for you, Rue," she pleaded, "a chance to get completely away from the city and its rush before the road trip. And we can be alone anytime," she lied, her fingers tracing the outline of his strong chin.

Jamey knew she was deceiving him horribly. She knew that there was little justification for the web of lies she was weaving around her every action, no matter how small. But to spend the weekend alone with him, given the secret knowledge that only she possessed, would be too dangerous. She had come terrifyingly close to revealing her secret to him several times during the past week, but she had held out. And she couldn't turn back now. It was too late. She couldn't face Rue's anger if he should discover the deception she was practicing.

"Okay, Jamey," Rue agreed at last. Reluctantly, but he agreed, then became more and more involved in planning the trip as his interest grew. Once he had made a decision, Rue rarely let anything stand in his way.

Jamey would have done well to remember how he had stormed into her life, rejecting her protests until he had won the response he wanted. Her only saving grace, had she thought of it, was that he didn't yet realize how thoroughly he had won.

Chapter Eight

Jamey drew her legs up, clasping her hands around them and letting her chin settle easily onto her knees, as she watched the flickering firelight make long shadows of the bodies clustered around its friendly warmth. Rue sat across from her on an old log, his guitar resting lightly across his thighs, the dancing flames casting changing patterns of light and dark over his relaxed form.

Rue's eyes were closed, and he listened with apparent pleasure as Steve's young voice filled the night air. Jamey's gaze swept over the length of him and rose to his face. Love dominated the soft brownness of her eyes as she watched him, imprinting each feature forever in her memory. As the last chord faded into silence Jamey looked away, loath to have Rue catch her staring at him. That would be too revealing.

"I swear, Steve, that song sounds better every time I hear it." Rue spoke quietly against the stillness of the evening.

A murmur of general assent rippled through the group of campers as Steve timidly accepted the praise. "Thanks," he said simply, quietly.

Understanding shone in Rue's eyes. Somehow he sensed the damage that had been done to Steve, recognized the overwhelming insecurity that ate at the youth. "Let's do one together," he suggested, moving over on the log to make room for Steve.

As Steve joined him he named a song that had been
a big hit for Mississippi River. Steve grinned his agreement. He was still so shy of the attention Rue gave
him, subconsciously certain that their growing friendship was too good to be true, and that any minute could
bring a rejection similar to those he had experienced
throughout much of his young life.

Pain shot through Jamey and she tensed, trying to
make the hurt be only for Steve and not for herself.
She loathed self-pity. Determinedly she pushed her
ugly thoughts away, the thoughts of the price she was
already paying for having fallen in love with Rue, and
forced herself to focus on the present.

Looking back at the two seated on the log, Jamey
succeeded in pulling herself into the here and now, but
still it hurt. It seemed that every moment brought
greater strength to a love she had tried so hard to deny.

Rue raised his guitar in capable hands, hands that
had molded her body to his, and the instrument became an inseparable extension of the man. His long,
sensitive fingers worked easily, quickly tuning each
string. Jamey cursed silently at the stupidity of being
jealous of an inanimate object simply because it was,
for the moment, the focus of Rue's world. She deliberately transferred her gaze to Steve as he followed suit,
checking the tuning of his own instrument and bringing it into accord with Rue's.

At Rue's satisfied nod, ten fingers began a race over
steel strings as they stretched to reach the chords of the
fast-paced song. Two hands strummed in unison, and
two throaty tenor voices evoked all the innuendos of
human joy as they sang. Jamey thrilled to the sound,
her pain of a moment before temporarily eased as she
joined her companions in clapping hands and moving
in place to the beat of the happy tune.

"Whew!" Rue grinned broadly at Steve as the song
ended, then moved into the beginning of another, sig-

naling the youth to keep pace with him. "Sing with us," he encouraged the group.

They sang for nearly an hour before Rue declared that his throat was parched, his look inviting Steve to join him as he set his guitar aside and stood, stretching tense limbs. Together, they went in search of liquid refreshment.

Jamey's love-sharpened perceptions were quick to register the meaning behind the look of determined satisfaction written across Rue's face as he draped a muscular arm over the younger man's shoulders. Her growing knowledge of Rue's nature sent a tingle of anticipation shivering up her spine. He had made a decision about something. And Jamey was willing to bet that the something was "Sweet Freedom," Steve's song.

Covertly she watched as Rue passed a cup of water to Steve, her mind only half taking in that the group around her was beginning to break up. She was far more interested in the intense discussion taking place only yards away, in the beaming smile that suddenly lit Steve's face.

"Did you hear me, Jamey?"

Jamey snapped her head around and encountered Meg's knowing grin. "I'm sorry. What did you say?"

"I said, I'll see you at the tent in a bit. Mac and I are going for a walk," she repeated. Her smile grew broader at Jamey's still dazed expression. "Tent, t-e-n-t, a portable shelter, usually of canvas stretched over a supporting framework of poles, ropes, and pegs," she intoned in a singsong imitation of her best teacher voice, teasing Jamey for her lack of comprehension. "Remember, we're sharing one."

"Oh... okay," Jamey replied dumbly, her attention finally focusing on the other woman's meaning. She still hadn't registered Meg's statement that she and Mac were going for a walk, alone together in the middle of the night. "See you shortly," Jamey promised.

Meg moved away, tossing her agreement lightly over her shoulder as she joined Mac where he waited beneath a towering tree. Jamey had already turned back to check on Rue and Steve. She missed the gentle linking of hands as two familiar figures moved off into the distance.

Rue's long strides were eating up the distance that separated him from Jamey. His expression was a study in pleasure. The feeling seeped through him at the thought of what he had just accomplished with Steve. Finding Jamey alone by the campfire only amplified his satisfaction.

Jamey's eyes followed his progress for a moment, then slid away to find Steve. The youth headed quickly toward the tent he shared with three of his peers, his arm lifted toward her in a silent good-night. She answered with a lift of her own hand, torn between the desire to talk with him about what had just transpired and her greater desire to have a few moments alone with Rue. They had been almost constantly surrounded by the others during the weekend, had found almost no time to be alone, and Jamey literally ached with the need to feel his arms around her, his lips on hers. There was no contest. Rue could tell her everything she needed to know about his conversation with Steve.

"Ah, alone at last," he drawled softly as he entered the circle of warmth cast off by the dying fire. He reached for her, his open arms inviting.

Jamey needed no second invitation as he echoed the thoughts that had been spinning through her mind. It seemed like years since she had last been held close in the protective comfort of his arms. She lifted her chin, offering him her lips, and he accepted the gift tenderly.

The kiss was long and deep, but Jamey sighed a quiet protest as his mouth left hers. The sound brought

Rue's head down again to take more of the sweetness she yielded so eagerly.

"God, Jamey," Rue said softly as he tilted her head against his chest, his fingers toying with the silken strands of her hair. "How can a simple kiss affect me so deeply?"

The question was rhetorical. Jamey knew exactly what he meant. She felt it too, a sort of nameless longing that started deep within her and screamed for release with each added second of contact. *What a fool I am,* she thought, but deliberately avoided pursuing the idea. She hesitated to follow its lead into the hinterlands of whether she was a fool for yielding to Rue's attraction or a fool for even considering leaving him.

"What did you and Steve talk about?" she asked quietly when her heartbeats had slowed to a more normal pace.

Rue laughed softly. It wasn't the direction he had hoped she would take, but it would have to do. She felt his cheek lift into a smile, moving against the top of her head as he lightly countered her question. "Curiosity killed the cat, little one," Rue teased. "I saw you sitting here squirming with your need to know."

"Well?" Jamey's lone word spoke volumes.

Rue's expression was serious when he answered. "Well, nothing. Steve has to think my proposal over, and once he's made his decision, he'll let the rest of us know what it is."

"But what was your proposal?" she prompted. Jamey stepped back, raising determined brown eyes to equally determined gray-blue ones.

"As much as I'd like to, I'm not going to tell you, Jamey," Rue said sincerely. "This is Steve's moment, and I won't take it from him by speaking out of turn." He paused, thinking. "All I'll tell you is that I had an idea I thought Steve would like, and I decided that tonight was the time to tell him about it."

Jamey didn't much care for the answer that was no answer at all, but she could do nothing about it. She recognized the firmness of conviction in Rue's voice and knew that no amount of cajoling would get any more out of him than he had already told her. She looked down, scuffing a sneaker-clad toe in the dirt, and Rue laughed softly at the action that revealed her perplexity.

"Come on. I'll walk you to your tent," he said gently, sliding his hand down to link with hers.

Rue pressed a quick kiss to her forehead as they came to a halt in front of the canvas structure. The sounds of someone moving around inside, getting ready for bed, indicated that Meg had returned. Her presence cut short their good-night. A light hug and a whispered "Dream of me" were all Rue left her with as he turned and moved silently toward the tent he shared with Mac. She needed so much more.

Jamey inhaled deeply and lifted the flap of the tent, all too aware that tonight was the last night of the camping trip. Tomorrow they would break camp and return to civilization, return to the single day left to them, all that remained to separate Jamey from a lifetime without Rue.

Meg turned as she entered, ready to speak, then stopped cold as she registered the sadness that clouded Jamey's eyes. She wasn't sure what she had expected, but not this—definitely not this downcast sorrow that bespoke an intense, overwhelming inner misery. Meg's heart wrenched inside her, and she reached out to Jamey in the only way she knew.

"Jamey, have you and Rue talked about what's happening between the two of you?" she queried gently.

Jamey's eyes flew up to meet the open honesty of Meg's green ones. "What do you mean, Meg?"

"Oh, Jamey...if I'm intruding, just tell me, but it's pretty obvious that you two are in love," she said sincerely, "and more than obvious that you, in particular, are awfully unhappy about something."

Jamey's thoughts were too chaotic to deny the truth of the other woman's words. Lord, was her love for Rue so apparent? And if it was, had he discovered it too? That would be the worst that could happen—for Rue to know, with absolutely no question, that she was in love with him. Her mind fairly reeled from the impact of the thought, and she opened up to Meg as she had opened up to very few people in her life.

"No, you're not really intruding." Jamey's words were spoken so quietly that Meg had to strain to hear them. She sat down on her sleeping bag, Indian style, waiting for Jamey to continue.

It was a moment before anything further came out. When it did, the words tumbled out on a choking sob. "But there's not much that can be said. I'm just dreading leaving Tennessee... and Rue." Jamey's lips trembled as her eyes lifted, swimming with tears, toward Meg.

The importance of her words registered as she caught the full force of Meg's confused look. Panic gripped her, sending an intense wave of near nausea rippling through her. "I mean... of course, we've talked about it, and we've made plans to see each other, but it just won't be the same," Jamey hastily lied, trying to ensure that Meg wouldn't accidentally let slip the news of her imminent departure in Rue's hearing.

"Oh." The word came out hesitantly. Something was wrong here, but Meg couldn't quite put her finger on what it was. "Mac said something about the possibility of your staying on as the administrator of the school. Why don't you?"

The implication that Meg had discussed the matter with Mac temporarily escaped Jamey. "I can't," she sighed, fighting back the tears that pooled in her eyes.

"I've already scheduled other consulting commitments, and you of all people must know how much work goes into developing a career in consulting," she went on plaintively, her quavering voice revealing the pain she felt.

"That's what Mac said. He told me you had consistently turned the position down." Meg pondered her next words before speaking. "But, Jamey, I don't understand why you would if that's the only way you can stay here with Rue."

Meg's words finally penetrated the ache. "You and Mac have discussed my relationship with Rue?" she asked, astonishment rising above her torment.

"Yes," Meg admitted a little sheepishly, "and more than that." Her eyes fell away from Jamey's startled stare, then returned. Renewed conviction filled her voice as she started again. "Jamey, I have to be honest with you. I'm very interested in Mac. As a man, I mean. And I know that he was interested in you for a time...before Rue. He told me, though he needn't have bothered. I knew that from the very first night when we all had dinner at Sperry's. But even then I was pretty sure your interest was in Rue. And when you refused to go to Nashville with Mac and me, I was certain. If you had felt anything more than friendship for Mac, you would never have encouraged him to go out with another woman, not even his friend's little sister," she added wryly. "And now I think I'm finally making some headway with him, becoming more to him than Damon's sister," Meg said wistfully, her eyes sparkling at the memory of the walk she'd taken with Mac, of the kiss they had shared. But she didn't mention the kiss to Jamey. She simply added, "Which is exactly what I intended."

Jamey's eyes rounded in wonder, her pain momentarily arrested. She was astounded by the freedom Meg seemed to feel to simply choose her man and go after him. It was worlds away from the approach she had lived with for twenty-six years, the careful avoidance of any romantic entanglements. She let the idea gel in her mind before commenting. "I like it," she mused.

"Like what?" Meg laughed nervously.

"I like you and Mac...together, I mean! I once told myself that there was a wonderful woman for Mac," Jamey remembered, her dampened eyes almost sparkling, "and you're here. I like it!" she stated firmly. The thought that this camping trip could be the start of something marvelous for Mac and Meg warmed the icy coldness that had surrounded her heart. But the dichotomy of her thought, wishing that Mac and Meg would get together even as she plotted a course that would surely destroy the bond that tied her to Rue, escaped Jamey.

"Thanks," Meg responded. "I had hoped you would feel that way, but I wasn't sure. And it still doesn't solve your problem. Are you sure you couldn't base your consulting work out of Nashville?"

The question brought it all back, all the pain that had been alleviated for the brief moment Jamey had spent looking into what the future might hold for Mac and Meg. She didn't want any more pain. She wanted to end this discussion. "I'll think about it," Jamey promised as she slipped out of her jeans and into her sleeping bag.

Meg accepted the end Jamey brought to their talk, and slipped quietly into her own sleeping bag. The even sounds of her breathing reached Jamey's ears. Meg had fallen quickly into a deep, untroubled sleep.

Jamey wasn't so lucky. She lay awake for hours, thinking and hurting. She tossed in her warm bag, silently hating the thoughts that held the blessed relief of sleep at bay. Finally, when the light of the approaching dawn began to filter through the flaps at the front of the tent, Jamey accepted that she would get no sleep that night. She rose quietly and dressed, then slipped out into the semidarkness of the early morning hour, moving stealthily toward the shore of the small lake.

Jamey didn't know how long she sat there, kept company only by the wretched, torturing thoughts that went round and round in her head. Honestly, at that point, she didn't care how long she had sat there. She only cared that some relief emerge from the hours of soul-searching. Communing with nature had proved no more helpful than talking with Meg or searching her own mind for answers during the long night.

She tried to focus on the dawning day, to escape the mental beating she was inflicting on her battered emotions. The day was dawning bright and clear. The sun stole up in the east, gradually nudging darkness from the lush greens of the Tennessee landscape, competing with the still visible moon. Rays of light slanted over the sleeping countryside, bringing definition to the scene and separating the brighter greens of the verdant turf from the deeper shades of water that lapped gently at the land. The brighter ball that was the sun set the vista ablaze with a million twinkling lights as its beams danced across the dewy wetness. A bird sang its morning call, and Jamey tilted her chin, eyes seeking the source of the trilling notes as she let out a weary sigh. But not even the breaking of a new day could still her thoughts for long.

Jamey had always considered herself to be forward-thinking, never one to dwell on the past. And, unquestionably, one who seldom cried. Yet her world since meeting Rue seemed to consist largely of shedding tears over some memory or some thought of her half-empty future that hurt too much to be admitted to even her own self, let alone put into words. She had spent the long night indulging herself in the freedom to think and to cry over her thoughts, subconsciously hoping that her actions would wash away most of the pain. They hadn't, and she turned her reflections to the career that demanded her denial of Rue.

Consulting generally left little time for developing strong ties. She had taken the temporary nature of her work for granted, she realized now, had lived in a fantasy world of false security. Jamey was usually gone from most places almost as soon as she had arrived, and she had relied on that transitory rush to keep others—especially male others—from touching her heart too deeply. Tanasie Basin had been unusual in the fact that her contract had held her here long enough to develop ties, to have her heart touched very deeply. And God, how those ties hurt! she thought bitterly as she vowed that her future contracts would all be short and sweet.

Silent tears slipped from her eyes again, and Jamey angrily dashed them away. *I won't cry any more,* she promised herself. *My course is set, and I'll damn well stick to it.* But her determination was no more effective in staying the vision that danced crazily before her eyes, rendering the breathtaking beauty of the sunrise into nothingness, than the scene itself had been in stilling her thoughts.

Time gave way, and Jamey was lost again to looking backward, forgetting the promising future that called to her. The vision shimmered in the air like a ghostly review of a well-remembered movie. Rue worked in tandem with Mac, organizing the chaotic group of eight teen-age boys and four excited adults. Rue sat astride the leggy roan gelding, at ease with the animal and with the acitivity, at home in the saddle. Rue taught the youths the importance of taking proper care of their mounts, overseeing the currying and grooming after the long ride. Rue teased Jamey and Meg about women's work as they set up the area that served them as kitchen over the weekend, then ducked and ran, laughing, as they called him a chauvinist and chased him away. Rue set up a rope swing for the boys to use to fly out over the lake, to drop into the cool water like great stones, then joined in the exuberant game himself.

The weekend had flicked through Jamey's mind with alarming speed, but slowed at the scene beside the lake. Rue's muscles rippled as he swung out over the lake, the sun glinting off his bronzed body as he dropped lithely into the water. His laughter rang out as he joined the youths in teasing and ducking each other. Then he emerged from the water like some avenging sea god, dragging Jamey to the swing for a turn, following behind her to steal a kiss underwater.

A kiss underwater. Jamey's fingers moved to her lips as she relived the sensual feeling. At that moment she had regretted talking Rue into the camping trip. If she hadn't, they would have been alone, their kisses free instead of fleeting stolen things whenever Rue was sure no one was looking. But someone had been looking, and they had teased them unmercifully about it.

Rue had accepted their teasing good-naturedly, their comments opening up a whole new world of manly discussion, and Jamey and Meg had stolen away as the sidelong glances of the youths suggested their discomfort at the women's presence. They had wanted to talk openly with Rue and Mac about women. They couldn't with two in their midst. Jamey would have given a lot to have known what was said in that discussion.

The flickering of moving pictures rolled on in Jamey's mind as Rue watched, wondering what had captured her attention so completely. He hadn't slept much, either. He had been too filled with wanting her, with hating the thought of leaving her for the time he would be gone on the road trip. He wondered what she would say to his idea, but hesitated before joining her, drinking in the sight of her as she rested her chin on arms that were folded across raised knees.

In profile, she might have been a very young girl. *My woman-child,* he thought, as his eyes traced each feature, then followed the line of her jet-black hair as it hung down her back in a single braid. It shone in the slanting rays of sunlight, reminding him anew of the song he had begun writing after their trip to the recording studio.

Jamey rocked forward slightly, then leaned back, catching herself with her hands as she extended her legs before her. Her jeans were molded to her slender form, the heavy shirt protecting her from the chill of the early morning air. Yet she shivered slightly and let out a long sigh that pulled Rue forward.

He moved quietly up behind her, squatting and placing a gentle kiss on her exposed neck. She hadn't seen or heard him, but she didn't flinch as the caress registered in her suffering brain. Somehow, it seemed right that he should be there, conjured up from the telepathic messages of her thoughts. Jamey leaned back against his knees as she turned a soft smile to him. He would not see her pain, she vowed.

"Morning," he whispered. "Enjoying the sunrise?"

"Yes," she whispered back to him, loath to speak in normal tones and shatter the fragile moment. It wasn't really a lie. She *had* seen it. It just hadn't been the focus of her thoughts, as Rue surmised.

"The others are still asleep," he said softly.

Jamey nodded. She was glad they were, glad of these few additional moments alone with Rue in this beautiful setting. The still of the morning combined with Rue's presence to soothe her, to give her the strength to solidify her thoughts and accept the wisdom of her plan. Yielding to her love for him would surely signal the end to her career, an end she couldn't accept. She would follow the course she had plotted, but for now she would yield to the sweet pleasure of pretending that she and Rue would go on forever, together.

Rue shifted his position, settling himself behind her, his long legs extending beside hers, one on either side of her. He took the full weight of her against his chest as he slid his arms around her. Jamey let her head fall back to rest lightly on his shoulder.

He kissed her ear, the simple action setting up a tingling sensation that thrilled her. She nuzzled closer to him, hugging the arms that held her.

"I had a good idea last night," he whispered as he breathed in the soft fragrance of her hair. "Why don't you talk to Mac about taking some time off, and come with us on the road trip?" His tone had been so sincere, but now he teased. "A couple of the other guys will be bringing their wives, so we would be well chaperoned."

Jamey felt the tension beginning to knot in the pit of her stomach, but willed herself to relax. She couldn't slip now, not in words or in actions. Closing her eyes, she answered the appealing invitation.

"I can't, Rue." Her sibilant tones held regret. "Classes start tomorrow, and there's simply no way I can take time off right now. It's a critical time for the school." Jamey held her breath, preparing for the lie that formed itself on her lips. "Next time," she promised.

"I'll hold you to that, you know," he said softly. "I think I knew what your answer would have to be this time. I understand how important your work is to you. Believe me, I understand," he sighed.

I hope so, Jamey thought, fighting back the tears that welled up in her eyes and the choking sensation that closed her throat. *I hope so, because that's the only thing that might prevent your hating me in a very short time.* She shuddered, and Rue tightened his hold around her.

"Cold?"

"A little. The air's nippy this morning." Another truth that didn't quite tell the whole story slipped from her lips.

The stirrings in the camp reached their ears. Reluctant to surrender the quiet moment, they rose. Rue stood first, offering her his hand to pull her up beside him. The movement carried her into his arms, and the bittersweet tenderness of his kiss was shattering to her unsteady composure. Jamey gave up all the yearning sweetness of her mouth to him in total surrender.

"My God, Jamey," he growled huskily, every muscle tensed at her response. "You choose the damnedest times to offer things you don't even understand." Rue broke the contact before it became too much for both of them, and literally dragged her back toward the campsite.

Breaking camp turned into a game, with Rue and Mac directing traffic as efficiently as they had at the outset of the trip. But this time the young men who worked with them were much more proficient in following their instructions. They had learned a lot on this trip and rode back into the stableyard at dusk happy, but tired. Their pleasure was in direct contrast to the bittersweet pain that swept through every fiber of Jamey's being.

THE ROSES were waiting on Jamey's desk when she arrived at Tanasie Basin the next morning. The card read simply, "Good luck! Rue." But the possibility of a double meaning escaped nobody. Were the flowers just for luck, or was their vivid red color evidence of a deeper meaning?

Jamey flushed beautifully at the teasing she received, her cheeks nearly as red as the petals of the roses, but underneath she sang a joyous song. Rue had said that he understood her dedication to her work, and he had sent her the precious flowers. He had never said so in words, but Jamey thought he might love her as deeply as she loved him. And if that was so, he would understand and forgive what she had to do. Wouldn't he?

That hope carried her through the day, through the excitement of seeing all her hard work result in the opening of a school designed to offer a realistic education to all the youths committed to Tanasie Basin. It speeded her motions as she made her way back to the cabin and to the final evening she would spend with the only man who had ever broken through the veneer of her determined independence.

Rue arrived at the cabin shortly after Jamey. Held gently in his arms was a tiny, wriggling puppy. Jamey saw him moving toward the cabin with his struggling bundle and forgot her exhaustion as she flew to the door, flinging it open to let them in.

"Oh, Rue! How precious," she breathed as her fingers stroked lovingly over the small dog's head. A tiny pink tongue licked at her. "Where did you find it?"

"I found *him* at the humane society, one of my favorite haunts. I couldn't leave him there," he said, adding to the puppy's lapping appeal. "He needed a home." Rue transferred his minuscule burden to Jamey's arms. "And I figured you needed someone to keep you company while I'm away. He's yours," he said softly, his words hinting at the time when he would return, at the new dimensions he expected his homecoming to bring to their relationship.

Jamey's eyes flew to his, and she couldn't for the life of her choke back the tears that filled them and began a slow course down her cheeks.

Rue misread the tears. "I'll be back soon, Jamey," he offered consolingly. "You'll see. Road trips never seem as long as the women who wait at home think they will at the beginning."

She had to let him believe that his words were a true reflection of her thoughts. To do otherwise would be to risk giving everything away at the last moment. Rue would be leaving the next morning. Tonight would be the last time they would ever be together.

"What's his name?" Jamey changed the subject, trying hard not to let herself care, trying to reject the feeling of longing that welled up inside her as the puppy snuggled into the safety of her arms. What would she do with this adorable, dependent creature? she wondered miserably.

"He doesn't really have a name yet," Rue told her. "And since he's yours, you have to name him. But I've been calling him Puppy Love," he teased as he reached out a long arm, stroking first the silky hair of the puppy's tiny gray body, then sliding his hand up to Jamey's shoulder as he drew her to him. Puppy Love squirmed between them as they moved closer together, squeezing him in their efforts to meld into one being.

Chapter Nine

"Jamey, what in the hell are you doing?" Meg's astonishment was apparent in her harshly spoken words.

Barely glancing up, knowing that if she did the anger and pain she felt would be written all over her face, Jamey bit out a smart retort. "What does it look like?" Even to her own ears, the reply came out sounding sarcastic and bitter, a response Meg didn't deserve. Jamey turned her back to the other woman.

Meg sighed and moved into the office behind her friend. She regretted the impetuous reactions that seemed to be so much a part of her nature, something inherited along with the flaming curls that cascaded to her shoulders. She started over, aware of the need to erase the bald irritation of her first approach.

"It looks like you're cleaning out your desk, like you're getting ready to leave and never come back." Meg spoke in a near monotone, with no inflection belying the question behind the unadorned observation.

"Right the first time," Jamey quipped. She didn't want anger between herself and Meg, but she had to keep the conversation light. It had been nearly two weeks since the camping trip, since Meg had startled a weakened Jamey into admitting her love for Rue Garrett, and just over one week since Rue's departure on the road trip. Jamey knew that she had to stand firm, that she couldn't let Meg read any more into her replies than the simple fact that she was leaving Tanasie Basin after having completed what she had been hired to do. "All the terms of my contract have been fulfilled, so I'm doing what comes next for a consultant. I'm leaving, clearing out to let you and the others get on with the business of running this school."

"But why, Jamey?" Life returned to Meg's voice, wiping out the monotonous cadence she had momentarily adopted. "You promised to think about staying on as administrator, and even if you've decided against that, I thought you were scheduled to be here until the end of the month."

"I was, but what's the point in staying?" Jamey asked reasonably, turning at last to face Meg. "I have decided against accepting the position of administrator," she admitted, "and my work here is done, so it's time for me to go. The break will give me an opportunity to settle in at home and to prepare myself for the jobs I've scheduled there."

Bright green eyes bored into her. "What about Rue?"

Jamey tensed in reaction to Meg's boldness. One of the things she liked best about the other oman was her direct approach, but she could have done without it at the moment. "What about him?" she asked, her tone flippant.

"Oh, come on, Jamey! That doesn't wash, and you know it. He's off on a road trip, a trip he would have canceled if he could, fully expecting you to be here waiting for him when he comes home. "So," she continued, giving up the struggle to deny the birthright of her red hair, "I repeat my earlier question. What in the hell are you doing?" The astonished anger that had permeated her voice when she had first entered Jamey's office returned.

Jamey folded her arms protectively in front of her, the action revealing her withdrawal. "Not you too,

Meg," she sighed, shaking her head in rejection of the confrontation. "I've already been through a heavy scene with Mac over this, and I just can't take any more."

"Can't take any more?" Meg's tone was sarcastic. "And just how is Rue supposed to feel when he gets back and finds you gone?" Fury at the thought of anyone taking a chance on destroying something as precious as what was growing between her and Mac spurred Meg's words.

Toes could never be as fascinating as Jamey pretended, looking down at her sandaled feet. "He's supposed to feel angry at first," she confessed, "righteously angry. So angry that he'll want to forget he ever met me." Undisguised pain crept into Jamey's voice at the thought of Rue regretting what they had known together, spilling over into her next words. "Then he's supposed to realize that what we had was a fleeting thing, a kind of summer romance that was good while it lasted but now has to fade into a pleasant memory."

"Boy, you're one of the world's best at kidding yourself, aren't you? If you think for one minute that Rue Garrett is going to let you get away with this, you're crazy! You seem to forget, Jamey, I know. I was with you on that camping trip, and I've been with you since. This is no fleeting summer romance you can simply turn your back on and walk away from. You just may be making the biggest mistake of your life," she said disgustedly.

"No!" The denial was ripped from Jamey's throat. "The mistake would be if I stayed in Tennessee a minute longer than I have to, stayed here where everything is a constant reminder of a love that can never be!" Pain tore away Jamey's facade of cool resistance, and the words that followed were terrifyingly honest. "Both Rue and I have demanding careers, commitments that leave no room for what we are together. Can't you understand that neither of us would be happy with the sort of relationship that found us on opposite sides of the nation as often as it found us together?'' she appealed. ''And that I can't be happy giving up a career I've spent years planning and training for?'' The last admission spent what remained of Jamey's will to fight. She turned away from the fire that flashed at her through Meg's eyes.

''God! Mac's right.'' Meg was relentless in her condemnation. ''You *are* a fool when it comes to your own emotions, Jamey. You're damn good at what you do, I'll give you that, but somehow you missed out on growing up emotionally.'' Tension crackled in the air as Meg drew a deep breath before hurling a final insult. ''The sad part of this whole mess is that your paucity of feelings doesn't hurt just you. You don't deserve Rue Garrett!''

Before Jamey could gather her wits to respond to the horrible declamation, Meg had turned and fled. She had stated her feelings clearly. She wasn't interested in listening to any more of Jamey's weak rationalizations.

Jamey sat down, trying to still the trembling that had invaded her legs. Slowly she worked at the miserable task of cleaning out her desk, her methodic actions belying the chaotic twisting of her thoughts.

A fool, Jamey pondered bitterly. *How right you are, Meg! All kinds of a fool for not nipping this thing in the bud before it became an ache I'll carry with me for the rest of my life. But never an emotional pauper. I've grown up in ways no one else could even begin to comprehend since meeting Rue—and I wish I hadn't! I'd rather never have known what it felt like to love than to walk around with the dead weight of my heart feeling like a cracked stone inside my chest,* she judged fiercely as she closed the center drawer of the large wood desk for the final time.

Jamey felt as though a page had been turned, inexorably closing the brief chapter that had brought love to

her life, as she made her way to the parking lot and to
the car that would carry her away from Tanasie Basin.
Mac, or one of his minions, would retrieve the car tomorrow, would pick it up from where she left it at the
airport. It was useless to hope that he would be there to
see her off. They were all, these people she had come
to care for so deeply, so angry at her defection that they
seemed only to want to cut her out of their lives. The
pain was like a knife twisting in her heart.

Tears blurred her vision as she glanced back and
found Steve watching forlornly from the window of his
dormitory room. Jamey raised her hand hesitantly in
farewell, then turned and quickly entered the waiting
vehicle. She had already said good-bye to him, had said
her good-byes to all of them. All that was left to do was
to pick up the crate Puppy Love would ride in on the
long flight to Oregon, to complete her packing at the
cabin, and to spend one last night in the cozy confines
that now seemed to hold more torment than promise.
Tomorrow she would leave it all behind her.

That realization sustained Jamey through the conclu-
sive motions of packing the few remaining items that
belonged to her. Most of the cabin's furnishings would
be left behind, left for Tom and Bonnie Martin's next
tenant.

Another ache took hold at the memory of her leave-
taking from Rue's grandparents. They hadn't believed
her lie that Rue knew of her return to Oregon. Perhaps
they knew him too well to believe that he would let her
go. Deliberately she pushed aside her remembrances of
the hurt reflected in their eyes as she had explained her
precipitate departure and offered her treasured plants
to Bonnie as a parting gift of thanks for all they had
done for her, denied that their taciturn acceptance of
both her gift and her explanation had been almost
more than she could bear.

Jamey lowered herself to the floor, sitting on crossed

legs as she reached for the blanket and began arranging it in the small cage. Puppy Love took a leave of absence from the war he waged against the bright red sock, cocking his head quizzically to one side as he watched her transfer his now familiar bedding to the strange enclosure. The comical expression brought a bubble of laughter to Jamey's throat, her first laughter in what seemed ages.

"Not to worry, little boy," she told the puppy. "I know what I'm doing." Soft brown eyes stared at her, almost questioning the truth of her statement. "I do, you know," Jamey assured both of them as she reached out to scratch the silky ears vigorously, then turned back to the incomplete job of making a comfortable haven for the little creature's long ride.

Her task completed, Jamey pulled the soft, shaggy body into her lap, stroking gently at his long, gray fur. "Puppy Love...what a dumb name," she muttered. "But you'll soon earn a real name," she promised as the little dog looked up at the sound of her voice.

The small gray mop snuggled against her, as though he sensed the upheaval taking place in both their lives and sought to give and receive comfort. Jamey hugged him to her as she continued in a low, husky voice. "You can't go on being known as Puppy Love forever, you know. Someday you're going to grow up to be a big strong dog, and what would your peers think if you had a name like that? Hmmm?"

A tiny pink tongue licked at her nose, reminding her of the man who had dubbed the puppy with the ridiculous name. Visions of Rue swam before her eyes, but she hastily quelled them. "Oh, no," she said aloud, "not this time, you don't." Jamey banished the images, looking back at the little dog as she stated firmly, "I'll just call you P.L. for now."

Jamey set the newly named puppy on the floor, rising quickly to make a final inspection of the cabin.

Everything was ready for her early morning departure, and she fled to her bedroom with P.L. trailing curiously at her heels.

As she snuggled under the light covering of the single sheet and reached out to flick the switch that cast the room into darkness, the puppy curled against her side. The warmth of the tiny body was comforting as mental and physical exhaustion combined to drag Jamey quickly into fitful, dream-riddled sleep.

"IT'LL be okay, P.L., I promise." Jamey said the words softly, pleadingly, as she slipped her trembling bundle into the crate and smiled tearfully up at the man who waited to take him away to the loading docks. The puppy's fear communicated itself to her. "He will be okay, won't he?" she asked the man, seeking calm reassurance.

"Sure," he said, his tone gentle as he comforted the very pretty lady who was entrusting him with a pet she obviously loved a great deal. "The hold is heated, and once those tranquilizers take effect, he'll probably sleep all the way to Portland," he added, revealing that he had already taken notice of her destination.

Somewhat reassured, Jamey looked back down at P.L.'s shivering form as sorrowful eyes regarded her miserably. "He doesn't think he'll be okay," she stated sadly. Tremors shook the tiny body, and P.L.'s tail was tucked firmly between his legs.

Jamey missed the interest that flared in the man's eyes as he watched her, glad the little dog's dependency was prolonging his contact with her. She wouldn't have cared if she had noticed the man's interest. She was beyond caring about anything at that point, but it might have given her some momentary relief from the pain that had numbed her—pain for P.L.'s almost palpable fear, and pain for her own fear at the irrevocable certainty that she was leaving. Her bags were checked, and there were now only moments left until she would board the plane.

"Oh, well," she sighed, "I guess I have to leave him now." Jamey checked her watch, already turning to make her way to the departure gate. P.L. yipped softly at her retreating form, and the sound wrenched at her heart. The poor little dog just didn't understand what was happening to him, any more than Jamey understood all that had happened to her over the past few weeks.

She paused, glancing back, and the man waved. "He'll be fine," he called. Jamey smiled tremulously in appreciation, then turned and broke into a run, her hand clasping her shoulderbag to her side to keep it from flapping uncomfortably against her hip. In her thoughts she compared herself to P.L. If she had a tail, she knew it would be tucked between her legs, the cowardly legs that carried her swiftly toward the waiting aircraft. Jamey was running hard from what might have been, running from an intense desire to change her mind and stay, to be waiting when Rue returned.

With her hair tangled wildly from her mad race, Jamey arrived at the gate breathless, gasping for air. She clutched at her chest with her free hand as a familiar figure loomed before her.

"Thought you might have changed your mind, Jamey," Mac said hopefully, his glance sliding from the disheveled mass of ebony strands to her eyes as he reached out a steadying hand.

Jamey swayed against him. "No. No, I haven't changed my mind." She denied his hope with a winded rush of words as her gaze moved past him to the still stances of Meg and Steve. That they had apparently begun to forgive her, had accepted her decision, and come to see her off meant so much. Tears of joy and sorrow fused together, and straightening, Jamey viewed her three friends through a shimmering haze. "But I'm so glad you're here," she choked out, a single teardrop tracing a revealing path over her reddened cheek. "I didn't think any of you ever wanted to see me again."

Meg moved forward, her eyes catching first Mac's and then Jamey's. "Oh, Jamey, no! We think you're making a colossal mistake," she stated firmly, "but that doesn't mean we don't love you." Meg closed the gap between herself and Jamey as she reached out to embrace her.

Jamey returned Meg's hug fiercely, ignoring the plea in her statement, then opened her arms to Steve. "Oh, Steve," she whispered, "you never told me what you decided to do with 'Sweet Freedom.'" She pushed back, her hands grasping the youth's slender shoulders as she stared soberly at Rue's young protégé.

"I still haven't made up my mind," Steve mumbled timidly, his eyes sweeping the floor at his feet. The action was revealing and Jamey knew he wasn't being entirely honest with her, but she didn't challenge him. Who was she to challenge anyone's honesty?

"You will, though," she sought his promise, "and you'll let me know?" Her tone questioned his intent as she waited for his eyes to meet hers.

"Yeah," he said softly, obviously uncomfortable as he tried to return her watery gaze. "I'll let you know."

"American Airline's flight two-seven-three, service from Nashville to Dallas-Fort Worth, is now ready for boarding at Gate Three." The voice that boomed over the public address system was impersonal, uncaring as it wrenched impassioned farewells from those who were going and those who were staying. "Please have your boarding passes available as you enter the aircraft."

Jamey's travels would take her first to Texas, where she would connect with another flight, then begin the last leg of the journey that would end in Portland, her home. She took one final look at the three tense figures, each of whom was so different, all of whom she had come to genuinely care for. "Keep in touch," she pleaded. Then Jamey turned and moved rapidly into the tunnel that linked the terminal with the opened door of the huge plane.

THE sound of the stewardess's voice was reassuring as she made the mandatory announcement about seat belts and smoking materials. It lent a familiar comfort to a world suddenly filled with unfamiliar sensations, sensations that were capped by a longing to stay even as Jamey reminded herself of all the reasons she had for leaving.

The rumble of the jet engines as the huge machine began the long roll down the runway was equally reassuring, and Jamey closed her eyes as they picked up speed, relaxing into her seat as the plane surged upward on a rush of power. She opened them again and reached for the book she carried in her purse as the aircraft leveled off and began its westerly flight. The decision was out of her hands now. Jamey was homeward bound, and she had every intention of putting Tennessee and Tanasie Basin and Rue Garrett firmly behind her—at least the tormenting segments that centered on Rue, making introspection too painful to allow.

The flight itself was uneventful. It was a beautiful day for flying, but Jamey paid little attention. She worked for a while at focusing her attention on her book with extreme dedication, but soon gave up.

The book was a tome on educational philosophy, and she had chosen it deliberately, thinking that nothing in it could possibly remind her of what she was leaving behind. But she had been wrong about that. The entire book was filled with reminders. If it hadn't been for her career, she would have stayed in Tennessee and let nature take its course. If it hadn't been for her career, she

would never have gone to Tennessee and met Rue, but
Jamey didn't think of that. She was too busy fighting
the memories that wouldn't let go of her troubled
mind.

Jamey changed planes, the necessary effort welcome, then turned with relief to the stewardess who
served the prepackaged meal with such style, grateful
for the diversion. After the meal she forced herself to
weave stories around the lives of her fellow passengers
in a move calculated to prevent her mind from continuing its steady slide toward thoughts of Rue. She even
talked for a while with the woman seated beside her,
but nothing seemed capable of stemming her wandering mental processes, and Jamey lapsed into silence.

She had battled her thoughts almost coast to coast,
and she sought release from them now by taking her
first conscious look out the plane's window as the captain's strong, deep voice announced the appearance of
the Cascade Mountain Range.

A patchwork world punctuated by the majesty of the
rugged peaks passed far below the belly of the massive
aircraft, and Jamey sucked in her breath. God's country!
Everybody seemed to say that, and to honestly believe
it, about their own little corner of the world, but Jamey
knew it to be true of the Pacific Northwest. She had
often thought that when God created the world, and
His long fingers reached the western side of the North
American Continent, He must have wearied of the
mundane chore of running His hands lightly over the
earth. And in His weariness of the plains He had just
created, must have decided to have a little fun and had
flexed and extended His mighty fingers time and time
again to form a region so filled with breathtaking, awe-
inspiring beauty that it simply defied human comprehension. Her eyes swept across the terrain of the
Willamette Valley and traced a path along the outline of
the craggy peaks. She picked out Mount Hood where it

rose majestically to the east of her home city, Portland, then let her eyes trail northward to another peak, Mount Saint Helens. The gaping hole left by the mountain's volcanic eruption was clearly visible.

Mount Saint Helens, of course, was in Washington, but the people of Portland, and other parts of Oregon as well, felt a bit of prideful ownership, and a wealth of respect, for the natural power of the smoldering volcano that had shot so much of its majesty into the sky. That majesty had returned to earth in the form of a powdery ash, and terrific amounts of the grayish matter had fallen over Oregon like some sort of demented snowfall. The ash was gone now, had been for some time, but the memory of the cataclysmic event would last for timeless ages in the minds of those who had witnessed it, as Jamey had, and in the stories they passed down from generation to generation. That memory would last as surely as her memories of another cataclysmic event, Rue's emergence into her life. But there was a difference. Her love for Rue would remain a closely guarded secret.

Jamey dragged her eyes away from the scene as the stewardess instructed her charges to fasten their seat belts and extinguish all smoking materials. The sheer power represented by the mountains had reached out to her, and she was reluctant to look away from the natural grandeur that had lent her a strength she had been lacking almost since the day she had taken Steve to Nashville for his audition with Rue Garrett and Mississippi River. How long ago that day seemed.

Her seat belt fastened, Jamey turned back to the window, gratefully accepting the deliverance the peaks seemed to hold out to her. The plane banked for its final approach, descending steadily as the sure hands of the pilot brought it into alignment with the distant runway, and Jamey felt more like herself than she had in what seemed years. A surge of pleasure rose in her at her homecoming. Here she would be surrounded by the strength of the mountains and by the brand of love she was accustomed to, a brand that encouraged her to hold fast to her rapidly growing career, to deny all other callings until that career was firmly established.

Tires squealed against the tarmac as the craft slowed, stopped, then turned for the long roll to the terminal. Jamey lifted her purse onto her lap, impatient now to be out of the plane and on her way. She tried to deny, even to herself, the pain of wondering when and how Rue would learn that she had gone. She tried to deny that she cared what his reaction to the news would be.

When the doors of the craft were finally opened, Jamey made her way as quickly as possible to the exit. She smiled pleasantly in return of the crew's farewell, then speeded her steps as she swung up the long gangway. A shiver of apprehension tingled up her spine, but was shrugged away as she told herself that there was no longer any reason to feel afraid. She had escaped, she thought—not heart-whole, but she had escaped.

"Jamey," her mother called as soon as she caught sight of the familiar figure emerging into the waiting area. Pride surged through her as she watched her younger daughter turn confidently toward her. Deanna Marsh missed the haunted look in Jamey's eyes that told of the new dimensions her experiences in Tennessee had brought into her life, but Duncan Marsh was quick to note that there was a definite difference in the young woman who hugged first one, and then the other, of her parents.

"It's so good to have you home, honey," Deanna Marsh said feelingly as her husband seconded her welcome by leaving his arm wrapped protectively around his child's slender waist. He had never thought of his determined, career-minded daughter as fragile, but the word sprang to mind as he watched her now.

"It's good to *be* home," Jamey responded huskily. "You can't imagine how good." The last was added quietly as she turned her head to gaze out the huge windows toward the strengthening splendor of Mount Hood.

"Missed your mountain, did you?" Duncan Marsh asked, and something in the tone of his voice arrested Jamey's attention. Was he remembering the times he had told the little girl she had been to look to the mountains for her strength? And comparing that little girl's actions to those of the now adult Jamey as she did exactly as she had been told so many years ago? It was a fanciful thought, but one that had Jamey's eyes seeking contact with her father's all the same.

"Yes," she whispered, striving for some bit of normalcy to right the topsy-turvy madness of the moment. "I've missed just about everything Oregonian over the past three months. This place is like no other on the face of the earth," Jamey vowed as she pulled her gaze away from eyes that seemed to see too much and turned to begin the trek to the baggage claim area. *Steady,* she told herself. *He can't possibly see into your soul, can't begin to know what's hidden there.*

Her parents moved to follow her, and Jamey slowed her steps to let them catch up, more certain suddenly of her ability to hide her new awareness of her womanhood, to hide the responsive stirrings she had locked away for so many years. "I have a surprise with my luggage," she promised teasingly, her words designed to create a lighter mood.

"What is it?" Her mother was still like a little girl when it came to surprises, and her words were filled with innocent curiosity.

Jamey laughed. "Well, Mom, I'm not sure how much you're going to like this particular surprise," she said, wishing she had prepared her mother more carefully for the advent of a new dog into the family. "It's a puppy!"

"Oh, no! Jamey, you didn't!" Deanna had never been able to understand how she could have spawned two children who were so fond of animals, and she was appalled that Jamey would bring a dog all the way from Tennessee to Oregon. Such behavior could only be a trait inherited from Duncan, she thought. It certainly hadn't come from her! Deanna liked animals well enough, but only as long as they belonged to someone else.

Duncan laughed heartily. "She did. I can tell," he assured his wife, his eyes twinkling at the evidence of Jamey's link with him. He sometimes thought that the only things she had inherited from him were her raven hair and her love of animals, and it pleased him that there were at least some things he could share with Jamey. In most ways she was almost totally Deanna's child, had been since birth. He had been away so much while she was growing up, building his own career as a journalist, that he had lost his chance to play a guiding role in her formative years. He regretted that loss deeply, wished for a way to reclaim the years as he joined in the conversation between his wife and child.

The three of them argued amiably about the various merits and demerits of animal ownership all the way to the baggage claim area, where the entire discussion was rendered moot by the sight of the wriggling body that yipped and pressed its nose against the wire at the front of the crate as soon as he spotted Jamey. P.L.'s small gray body was a study in perpetual motion as he waited for her to open the door and set him free, and once out, he snuggled into her arms as though he had at last reached a safe haven, making all of them laugh at how quickly he seemed to accept his crosscountry move. It was as though he was saying location didn't matter. Love and trust and the warmth of human contact were all he cared about.

"What's his name?" her father asked, his fingers lightly stroking the small gray head.

Jamey looked up and grinned. "P.L., which stands for—"

"You're an absolute nut, Jamey," Deanna interrupted, laughing. "Imagine your naming a dog for that tiny town where we used to live in Washington." She was referring to Pe Ell, Washington, and indeed they had once lived there, but the thought had never entered Jamey's mind until now. She had been far too young to have remembered the place, or to have attached enough sentiment to it to have named anything after the small city.

Now, however, she grasped at the name as though it were a lifeline. She could hardly believe how close she had come to telling her parents what P.L. really stood for, how close she had come to revealing the secret pain she intended to share with no one. "Well, all I can remember of Pe Ell is that the sky always seemed to be gray, so when I saw this little critter, it just seemed like a natural," she laughed, the sound expressing as much relief as it did humor.

Both her parents laughed and agreed with her that the colors were almost identical. Still chuckling at her naming of the small dog, her father retrieved her luggage and the three of them made their way to the car. Her mother relented enough to offer grudgingly, "Well, he is kind of cute."

Jamey chuckled at the comment as she settled into the backseat with the newest member of her growing animal family, then looked up as her father pulled into the line of traffic leaving the airport. She stared blindly at the other cars, wondered where all the people they carried were going, wondered where Rue was and what he was doing.

"Would you like to come over for dinner tonight?" her mother asked, snapping Jamey's pensive contemplation of a topic she had vowed to avoid.

"No thanks, Mom," she answered quickly. "I think I should get settled in at home, and introduce this little scamp to Digger and Charlie before I start spending very much time away from the house." It was the only excuse she could come up with. She couldn't just announce that she preferred to be alone.

"Well, I didn't know you would be bringing another dog home with you," Deanna said in mock disgust, "but I did expect that you would prefer to spend your first evening settling in and renewing your acquaintance with the two you already had," she reminded her half teasingly. "So I brought some papers with me that Paul thought you should look over." She reached into the glove compartment of the car and, turning, passed a parcel to Jamey in the backseat.

The packet contained the contracts for the two consulting jobs Jamey had instructed Paul to accept for her, contracts that only needed her signature to be legally binding, and offers for two more jobs that Jamey was as yet unaware of. Her eyes widened as her tired mind absorbed the meaning of the additional papers, and she groaned.

"Oh, Jamey, I thought you would be happy! One of those contracts is for a seminar on discipline at Mac-Laren," her mother said, making reference to one of the two large juvenile facilities located just outside Salem, the state capital, where Jamey had first become interested in working with delinquent youths.

Jamey quickly stifled her groan. "I'm just tired right now, Mom. I'll look these over later tonight, after I've had a meal and a hot bath, and enough time to collect the parts of me that think they're still somewhere between here and Tennessee," she assured her mother calmly, tucking the papers back into the folder. Jamey knew that the part she spoke of was her heart. She felt as though pieces of it had been strewn all across the vastness of the nation.

Duncan Marsh brought the car at last to a smooth stop in Jamey's driveway, then helped her unload her luggage and carry it into the house. Her parents stayed with her for about an hour, talking easily about Tennessee and Oregon and how good it was to have her home, then left after extracting a promise from her that she would come over to spend the afternoon with them the next day.

Jamey felt selfish, but she was relieved when they left and she could busy herself with the chore of settling back into her very own home, letting the familiarity of the place ooze into her being and comfort the ragged feelings that were the product of her long trip and the constant battle of trying to ignore the images of Rue that pushed at all the other thoughts in her mind, trying to take over.

She shoved the thoughts away again and focused on P.L. as he snooped around the house, sniffing at the interesting, unfamiliar scents he found. The sight of the puppy reminded her of one of the excuses she'd given herself for her eagerness to return to Oregon. Digger and Charlie, she thought, silently mocking her own forgetfulness. They would be waiting impatiently in the fenced backyard, sure because of the now familiar routine of being retrieved from the kennel and returned to their home by Duncan that Jamey was in the house.

The antics of the two large dogs as they vied for her attention and tried at the same time to figure out the tumbling ball of gray fluff that had followed her into the yard were amusingly reassuring. Digger, huge and black, half Irish setter and half Lab, had earned his name for obvious reasons, costing Jamey a great deal of work in the process. Charlie, a Samoyed, had been so named because of her clumsy mistake in knocking over a bottle of perfume that bore that name. She had pranced around reeking of the concoction for weeks afterward, and the experience had destroyed Jamey's liking for the fragrance. She wrinkled her nose at the memory, wondering idly what P.L. might do to earn his permanent name. She couldn't keep calling him P.L. The abbreviated name evoked no memories in her of Pe Ell, Washington. It evoked only painful remembrances of the man who had given her the little dog...and of the too-short time she had given to her love for that man.

Jamey turned and moved briskly back into the house, trying to leave her thoughts behind her as easily as she left her dogs. She focused her attention on unpacking, aware that she was tired but in need of activity to fill her time and her mind. The chore was completed all too quickly, and Jamey turned her thoughts to food, realizing that all she'd eaten that day was the meal served in-flight between Texas and Oregon.

She really wasn't all that hungry, though. She was far more in need of a rejuvenating soak, she thought as she moved to the bathroom and started the water running into the tub.

Jamey slipped out of the light green pantsuit she had worn for so many hours that it felt like a second skin, tossing it into the hamper before easing her tired body into the deep water. She relaxed, leaning her head and shoulders against the back of the tub, allowing the warmth of the liquid to ease away her tensions and soothe her weary muscles. The feeling was delicious, and Jamey nearly fell asleep right there. But the slapping of the water as she slipped sideways in her lethargic state woke her fully, and she lathered herself and emerged from her bath feeling more energetic than she had in hours.

She hummed a light tune as she threw together a salad, then moved to the table with her simple meal and the packet of papers she had promised her mother she would review and consider. Jamey signed the two contracts she had already verbally committed herself to and slipped them into envelopes, ready for mailing, then turned her attention to the other offers. One, as her mother had said, was an offer that would require her to return to her old stomping grounds to present a seminar on discipline for the teachers currently working at MacLaren. The other was an offer that would require her to present a three-day training session on teaching remedial reading for the staff of a nearby school district. Remedial reading had long been a pet concern of Jamey's, for if kids couldn't read, how could they hope to do well in other academic pursuits?

Jamey wavered for only a moment between her opposing options. She knew she had earned the short vacation she had carved out for herself by completing her work at Tanasie Basin ahead of schedule, still felt she might need the time in order to come to grips with the pain of leaving Rue. But on a wave of confidence inspired by the fact that she really had followed her plan, had followed it and returned to Oregon, decided to accept both proposals.

Her confidence grew stronger as she thought of how rapidly her career was developing. More and more job offers were coming ever more quickly. The feeling followed her as she cleared away the few dishes she had used, washed them, and returned them to the cupboard, then retired to her bedroom on the thought that a good night's sleep was probably all she needed. *Maybe,* she thought as she slid into the comfort of her very own bed for the first time in more than three months, *getting over him won't be as hard as I had thought it would.*

Sleep claimed Jamey quickly, but it wasn't the healing sleep she had hoped for. Her rest was interspersed with a series of painful dreams, with Rue at the center of each theme. She slept fitfully, tossing and turning as pain piled upon rejection and burning anger.

The night was shattered by Jamey's piercing scream as she jolted into wide-eyed wakefulness from a nightmare so real that she could almost feel the heat of the flames that had threatened to consume her as she tried to reach through them to Rue. She drew her legs up and huddled against the headboard, her balled fist crammed against her trembling lips, too terrified to take the risk of closing her eyes and finding herself again in the burning building. It was impossible to remember whether she had been fighting to save Rue from the searing flames or he had been fighting to save her.

Rising, Jamey moved quickly away from the bed, its softness no longer warm and welcoming. She padded shakily to the back door and whistled softly. All three dogs came at her quiet command, but only P.L. was allowed through the door. Digger and Charlie were both far too large to be house dogs, and they provided no link with the object of her tortured thoughts.

Jamey retraced her steps and curled onto the brown couch in the living room, hugging P.L. to her as she fought the memory of the vivid nightmare. But it had been too real, and the images it dredged up were so painful that Jamey could only sit and stare. Her brain refused to function, subconsciously protecting her from the agony she now had to face.

Finally her thoughts began to gather in a numbing pattern. By leaving Tennessee in so cowardly a fashion, she had chosen her career over love for all time. Rue would soon discover her deception, would know of all the lies she had told, and the love he felt for her would be completely destroyed. Rue...the man she loved, but had turned away by her own weak actions.

In the small hours of the morning Jamey concluded that her decision to accept the additional contracts had been the right choice. She would have to keep herself as busy as possible in order to avoid a repeat of the last night. Taking time off now for a vacation would have left her with more time than she wanted to think of all the things she was trying so hard to forget. She hoped for more offers of work. She would not allow herself to dwell on memories of the handsome, gentle man whose face had been twisted with pain in her dreams.

Chapter Ten

"Damned stupid weeds," Jamey muttered in irritation as she tugged at the ridiculously stubborn patch of unwanted greenery that had sprung up where the driveway met the walk leading to her front door. She was too hot, too tired, and more than a little disgusted. It seemed she had hardly had five minutes she could call her own over the past two weeks, and now that she did, nothing was going according to plan.

Jamey had accepted and completed the two surprise consulting assignments and had worked in three additional mini-seminars as well. Between research and preparation of her topics, travel time to and from the job sites, and the drain of the actual presentations and question-and-answer sessions themselves, she had managed to so regiment her time that she was now thoroughly exhausted. She had achieved little with this much needed weekend break other than tired, aching muscles that were well matched to her tired brain, a brain that refused to let go of thoughts of the one person she wanted to forget.

That was the true source of Jamey's disgust. It rankled that no matter how hard she had worked, how far she had pushed herself, she still hadn't succeeded in putting Rue Garrett from her mind. Memories of his gentle loving popped into her head at the oddest moments, his image filled her dreams, and she often found herself wondering where he was, what he was doing. She had heard nothing from him since she had left Tennessee.

The dead silence of the past two weeks had surprised her. She wasn't sure how she had expected him to react to her cowardly departure, but simple common sense had told her to expect some contact—at the very least an angry phone call. But there had been nothing. Perhaps she had been right, she thought, choking down the burning nausea that rose inside her. Perhaps Rue, having discovered her deceitful lies, really did hate her now, hated her and regretted the day he had met her.

Jamey bent to her task with renewed fervor. Today's toils had been intended to relieve her mental exhaustion and to finally dispel her thoughts of Rue, but the job wasn't living up to her expectations. If anything, she was spending even more time dwelling on things best forgotten, so she forced her attention to the weather.

Indian summer was dragging on too long, she reflected peevishly as she yanked again at the weeds that should have been going dormant by now instead of clinging to the earth with rigidly grasping tendrils. The vinelike plants refused to cooperate with her efforts to dislodge them, just as her thoughts of Rue did, and she sat back in defeat, wiping the loose particles of dirt that clung to her hands onto the sides of her ragged denim cutoffs.

Perspiration trickled down the valley between Jamey's unencumbered breasts, tickling her, and she reached up to rub idly at the bothersome spot with her fingertips. Her labors had caused the material of her light blue halter top to shift into an uncomfortable position, and she transferred her fingers to the elastic banding that held it in place, readjusting the tension of the fabric.

Rue would have returned to Nashville sometime yesterday, she remembered. Even now he could be

walking casually along some southern street, passing
strangers who, unless they happened to recognize him,
cast uncaring eyes on his beloved form.

"No, no, no," she moaned, rejecting the wishful
thinking that had her walking down the street at his
side. She had made her decision, and still believed it to
be the right one. And, if nothing else in all of this could
be looked upon as a blessing, at least her tears seemed
to have dried up. It had been a long time since she had
cried over her final choice.

Jamey reached for the trowel that lay on the ground
at her side, then attacked the noxious plants with a vig-
or that revealed her efforts not only to accomplish at
long last the weeding she worked at so strenuously, but
also to accomplish the task of thinking of something,
anything, other than Rue Garrett. A segment of the net-
work of greenery finally began to yield to her exertions,
and Jamey was so intent on winning the battle against
the weeds that she was barely aware of the car that
pulled into her driveway.

Barely aware wasn't unaware, though, and she shook
back her mane of raven hair, looking up with a grim
expression to determine who was paying her this un-
timely, unwanted visit. The sun glinted off the wind-
shield of the car, making it impossible for her to tell
who drove it, and the car itself was not one she had
ever seen before. On the thought that it must be someone seeking directions to some other house, Jamey
rose and walked briskly toward the small yellow vehicle, the trowel held loosely in her hand.

As she approached the driver's side door Rue swung
it open and stepped out. Barefoot and in her oldest,
grubbiest clothes, Jamey felt smaller than ever as he
emerged, towering over her. But she didn't care. Her
overtired mind forgot to question his presence, forgot
everything as she stood, transfixed by the sight of
him. Her eyes moved hungrily over the reality that

was so much more satisfying than the memory. She smiled, bemused, as she took in the boots, the casual jeans, the open-necked plaid shirt of muted greens, the gold chain around his neck that was the only evidence of his success, then lifted her eyes to his face. Her heart began to trip frantically as she encountered only coldness.

Rue's gray-blue eyes were filled with storm clouds. There was no answering smile to lift the corners of his mouth, and Jamey's smile died instantly. His features might have been chiseled of granite.

In the few seconds that had passed, Rue had assessed his opponent and was ready for any action she might take. His still stance reminded her of the first time she had met him, when she had refused to stay and have dinner with him, and she thought again of a jungle cat stalking his prey. But this time there was a difference. Rue made no move. He waited patiently, biding his time. He would let his prey make the first move.

Jamey's mouth went dry as she realized she wasn't up to the battle Rue's stony expression promised. She had already given away too much by staring at him so bemusedly. Surely he had read the longing, loving message she hadn't even thought to hide. The trowel dropped unnoticed to the ground as she took a step backward, away from the threat his very presence implied, then spun around and ran as fast as she could toward the open door of her house. If she could reach it in time, could close it against him, she would be safe, she thought wildly as her memory caught up with the here and now. This was no gentle, loving Rue come to woo her as he had in Tennessee.

She gained the steps, already reaching for the handle as she crossed the portal, but a booted foot was thrust quickly into the path of the slamming force of the heavy wooden door. A strong, muscled arm reached out, pressing firmly against the panels that, once closed. would deny him access to the explanation he meant to demand.

Jamey reeled back, her inferior strength no match for the power of the arm that sent the door crashing into the wall behind it. The sound of wood slamming against wood cracked out like a pistol shot, and Jamey's already hammering pulse increased until she thought she could hear the blood singing in her ears as it was pumped madly around her body. Rue was pleased by the reverberating sound that echoed through the house. It was a reflection of the strength of his feelings.

The door was still vibrating from its impact against the wall as he stepped into the entryway and reached for Jamey, grasping her by the arms in a viselike grip that it would have taken superhuman strength to deny.

"What in the hell do you think you're up to, Jamey?" he ground out, his tones low and deceptively quiet.

Eyes that had rested momentarily on the fingers that grasped her arms so tightly, fingers that gripped bruisingly hard, flicked up to meet the jarring impact of eyes that flashed fire. Her brain refused to send a logical answer to her lips. "Nothing!" she squeaked out, then found more of her voice. "I'm not up to anything," she said frantically, her quivering tones revealing her panic.

"The hell you're not!" he snapped. "You let me believe you were in Tennessee to stay," Rue accused, his tone questioning every lie she had ever told him, "and that we had something special together. My God, Jamey, the first week of the road trip was bad enough, aching for the sight and feel of you, but it was at least bearable because I knew you were waiting for me... and I had your promise that you would be with me on the next trip," he added, the timbre of his voice dropping to an ominously low pitch. His next words came out on a rasping whisper as he continued. "The last two weeks were sheer hell for me and I probably made them hell for the rest of the group because I couldn't keep my mind on work. After Grandma's call to let me know what you had done—a call that should never have had to be, Jamey!—all I wanted was to get away, to get to you and find out what was going on.'' Remembered pain mingled with the anger that spurred him on. ''You have a lot of explaining to do, lady,'' he threatened, his eyes pinning hers.

Jamey groaned. This was far worse than any contact she had imagined. Rue was angry, yes, but it was an anger so controlled that she knew he would stay with her, battering at her defenses, until she had somehow satisfied his need to understand. Since leaving Tennessee, she had wished that she had stayed to face him honestly, had explained openly the reasons that demanded their denial of what they felt for each other, or that she had been honest with him from the beginning. Lies and deception had never played a role in her life before, and she was a miserable lump of confusion as she searched her rioting mind for words that could somehow reach through the quiet fury to the gentle core she knew rested in the heart of this man she loved so much.

''Is it Paul?'' Rue asked suddenly, viciously, cutting across her thoughts.

A bubble of near-hysterical laughter rose to Jamey's lips at the idea that Paul Cameron, her aging mentor, could ever come between her and Rue. The bubble burst and, with it, Rue's rigid control over his anger. Her laughter fanned the low-burning flames of his fury, shattering the fragile hold he had fought so hard to maintain. He dropped his hands away from her arms, his movements so contained that even the air around them seemed charged with danger. He wanted to shake her—hard!

''Damn you, Jamey! Is it?'' That she might have

added that final deception to all the others she had woven so carefully was more than Rue could stand, and he was gripped with a powerful urge to hurt her. He wanted to hurt as he had been hurt, to wring from the raven-haired defector the truth behind her flight.

"N-no," she wrung out, the mental anguish that laced his words breaking through her own pain. "It's n-not Paul... or anyone else," she admitted, tears of fear and frustration blurring her vision. How could she possibly explain this to Rue?

"Then damn it, what *is* it?" he demanded. "And who is this Paul?" The sight of Jamey's tears made him angry with himself—not that he had made her hurt mentally, she deserved that, but that he had come so close to attacking her physically. He lifted his hands toward her again, but dropped them away before touching her, unable to trust his control until he had heard her answer. Never before had he been so consumed by the desire to do violence to another human being, and he moved back from the woman he loved, the woman who had driven him so close to the edge.

Jamey rubbed at her arms, at the reddened spots where his hands had gripped so hard. The action was as much protective as it was an effort to ease any pain Rue might have inflicted. Like his, her pain was an emotional torment, and she dropped her eyes to study the floor. Quietly she explained who Paul Cameron was, explained the long road of study and planning that had brought her to her present growing success as an educational consultant, explained Paul's role in that success. Her voice shook as she delved into the confused muddle that had brought them to this impasse, and Rue at last began to understand Jamey's dilemma. With her eyes cast down, she missed the relaxing of his shoulders that signaled the easing of his anger, but her ears picked it up as he questioned her further.

Rue watched her as she stood before him, eyes still

downcast and arms still hugging her body protectively. "Jamey, do you love me?" The words were spoken quietly, a little uncertainly.

Her eyes flew up to meet his. How did she answer that, she wondered crazily, when the truth made not one whit of difference to the decision she had made? But Jamey had learned her lesson. She was through with lies. "Y-yes," she admitted shakily, softly.

"Say it, then," he ordered in tender tones. The gentle man she had sought emerged from his furious shell, and Jamey's heart was in her eyes as she obeyed.

"I love you," she said, the simple phrase a heartfelt vow.

"That's all I needed to know," Rue whispered as he quickly closed the gap that separated them. He reached for her, this time with gentle intent.

It wasn't all he needed to know, but Jamey moved to meet him, her need to feel his touch rising above the need to complete her explanation. She stepped into Rue's arms, and all the loving she felt was offered to him through the tender yielding of soft, sweet lips as they were met hungrily by the force of his as he took all she offered, then demanded more. A silent tear rolled down her cheek, and the salty taste of it was manna to Rue's questing lips.

"Oh, God! How I love you, Jamey," he whispered between kisses, his hands beginning to demand far more than his lips had.

Pressed fully against him, with only the brevity of her cutoffs and the thin material of her halter top protecting her sensitive skin, she gloried in the hardness that revealed his heightened need of her. And in that moment Jamey took a giant step toward growing up. Without even being consciously aware of the momentous decision she was making, she chose to give herself fully to the need that raged within both of them, to trust that their love would survive the test of time and distance until her career was well established and she could join him, could marry him if that was what he wanted and live with him in Tennessee. But for now, she would hold nothing back. She would share everything with him on those occasions when they could be together. It didn't occur to her that Rue's plans might be far different from those she made so lovingly, so hastily.

Rue sensed her surrender. He lifted her in his arms, reluctantly dragging his lips from hers to question silently with his darkened gaze.

"Second door on the left," Jamey whispered, love shining at him from eyes that had dilated with emotion, smiling from lips that were softly swollen from the heat of their passion. Rue's lips found hers again as he carried her slowly to the room she had indicated, then lowered her gently to the inviting bed, moving to join her at a leisurely pace, as though they now had all the time in the world.

His hands were sensually coaxing, teasing an ever-increasing response from her as he removed first her halter top, stopping to nip lightly at her taut nipples, then slid his hands down to work provokingly at the snap and zipper of her cutoffs.

Jamey's fevered wonderment was evident in the gleaming depths of her brown eyes as she reached out to him, her fingers trembling as she tried to unfasten the buttons of his shirt. Her progress was slow, and she lay beside him naked before she had even undone the third button, but Rue helped her. He discarded his shirt, and she wondered how she had ever managed to leave him, even for two weeks, as she tangled her fingers in the familiar coarseness of the burnished hairs that curled over his chest.

Rue's eyes swept over her nude form as he released the buckle of his belt, and he groaned and reached for her again after dealing with the task of removing his pants, the only barrier that had remained to prevent the union that would bond them together irrevocably.

"Love," he moaned in a low, husky voice, "you're so beautiful. I don't think I could have stood it if you had told me you didn't love me," he confessed. "But I had to know and I had to be with you, to hear your answer and read the truth of it with my own eyes," he added feelingly, revealing the reason for his lack of contact with her over the past two weeks.

"I love you," Jamey whispered, and the words became a magical litany of mutual passion as he gave her answer for answer.

Trails of fire were blazed by questing lips and exploring fingers as Rue urged her body to an intense, demanding need, and Jamey was nearly demented with longing as he shifted his weight further onto hers. She sought to give pleasure for pleasure with fingers that no longer trembled, wanted only to become one with him, to know fully the brand of his possession.

The need for words had long since died, had given way to the rising urgency of a need more basic when Rue finally moved to take her, to join himself with her in the final bond. And the momentary pain that brought a gasp from Jamey's lips could never have competed with the greater joy she felt at his possession of her, hers of him. She moved with him through the cadence of love to spiraling heights she'd never imagined, descended with him to a shining euphoria.

In the aftermath of their lovemaking, hands still sought. He held her gently, one hand lightly caressing the softness of her cheek as his gaze held hers. She moved her own hand wonderingly over the taut muscles of his stomach and upward to his chest, awed by the intimacy of their silent communion.

"How soon will you be ready to go back to Tennessee with me?" he asked softly, lovingly, as he bit gently at her delicate earlobe.

Jamey tensed beside him, her fingers stopping their sensual task. *Oh, God,* she thought, *he still doesn't understand.* She lifted her hands to cup his beloved face between sensitive palms, her eyes seeking his as she sought to explain. "Not for a while," she whispered, clinging to him as he began to pull away from her. "Not until my career is so firmly established that I can be more selective about the contracts I accept."

Rue's hands left her body. His jawline was tensed and his eyes clashed with hers in disbelief. "What do you mean, not until your career is firmly established? How much time are you talking about?"

"M-maybe two years... or one, if I'm really lucky," she said shakily, her body aching in its desire to have him return to his tender caresses. "But until then, we can see each other as often as possible, Rue," she offered pleadingly. "Both of us travel so much, and our paths are sure to find us in the same area fairly often, especially if we plan it that way." Each word became more urgent as she sensed his withdrawal, and she clasped her hands behind his head to try to pull him back to her.

"What are you offering me, Jamey?" he asked, the words coming out harsh and insulting. "I'm offering you my love... and marriage," he added, almost callously, as he regarded her with contempt.

"All of me," she whispered, her conscious mind rejecting the coldness that invaded gray-blue eyes that had been warm with love and sated desire only seconds before. "All of me, but without marriage... at least, not yet."

"All of you," he pondered bitterly. "Don't you mean scattered bits and pieces of you, whenever you can fit our love into your busy schedule?" he asked sarcastically. Rue pulled her hands from him, rejecting her physically as he rolled away from her and stood up, already reaching for the pants that lay in a crumpled heap on the floor.

Jamey sat up, her rising frustration at his refusal to understand making her forget her own nudity as she lashed out at him. "That's not fair, Rue! You have your career, so don't ask me to give up mine! All I'm asking for is time—enough time to establish myself—with nothing held back between now and then!"

Rue shook his head sadly. "No, Jamey, time isn't all you're asking for. You're asking me to put our love on a back burner, to let it become something we drag out when it's convenient," he said tersely, "and that's holding back too much. It's simply not enough," he added derisively as he buttoned his shirt. "Care to tell me why you couldn't manage your career from Tennessee as easily as you can from Oregon?"

"Because all my contacts are here," she snapped heatedly, then relented a little. "Oh, maybe I could manage my work from Tennessee," she admitted grudgingly, "but the move would only make it all that much longer before I was truly established," she avowed. "And what about children, Rue? We would want children, and that would really destroy what I've worked so hard for."

Jamey had trouble with her final statement. Visions of a small face, so like Rue's, swam before her eyes, and anger rose at her inability to shake away the image. She wanted his child, she realized, wanted it with an intensity that was almost overwhelming as she fought to quell the desire. That was something she *had* to deny herself for now, but she wouldn't be able to deny it if she returned to Tennessee with him, married him, and lived with him daily. It was her own desire she would be fighting, she knew, a desire far greater than his.

Rue's tones were bitingly sarcastic. "For an intelligent woman, you certainly are stupid at times. Your body could be beginning the process necessary to carry our child right this minute," he growled, raking his fingers through his hair. "God! I almost wish I could know that it was," he said, his voice full of the hurt she inflicted. "But I doubt it. We both know how unlikely that is, don't we?" Sarcasm returned to blot his pain as he continued. "Medical science has come up with an absolutely amazing little concoction called birth control, Jamey. And, while the idea doesn't exactly thrill me, we could surely wait a couple of years before having children." His expressive eyes impaled hers as he tucked his shirttail in and tightened his belt, waiting for her response.

Stark terror gleamed in Jamey's eyes for a second. How could she have been so stupid? She'd never even considered the possibility that she could become pregnant! But Rue was right, she thought wildly. He had to be right! It was highly unlikely. She wouldn't acknowledge the possibility with words. She might want his child, but she couldn't have both that and her career.

"No, I can't go back with you yet," she said, her tone defiant. Jamey felt as though she were moving perilously across a tightrope that was badly frayed at one end, a tightrope that could snap and send her plunging downward at any moment. "I love you, but I just can't throw away everything I've worked for," she finished acidly. The memory of the many times she and her sister had cried because they felt responsible for their mother's bitterness, felt guilty that she had been forced to care for them instead of pursuing the career she claimed she had wanted so badly, wove its way into her battered consciousness. She jammed her hands over her ears, trying to still the parental voice that loomed from her past.

"Can't you take what I'm offering?" she asked frantically. Pride was cast aside, and fear infused her voice as he began to walk away from her.

Rue paused, turning back to her. He didn't want to walk away, felt as though he was walking away from a vital part of his being. But it was his only hope of jarring her into understanding what she was doing to them. "It's not enough, Jamey," he repeated, "and it's not love as I know it."

Suddenly the impulse to wound, mortally if he could, was too strong to resist. He wanted to leave her with at least as much pain as he was taking with him. "What you're offering me is a cheap imitation of what I've asked of you. I never wanted parts of you—bits and pieces tossed out like morsels to a hungry dog," he added bitterly. "It's always been all or nothing and, thanks, but I'll take nothing!"

He spun on his heel, long strides carrying him out of the room as he flung back a final threat. "You know where to find me if you come to your senses, Jamey. Just don't leave it too long. I don't plan to wait for you."

The sound of the door quietly closing behind him echoed through her despairing mind, and unadulterated pain splintered through her body. Jamey scrambled from the bed, tripping as she ran toward the front door. "Rue," she called, his name a hysterical plea as she stopped at the end of the hall, her nudity remembered. She couldn't catch up with him, couldn't call him back to discuss their differences rationally. He was already gone.

The motor of the small yellow car droned fainter and fainter in her ears as it carried him away, leaving her with an ache far greater than the one she had carried with her on the long flight when she had so sneakily left Nashville two weeks earlier, an ache that left her nearly doubled over in its intensity as she recognized what she had done. Rue was gone. She knew he wouldn't be back.

Numbly Jamey stumbled back to her bedroom. Why was it that her brain always seemed to fail her when she needed it most? she wondered abstractedly. Shock had taken over, and she could make no sense of her chaotic thoughts. Lethargically she pulled her cutoffs and halter top back on, uncaring that scalding tears were beginning to slip from her eyes, sliding over her cheeks and leaving a salty taste in her mouth as she gulped for air.

Jamey cried until no more tears would come. At first she moved restlessly around the house, clutching her arms around her midriff as racking sobs shook her slender body. But she finally settled in the living room, curled into a miserable ball in one corner of the brown modular couch, and waited until her sobs had subsided into nothing more than a deadened feeling of stark emptiness and loss. She sat there for hours, staring at nothing in particular, caring about nothing at all.

That was where her father found her when he dropped by late in the afternoon. He entered through the unlocked door when she failed to respond to his repeated ringing of the doorbell, and was stunned by Jamey's vacant stare as she turned her eyes toward him.

"Jamey! What is it, honey? What's the matter?" His worried tones penetrated her lethargy.

"It's okay, Dad. It's all over," she answered, rising to look out the picture window toward the mountains it framed.

Duncan Marsh's thoughts raced back to the fragile tragedy he had imagined he sensed in her when she had flown in from Nashville. He had never questioned her about that feeling, had decided it must have been the product of his own overactive journalist's imagination as he had watched her throw herself into her work over the past two weeks, had watched her push herself to her capacity. Jamey had always been a hard worker, and her actions had gradually come to seem normal to him. But now he knew they weren't.

"What's happened here, Jamey?" He pressed for an

answer to his question, moving across the room and gripping her shoulders from behind as he sought to force a response from her.

Jamey turned toward him then, unable to stop the tears that welled in her eyes at her father's concern, unwilling to tell him of the agonizing loss she felt. "I guess I've just been working too hard," she mumbled, shrugging her shoulders.

"The hell you have!" he spat, his inability to get through to her spurring him to fearful anger. "Jamey, what's wrong?" The question was paternally authoritative, demanding an honest response, but his hands were gentle as they moved lower to draw her into comforting arms. "Has someone been here with you? Someone who's caused this?"

Jamey trembled at the accuracy of his guess and stared at the top button of his shirt for a long moment before lifting her stricken eyes back to his. "You don't know him," she groaned, aware that her father would demand more of an answer now than she wanted to give him. She might be twenty-six, an adult, but she was still his child, and someone had hurt her.

"I soon will," he barked. "Who is he?"

"Oh, Dad, it doesn't matter," she choked out, the tears that had welled in her eyes beginning to spill from them. "He's just a man I met in Tennessee, a man who thought he had a right to follow me home and demand an explanation for what I was doing here," she sobbed, her words adding to her father's anger and confusion.

"Jamey, you're not making any sense. Come into the kitchen," he ordered, leading her by the hand when she made no move to go there on her own.

Jamey sat down at the table, watching as her father opened the refrigerator and filled two glasses with iced tea, then returned the pitcher to its shelf and closed the door before turning to carry the drinks across the room. She registered his movements mechanically as he placed a tall glass in front of her, then moved to seat himself.

"Now, tell me what's going on," he demanded as Jamey sipped at the refreshing liquid.

Suddenly, inexplicably, she wanted to tell him, to share her pain. She wanted to ease the burden of her torment.

"Oh, Dad, I've made such a mess of everything," Jamey said miserably. Her knuckles were almost white as she gripped her glass tightly and began to reconstruct her story.

"You remember the young man I told you about? Steve Carlson, the one I was helping with his music?"

Her father nodded, prompting her to go on.

"Well, through my work with Steve, I met Rue Garrett," she continued, her voice growing strangely quiet as she explained who Rue was, explained his importance in her life. As she spoke, her eyes fell away from her father's and she stared blindly at the patterned tablecloth, her fingers clenching and unclenching around the glass she held.

"Dad, I didn't want to fall in love with him! I didn't mean to," she moaned, blinking hard to hold her tears at bay as she lifted her eyes once again to meet her father's. "And I didn't mean to hurt him, to hurt either of us," she added, then told him of the lies and deceptions she had practiced, lies and deceptions that had led to her cowardly departure while Rue was out of town on the road trip that had left her the freedom to make her escape without offering him any explanation for what she was doing. "I just did what I thought was best by leaving while he was on his road trip," she sobbed, "because I know careers and marriage are impossible to mix successfully, and I'm not prepared to give up my work. Look what taking care of Samantha and me did to Mom's career," she said plaintively.

It wasn't the first reference Jamey had made in her

lengthy monologue to guilt feelings that could only have been carried over from childhood. But still her father sat quietly, listening and watching and occasionally squeezing his daughter's hand to show his support. His thoughts were another matter. The guilt feelings Jamey expressed made him fully aware of the role his wife had played, however inadvertently, in Jamey's foolishness. At least, he thought, that role had better have been inadvertent. He would deal with Deanna when he got home. For now, he had to deal with his very confused daughter.

"At least it's over now," Jamey said finally, idly tracing the line of a leaf on the tablecloth pattern with her index finger. "At least now we can both begin the healing process," she said so quietly that the words were almost inaudible. All she had left out, the only part she wanted to share with no one, were the moments of shared intimacy, the thought that she might be carrying Rue's child.

"Jamey." Duncan spoke at last. "You know that your Rue had every right, every *reason,* to follow you here and demand an explanation, don't you?" he asked, accepting her halting nod as affirmation. "You deceived him terribly, more horribly than I can understand when I consider that I've never known you to lie before," he added gently.

Jamey looked down again, and her shoulders shook slightly as she reacted to her father's words.

"God!" he said suddenly. "Given the same set of circumstances, I'd have done the same thing. I might have done worse! Even though I know, as Rue must, that you never meant to cause either of you such pain," he said feelingly.

His memory had taken him to an earlier time, a time near the beginning of his marriage to Deanna, when Jamey was just a child. A time when he and Deanna had known similar problems. But those problems had been resolved by time, as evidenced by the fact that they were still in love and still together after nearly thirty years.

"Jamey, do you still love him?" her father asked gently.

"Yes," she whispered, "I'll always love him. But it's too late. He all but told me so when he left this afternoon." Though the words were spoken quietly, there was a firmness about them that was reminiscent of the old Jamey, the confident young woman who had left for Tennessee untouched by love. Already she was sliding the protective barriers back into place, raising them high to hide her real feelings from the world, and—if she could—from herself.

In that moment Duncan Marsh was reminded of the self-possessed young woman his wife had been, and he sought to warn his child, to smooth the rocky path she seemed to choose. "Honey, you better do some powerful thinking before you accept that as final. If you truly love Rue Garrett, and I think you do," he said, watching as she flinched, "your career won't mean much to you as time passes. You'll learn to hate it for coming between you and your heart." He almost stopped there, but went on, the words that followed a loving request. "If you'll only ask your mother, I'm sure she'll tell you openly that, given the chance to live her life over, there are few things she would wish to change. And that our marriage is *not* one of those things."

The warning was unwelcome to the young woman who had already withdrawn behind a wall of cool self-sufficiency. "No, Dad," she rejected his counsel, "it's over. Let it die."

Jamey rose and carried her glass to the sink, rinsing it before turning a composed, almost expressionless face toward her father as he moved to the door. He could think of nothing more to say that might touch a vulnerable spot in the heart of the seemingly self-assured Jamey as she walked with him to his car.

SEPTEMBER bowed gracefully to the cooler temperatures of October, and Jamey went through the motions of living her life as she had before meeting Rue. Time had proved them both right. No child grew inside her, and Jamey vacillated between a feeling of relief and a sense of desolation at the finality of that truth.

Outwardly she was the determined career woman she had always professed to be, calm and imperturbable as she added ever more experience to her growing reputation as a successful educational consultant. She seemed as cool as the autumn climate that moved steadily toward winter.

She couldn't help it that inwardly she was a mass of uncertainty, or that her father's words kept repeating over and over in her memory, always followed by Rue's final threat. She couldn't help it that her eyes lifted with increasing frequency to the mountains, seeking to borrow more and more of their strength. Her success in her chosen field seemed at times an ephemeral whimsy, so much chaff to be blown away by the winds of time, time that weighed heavily on her mind.

The month dragged on, drawing inexorably toward its end, toward another month, and then another, an endless calendar of empty days that would grow into empty years. Only Jamey could choose to take the risk that might put an end to the void of loneliness that stretched before her.

She had heard from Meg twice and, indirectly, from Mac through the words Meg had written. Steve had written once, a short letter scrawled in his teen-age hand, a letter that thanked her for her help and told her that her young friend missed her. She had ripped the envelopes open when they arrived, reading each letter rapidly, eagerly, hoping for some word of Rue. But there had been none. Nor had he contacted her in any way. It was as though he had ceased to exist as a part of her world—at least, in the minds of Meg, Mac, Steve...and Rue. It was over. Why couldn't she let it go?

Chapter Eleven

"Jamey, come in here for a minute, honey," Duncan Marsh called from the den where he sat watching TV. It was the last Saturday in November, and Jamey had spent most of the day with her parents. She often spent her Saturdays with them these days, and sometimes her Sundays as well.

Though she didn't know it, her father had recognized her actions for what they were—a yearning for protection as she tottered on the brink of the most vital decision of her life, like a child clutching at her mother's skirt on her first day at school. He smiled at the analogy. It was time to push the fledgling from the nest, he thought, time to discover if he was right that she looked so often to the hills in a silent prayer for help as she struggled with her conflicting desires. He wanted to see for himself her reaction to the program that filled the screen of the television.

"What did you want, Dad?" Jamey asked easily as she came through the door and into the room, drying her hands on the dish towel she had been using as she helped her mother clean up after their evening meal.

"Look," he said, his hand indicating the screen as he kept his gaze riveted on her face. "Rue Garrett is hosting this country music special that was filmed in Las Vegas last summer."

Jamey paled, her eyes turning to the moving images

against her will. Had she had any idea that this was what her father wanted, she would have ignored his summons. She had known that the program was being aired tonight, had known that it was being shown a month later than initially scheduled because the fire had both damaged some of the original footage and delayed completion of the filming. She had known because Meg had mentioned it in her latest letter, the third she had written since Jamey's return to Oregon, but the only one with any reference to Rue. The letter had also contained a magazine item, a clipping Jamey hadn't read because she knew it was about Rue, suspected it chronicled his appearance in tonight's special. And she had deliberately avoided the temptation of watching, afraid to see Rue again, even so remotely. But the smiling face that filled the screen drew her eyes as the camera zoomed in for a close-up shot, and she dropped hypnotized to the arm of the patterned sofa where her father sat. The dish towel fell to the floor beside her.

Rue smiled at Jamey, and at countless other viewers, as though he would communicate to them all his joy in living. His smile was like a caress, a caress she felt as vividly as though he had actually touched her. The even whiteness of his teeth dazzled her as her gaze locked longingly on the mouth that had moved so sweetly, so demandingly, against her own.

Jamey wanted to protest the action as the camera panned back, and her hands were clenched into tight fists as Rue ceded his claim to the blinking eye. Someone else moved onto the screen, but Jamey's eyes followed the casual strides of Rue's progress as he walked off-stage resplendent in full evening dress. She sucked in her breath, awed by the sheer male beauty of him, unaware of the revealing sound she made as she tried to memorize the black and white perfection that he wore as easily as the jeans she had seen him in so often. Even on TV, Rue exuded a potent masculinity that almost screamed to her, and Jamey's expression was oh, so revealing.

Duncan cleared his throat, seeking her attention now that Rue Garrett had disappeared, satisfied by his daughter's reaction. She was by no means over the man. She was as affected by him today, as in love with him right this minute, as she had been on the day the man had left her, alone and in torment.

Jamey turned to her father, her eyes large in her face, and sad. She rose and started toward the door, prepared to walk out on him before he could comment on her reaction. She knew what he would say. But her mother stood in the doorway, her eyes flicking nervously from Jamey to her husband, and Jamey stood still. Instinct flashed a warning that her parents' actions were contrived, carefully planned.

"Would you please sit down, Jamey?" her mother asked, the casual question seeming to lend her courage as she moved into the room. She waited for her daughter to seat herself, grimaced at the exasperated sigh Jamey emitted as she obeyed, then quietly crossed the carpeted floor to seat herself within the protective comfort of her husband's enveloping arm. His nod encouraged her.

Deanna inhaled deeply. "Jamey, your father has told me something of your experiences in Tennessee," she started, avoiding any direct mention of the word *love* or the name of the man involved. She swallowed hard. "He seems to feel that my having told you and Samantha of my frustrated hopes for a career in photojournalism has made a difference to your decision," she said, again refraining from direct communication. Her discomfort was terribly apparent, as was her daughter's.

"Mom," Jamey interrupted, "this isn't necessary. As you imply, my decision has been made, and I'm—"

"Wait a minute, Jamey, I haven't finished," her mother stated firmly, taking control with more confidence than she felt. "This is something I want to say—no, *need* to say," she amended, "and I'd appreciate it if you would do me the courtesy of listening."

"All right," Jamey conceded grudgingly, intensely uncomfortable as she waited for words she didn't want to hear, words she feared.

"When you were a little girl, I know I gave the impression of being a very bitter woman. In many ways, I was," Deanna confessed. "I had chosen to marry Duncan, chosen it consciously, but hadn't really believed that marrying him would mean giving up my career, even though I had agreed that I'd rather be with him than have any career in the world." She glanced at her husband, a small smile adding to the love in the look she gave him, then turned back to Jamey.

The air around them seemed to vibrate with feeling as Deanna continued. "I had been good at my work, hoped to become a noted photojournalist, but willingly set those hopes aside for love of your father. Unfortunately," she added with another sidelong glance at the man whose fingers tightened reassuringly on her shoulder, "Duncan's career kept him away so much that I began to feel jealous, not only of his work but of his freedom, and whether I meant to or not, I'm afraid I took it out on you two girls," she admitted, her eyes falling to her hands where they rested in her lap. "For that, I want you to know that I'm more sorry than I can ever say," she stated sincerely, looking again at her child, "but I also want you to know that other than that short time when I was eaten by my own rotten jealousy, I have never regretted marrying your father. I love him," she said softly, her eyes locked firmly with Jamey's, "and what he and I have shared is worth far more to me than any career goals I might have achieved. I mean that." The words were full of promise, honestly spoken.

Duncan reached over and took his wife's hand in his

own as her last statement hung in the air, lending his support as she sought to undo whatever damage lingered in their daughter. Jamey had been so small, so young, during those troubled times, that it didn't seem possible she could have absorbed so much of her mother's negative feelings, yet somehow she had. Somehow the child had become an adult who thought she should be able to dictate her every move, every emotion, should plot her life according to some master plan that only she controlled. And the effort was tearing her apart before their eyes.

Jamey watched as her father's hand tightened over her mother's, and her own hand flexed as though she too would reach out for support. But the only hand that could answer her need was far away, thousands of miles away.

"Thank you, Mom," Jamey said quietly as she clasped her hands together, forcing them to behave. "I needed to hear that, I guess, and I'll admit that I've wondered how you and Dad could seem so happy when my memories kept reminding me of how *un*happy I had thought you were." Jamey paused for a long moment. "But it really doesn't make any difference to my situation," she sighed, "because it's far too late for me to think of going back to Rue. He made his feelings very clear the last time I saw him, and that was nearly two months ago. It's just too late," she repeated sadly, her eyes falling away from the contradiction that flared instantly in both her parents' faces. Two months that had seemed more like two hundred years, she thought tiredly, but said nothing more.

"I'm not sure it's ever too late for love, Jamey," Deanna said softly, tempering the harsh denial her child's words had triggered. "If your Rue really loves you, it won't be too late. Why don't you call him?"

The idea of calling Rue made Jamey feel literally ill. What would she say to him? I'm sorry to bother you,

Rue, but I've changed my mind, and I was just wondering if you were still in love with me. Her hands moved to her stomach, willing the fluttering sensation to go away, and she laughed a little crazily. "No, Mom, I wouldn't have any idea what to say to him. And, in any case, I'd never call him. I'd just show up on his doorstep and hope for the best," she said, trying to make light of her remark, trying to joke her way out of the tense moment.

"That might not be a bad idea, honey," her mother agreed hopefully.

Jamey shook her head slowly, negatively.

"Well, just promise us you'll give it some thought," Deanna requested pleadingly. "I don't think I could bear to feel that I was even partially responsible for your making the wrong choice about this, Jamey."

Give it some thought . . . give it some thought. . . . How could I not give it thought? Jamey wondered miserably an hour later as she drove her small car toward the house that had long since ceased to feel like home to her. Her brain was spinning with her efforts to connect her memories of Rue with the words her parents had spoken, spinning so rapidly that it took her some time to realize that her fingers were tapping against the steering wheel in rhythm with a catchy, familiar tune. "Sweet Freedom!" And being sung by Steve! At least, it certainly sounded like Steve, Jamey thought as she quickly pulled to the side of the road and turned the volume up, shaking with reaction as she listened intently.

The song ended. "That was 'Sweet Freedom,' a single released early last week by the newest of Nashville's new voices, Steve Carlson," confirmed the announcer. "Steve obviously possesses a freshness of style that enhances what appears to be natural talent, but there's an interesting sidelight to the story of this release. It's rumored that, in an unprecedented move by a talent of such stature in the music world, Rue Garrett has provided the backing that enabled the previously unknown *boy* to cut this record," the disc jockey continued, his stress on the word "boy" a highlight that Jamey knew Rue would never have sanctioned. "Interesting," the man said mysteriously, implying the question: Why?

Jamey was stunned, and it was several minutes before she could drive on. She'd quit listening as the disc jockey moved on to other topics. Once again her brain was trying to opt out on her, and the only sense she could make of what she had just heard was the singing joy she felt at the sure knowledge that Rue's interest in Steve had never been merely a ploy to keep her near him. He had truly believed in Steve's talent and had helped him begin the long road to musical success in a way that Jamey could never have achieved. Her heart soared with the love that welled up inside her, and she would have given anything if she could only have seen Rue and Steve at that moment, could have shared her happiness with them.

Why not? The tiny voice niggled at the back of her mind, reminding her that planes traveled both ways. But she stilled the voice. No. If they had wanted to share this with her, they would have. Rue had probably made it clear to Steve that he wanted nothing more to do with Jamey Marsh.

As quickly as she answered that question, the voice inside her raised another. The clipping Meg had enclosed in her letter. Why hadn't she read it?

"Because I was afraid to," Jamey whispered, unaware that she answered the voice aloud. *Because I read part of the first sentence, and once I came to Rue's name, I knew I couldn't read any further. I couldn't face whatever it was that Meg considered important enough to include with her letter, a letter that made only fleeting reference to the special that was shown on TV tonight,* she admitted silently.

Jamey pulled into her driveway. Her actions as she left her car and moved toward the house were rapid. She knew exactly what she had to do. In her haste Jamey left the front door open, her attention focused only on the experience that lay before her.

Two days earlier she had gone into a department store looking for shoes, but her errant feet had carried her first to the record selection displayed near the entrance. She had left the store without the shoes she sought, carrying under her arm the album she had purchased instead.

The face on the cover of the album was achingly familiar... Rue's face. And Jamey had been unable to resist buying the album, as unable to resist buying it and bringing it home as she had been to open it and listen to it once she had got it there. She had stared at the face on the cover for long minutes, had read the album's title, *Raven's Flight,* and had shoved it quickly to the back of her record cabinet, jerking her hand away as though she had been burned. Rue had referred to her raven-colored hair so often. She had flown away from him. Jamey had been terrified of hearing the words and music Rue offered to his public, too terrified to risk listening and having her speculations confirmed.

Now she ripped the cellophane from the jacket of the album and, with shaking fingers, pulled the disc from its protective covering. The record slid easily onto the turntable. Jamey turned the machine on and moved across the room like an automaton, surprised to see the front door still standing open. She closed it quietly, then sat, accepting Rue's music as it seeped into her.

The tenor voice shimmered in the air, publicly exposing Jamey as a coward, a frightened young woman who had turned her back on love and whose bleak future promised only cold and bitter loneliness. There could be no doubt that the album's title song was the musical story of her defection.

Jamey's first reaction was anger—an intense, burning anger that Rue could have done this, could have made their story public. But as the song drew to an end, and the strong, throaty voice evoked the blessings of the gods, her anger dimmed. The right to share his feelings was something no one could take from him...and there were few who would ever know of the truth that rang from his words, she thought sadly.

"Pray God that Raven's flight will bring her safely home." The final phrase of the song haunted her as the album played on. What had he meant by that? Was he wishing her some measure of happiness as she acted out her life a continent away from him? Or was it a prayer for her return?

Jamey shivered at the possibility. It couldn't be a prayer for her return. He had made his feelings abundantly clear when he left her. It was too late.

Lifting her purse from the floor, Jamey opened it and pulled Meg's letter from inside. She had to know what Meg had considered so important that she had included it with her letter, even though she must have suspected that Jamey would resent the intrusion. The clipping fluttered from the envelope as she fumbled clumsily with the papers and Jamey reached out, grasping it before it hit the carpet, then lifted it and began to read.

"For the past several years, Rue Garrett and Mississippi River have evoked in us all a broad range of human emotion, from the heights of joy to the depths of deepest sorrow. But always, there has been distance. One could separate the singer from the song.

"In their latest album, however, that division seems nonexistent. 'Raven's Flight,' the song from which the album takes its name—and, indeed, every cut on the album—feels more like a journey into one man's private hell than a mere listening experience. For anyone who has ever lost what they believed to be a true love, the album will rekindle every thought, every feeling, and every moment of aching loss. If you're looking for a very real slice of life, musically rendered, buy this album and pour yourself a glass of your favorite wine. Then settle back and listen."

Jamey's eyes filled with tears as she read the words. Few would ever know of her part in the existence of the album, but the writer of the brief critique was right. Everyone who listened would recognize the sincerity of Rue Garrett's emotion as he sang. Then her eyes fell to the tiny italicized postscript that was almost lost between the statement about Rue's album and a description of yet another musical offering.

"P.S.—If you're listening, Raven, pray God your flight really will bring you home again."

Chills rippled over Jamey's body, raising goose bumps as her tears slid freely down her cheeks and dripped onto the paper she clutched in her hand. The stereo arm lifted and swung back from the record, then returned, settling its needled head gently into the grooves at the beginning of the disc. She had forgotten to set the player to shut itself off automatically. She didn't move to do so now. Jamey listened as the songs repeated themselves over and over, and she ached with a purely personal pain as Rue's intensity reached out to her time and again, willing her to share his hurt.

Gradually his sorrow became a living part of her, an emotion that could only be whole when shared by two. The ache shattered into fragments of fear—fear that her almost complacent acceptance of both her decision and Rue's parting statement as final could only equal, in the end, the cold and bitter woman alluded to in "Raven's Flight." And suddenly she knew what she was going to do. Raven *was* going home, home to Tennessee...and to Rue—if he still wanted her.

For the first time in her life Jamey acted with no firm plan to guide her, acted solely on instinct. She booked a flight for the coming Wednesday, felt pleased with herself at her decisive action, and inordinately pleased with the airline for having agents available twenty-four hours a day. Mentally she reviewed everything she could think of that had to be arranged. Really, she thought, there wasn't that much to be done. There were no consulting contracts to be canceled. Only the dogs and the house remained as major obstacles in her rapidly diminishing list of items that absolutely had to be dealt with before she could go.

And, as it turned out, both were handled with far more ease than she could have hoped for, Jamey thought several days later as she stood once again with her parents in a waiting area of Portland's air terminal. The three were linked, holding hands in a triangular formation. They talked quietly, their voices lowered, saying their farewells.

"Let us know what happens, Jamey," her mother whispered as the flight was called. She whispered because she was afraid she would burst into tears at any moment, tears of joy and sadness at the same time. Both she and her husband were convinced that Jamey had made the right decision. But that made it no easier to say good-bye to their child. Not this time.

"I will," Jamey promised softly, her own tears not far away. "And thanks again for taking care of the dogs and the house for me," she added as her hands were released and she stepped into her mother's embrace. She still found it hard to believe that not her father, but her mother, had offered to keep the dogs until she knew whether or not it would be necessary to make arrangements for them to be sent to Tennessee. That had been an unprecedented move in the life of Deanna Marsh, and one that had been greeted with astonished pleasure by both her husband and her daughter. But, as Deanna had smilingly commented, Digger and Charlie and P.L. would all be much happier with her and Dun-

can than they would be in a kennel. Jamey had gratefully agreed with the pronouncement and had thank-
fully accepted their assurances that they would see to
anything that needed their attention at her house.

Jamey hugged both her parents fiercely as the placid,
anonymous voice made the final boarding call for her
flight. Then she turned and moved into the same tunnel she had emerged from two and a half months earlier.

Again she felt the power of jet engines as the plane
surged upward into the blue sky, accepted the easing of
her tension as the aircraft leveled off to soar miles
above the earth. Her heart soared with it as she brushed
a speck of lint from the fabric of her designer jeans,
then smoothed the material of her bright red cowl-neck
pullover before glancing out the window. The snow-
capped peaks of the Cascades glistened, and Jamey
mouthed a silent good-bye to them. As odd as it
seemed when she was flying away from the place of her
birth, she felt as though she was finally going home.
She wanted to spur the plane on, to somehow make it
go faster. It was almost impossible to believe that they
were moving at a rate greater than five hundred miles
an hour, she thought, smiling as she imagined herself
whipping the huge jet, manipulating it to even greater
speed.

Two long flights later Jamey emerged into the shining newness of Nashville's Metropolitan Airport, a
captivating figure who looked as though she belonged
in the country music capital of the world. Many eyes
followed the progress of her slender form, male eyes
admiring and female eyes almost envious as they
watched the confident way she moved toward the desk
of the car rental agency. Jamey was unaware of the
inspecting eyes. She was once again masking a sudden
shyness, a burgeoning uncertainty, behind an aura of
cool self-possession. She smiled serenely as the keys

to a small Ford were passed to her, then turned to collect her bags and make her way out into the crisp late-November air.

What next? Jamey asked herself. She chewed at her tender lower lip, a sure sign of her growing uncertainty, as she turned the light blue car north on Briley Parkway, then west on Interstate 40. She drove toward downtown Nashville, her mind awhirl with questions.

Could she really just show up on Rue's doorstep, unannounced? What would his reaction be? Would he welcome her—or reject her coldly?

As suddenly as she had decided to return to Nashville, Jamey changed her plans. She simply couldn't follow through with the intent that had seemed so right until this minute. She couldn't risk Rue's rejection, she thought with a shudder as the last words he had said to her—"I don't plan to wait for you"—echoed through her mind. She changed lanes, exiting the freeway as her eyes scanned the surrounding area for a place to stay, a hotel or motel where she could rest and collect her now scattered thoughts. But as she pulled into the parking lot of the Tudor Inn, a new plan was already forming, waiting for her to carry it out.

Impatience marked Jamey's actions as she let herself into the room. She moved quickly to the phone, not even bothering to glance around at the comfortable styling of her temporary quarters. She dialed the numbers with no hesitation, dialed from memory the series of numerals that would link her with Rue's penthouse apartment. She had never before called Rue, but the small card that rested safely in her wallet had been read and reread so often that the numbers on it were printed indelibly in her memory.

The ringing in her ear seemed to go on forever, unanswered, until Jamey finally returned the receiver to its cradle, defeated. Doubt hovered over her, and only the memory of the final phrase of their song, "Raven's

Flight," boosted her courage as Jamey reached again for the phone.

This time the ringing stopped almost immediately, a familiar male voice responding to her call. "Hello," the man said firmly.

"Mac?" she questioned, then rushed on. "This is Jamey," she identified herself, wanting to get pleasantries out of the way as quickly as possible, wanting to know the answers to her uncertainties.

"Jamey!" he responded eagerly. "Where are you?"

"Here...in Nashville, I mean," she explained. "Do you know where Rue is?" she asked baldly.

There was a slight pause before Mac confirmed the worst of her fears. "Yes, I think so," he said hesitantly. "I believe he said he would be in Atlanta until the end of the week...but then he'll be back here for a concert on Saturday night," he added hastily.

Jamey's unvoiced disappointment was evident as she accepted the reality of Rue's absence, then went on to question timidly Mac's opinion of the wisdom of her plan to see Rue.

"Oh, Jamey," Mac sighed. "There are no guarantees. You know that, honey," he continued avuncularly. "But the only way you're going to find out is to follow through with your plan to see him. Only Rue can answer your questions," he assured her. "You hurt him badly, and I frankly have no idea what his reaction will be. He never mentions you anymore, and doesn't allow anybody else to, if he can stop them," he added, his words eliciting an incredibly sharp stab of pain in the region of her heart.

Jamey's silence stretched between them for a moment. Then Mac, with impatience edging his tones, went on tersely. "God, you've been gone for nearly three months, Jamey! What did you expect?"

"I guess I didn't know what to expect," she admitted quietly, no longer sure of herself at all, no longer sure of anything. She should have remembered the time lapse between the recording of a record and its release, she thought. She questioned Mac about the Saturday concert, then talked with him for a moment about Steve and Meg before ringing off without telling him where she was staying, or even *if* she would stay until Saturday. But she knew she would still be in Nashville when Rue returned. Her decision had been made and, no matter how much it might hurt, she had to see him again, had to learn the truth of his feelings from his own lips.

The two days that followed were more miserable than Jamey would have believed possible. One minute she was sure that everything would be fine; the next, she was plunged into deep despair at the absolute certainty that Rue would coldly turn her away. She wavered constantly between the two feelings as she wandered through the streets of Music Row, memory swamping her as she passed by the recording studio she had visited with him. And, as she purchased a ticket for the concert Mississippi River would present on Saturday night, a special two-hour concert that would be held at Opryland as a benefit to raise funds for a halfway house for runaways and incorrigibles, her heart swelled again with love and pride.

Her discovery of the purpose of the concert had sent a tingling sensation rippling up Jamey's spine, had raised even more questions that only Rue could answer. But even this evidence that Rue's involvement with Steve was important to him seemed to cut her further out of his life—out of the lives of all her friends. Doubts festered in her mind, and Jamey cast aside any thought of further contact with even Mac or Meg or Steve. She suspected that they had tried to find her after her brief call to Mac, but was relieved by her memory of the conversation. She remembered every painful word. She knew she hadn't mentioned where she was staying.

Perhaps she would stay in Tennessee only long enough to see Rue one last time. anyway, she thought in the depths of her depression, to attend the concert and see the real flesh-and-blood Rue instead of merely pictures or pieces of film. Her heart rejected the idea that she might leave without talking with him, but her mind clung to the plan. It wasn't a very comfortable plan. In fact, it didn't comfort her at all as she settled into the lonely double bed in her lonely room, waiting for sleep to erase what remained of Friday.

JAMEY waited until the last minute before slipping unnoticed into the huge auditorium. She had intentionally arrived only moments before the performance was to begin, determined to avoid even the remote possibility of running into Mac or Meg, or anyone who knew her. She had suspected that they would attend the concert, and her suspicions had been verified upon her arrival by the sight of them looking around anxiously before finally entering through the wide doors. She knew they were looking for her. She was grateful for the darkness that made her simply one of a sea of nameless faces as she made her way to the carpeted pew she chose so carefully from the few that still had open space. The seat was as near to an exit as she could find.

Like every other female at the concert, Jamey was dressed in boots, jeans, and western shirt. That too had been deliberate—as deliberate as her choice of a back row seat. She wanted nothing to set her apart from any other fan. And, other than the fragile sadness that had settled around her like a cloud, adding to her elusive beauty, she had succeeded. She gave every appearance, outwardly, of feminine serenity. Inside, her blood pressed frantically against her nerve endings as she strove to maintain the delicate hold that kept her from running from the auditorium, from running in fear of even the sight of Rue Garrett.

Then the moment was gone. Rue strode onto the stage, followed by the members of his band as they waved to the crowd, returning their greetings with broad smiles. Each of the men moved to his own instrument, lifted it and stood poised for the action that would begin at Rue's signal.

Rue's eyes scanned the crowd, then he swung his guitar up and the specially designed room was instantly filled with sound, sound that dipped and soared as Mississippi River ran through a medley of familiar melodies. Jamey's eyes sparkled with emotion, all thought of running banished, replaced by her memories of the time he had played for her alone.

For long moments Jamey was unable to tear her eyes away from Rue's face. At last she let her gaze slide down the length of him. So casual, she thought, her glance passing lightly over the plaid shirt that was topped by a leather vest, then to the customary jeans that outlined his lean, muscled lines, and to the booted foot that kept time with the rhythm of the music. The booted foot became still, and Rue's voice interrupted her yearning inspection.

"The boys and I want to welcome you all to this concert," he said as the music continued at lowered decibels around him, enveloping everyone in the room with its invitation. "As you know, it won't be fancy— just us and the music," he added, the crowd held easily in thrall of his comfortable, receptive presence.

Rue went on to explain briefly the reason for the concert, thanked the audience for their support of the project, then introduced his special guest.

"You may have heard a new single that was released a few weeks ago," he began. "That single is the product of a very talented young man whom I've been privileged to get to know over the past few months, a young man who taught me that some songs are destined to be sung by only one person. Folks, meet Steve Carlson, singing his first release, 'Sweet Freedom.'"

Jamey had moved to the edge of her seat, pulled there by Rue's introduction of Steve, held there by the youth's loping stride as he advanced across the stage, trying to emulate Rue's easy style. A shy, endearing grin split the lad's face as he lifted his guitar into his hands, and Jamey almost relaxed. Then the opening strains of "Sweet Freedom" reached out to her, opening up a Pandora's box of remembrances as she lost herself to time gone by.

The deafening thunder of applause that rose at the end of Steve's performance was music to her ears. It cut across her memories, assuring her that her young friend's talent had been recognized and accepted. The road was clear before him, if only he could handle the public adulation that would almost certainly follow his introduction to a waiting community of fans by one of their best-loved country singers.

Steve remained onstage after his solo performance, backing Rue musically along with the rest of the band, and Jamey's eyes occasionally traveled the short distance to where he stood. But most of the time her gaze was locked avidly onto Rue's long, masculine frame as he sang song after popular song. How she loved him, she thought as an intense, involuntary response invaded her, weakening her resolve to leave without him ever knowing that she had at last followed him here.

Two hours had never passed so quickly! Jamey was sure of that as she realized that the performers were sliding into the final song of the show they had planned. She watched as Rue set his guitar aside, as he slipped the microphone from its stand and moved forward on the stage. She waited, as breathless as anyone else in the audience, as the opening strains of music paved the way for Rue's clear, tenor voice to rise to meet haunting chords.

Jamey groaned, unaware of the throaty sound she made, as her public humiliation began. She had known it would come, but she hadn't believed it would hurt so badly. She closed her eyes and sank limply against the carpeted pew as Rue began "Raven's Flight." His tones were so firm, so sure, as they reached through his own agony, and she opened her eyes again to find his face as he poured out the story of their ill-fated love. Rue's eyes were closed, his head tipped back as though he would close himself away from the throng before him and shut himself away to relive the pain that had given birth to the song, and the feeling of shared pain rose in her anew with an overwhelming intensity. A hush had fallen over the crowd of thousands as they too felt the agony of lost love. But for Jamey, there existed only two people in the vastness of the auditorium.

Jamey rose slowly from her carefully selected seat. Her subconscious mind accepted the risk that failed to register at any other level as her feet carried her forward, down the long, long aisle that stretched between her and the one man for whom she was willing to alter her meticulously plotted life. She was aware of nothing except the love that pulled her, like a puppet on strings, toward Rue Garrett.

Meg nudged Mac as Jamey passed them by. Mac looked up, smiled, and nodded. He reached over and took Meg's hand in his own, contented with the love they shared, grateful that they would never have to endure the agonizing pain that Rue and Jamey had known. He squeezed the hand he held and turned to Meg with a smile as the murmurs of the crowd grew. More and more of them were becoming aware of the raven-haired woman who moved so intently toward the stage.

Jamey walked on gracefully, still unaware of anything other than her goal. She neared the stage, and as though on cue, Rue's eyes opened. His concentration had been penetrated by the rippling murmur that reminded him of the audience he had left behind as he lost himself to the story he told. Movement captured his attention. The leonine head turned toward the source of the movement, his eyes seeking.

The music seemed to swell behind him as recognition flared in his eyes. Rue moved across the stage as slowly, as gracefully, as Jamey moved toward it. He descended the short flight of steps that led to the floor of the auditorium, and his free arm extended in invitation and slipped gently around her waist as she joined him. Gray-blue eyes locked with deep brown ones, and love flashed between them as though on a current of electricity.

"Thank God that Raven's flight has brought her home to me." Rue changed the final words of the song, the new words at last penetrating the trance that had pulled Jamey forward. She registered the new words, but meaning eluded her as her conscious mind took over, exposing to her the action she had taken, the risk she had taken. Her slender body went rigid beneath Rue's fingers, and she pulled back. But the strong arm of the man who held her tightened, pulled her firmly to his side as he refused to relinquish his hold, and most of the festering doubts that plagued Jamey's mind were banished as she raised her eyes pleadingly to Rue's. Her eyes encountered love...and strength, a strength that enveloped her as the arm that held the microphone was lowered to her waist.

The cold, hard metal of the microphone was unfelt as it pressed against her back. Jamey felt only the warmth of Rue's loving presence as his lips lowered steadily toward hers, the now silent audience forgotten again as they welcomed each other home.

Cheers erupted, ringing throughout the massive auditorium, as the crowd finally understood the certainty of what they were witnessing—Raven's return. They added their welcome to that of the man who held her so tightly, and Jamey's cheeks flamed as Rue lifted his mouth from hers, turning back to the audience without letting her go.

Rue grinned at his fans, then looked back down at Jamey, love and humor mingling in the sparkling gray-blue of his eyes as he noticed her reddened cheeks. Then his hands slid away from her, and for a moment Jamey felt deserted. But her desertion was ended quickly as Rue extended one hand toward the cheering crowd, the other down to grasp her smaller hand as he led her up the steps and onto the stage.

Rue spoke into the microphone. "I'm sure you'll excuse us," he quipped as the cheers began to turn to laughter at his easy handling of the moment, "but this public moment is about to become very private."

Hank moved forward and caught the microphone as Rue tossed it easily to him, then turned to the rest of the group with a grinning nod. "Raven's Flight" soared to the rafters as Rue ushered Jamey quickly from the stage and into the relative privacy of a dressing room.

In the dressing room he turned Jamey into his arms again for a brief moment, simply holding her before stepping back to catch her eyes firmly with his. Long minutes passed slowly as he stared at her, drinking in the sight of her as though he was still uncertain that their moment could last.

"No strings this time?" he asked finally. His voice was husky with emotion.

"No strings," Jamey promised, her brown eyes twinkling up at him.

"Your career—"

"—plans have changed a bit," she interrupted the question. Her heart was in her eyes.

And then she was in his arms, bewitched again by

the feeling of Rue's body pressed hard against hers as he held her, by the sweetness of his kiss as his mouth explored hers. The room seemed to spin, to turn slowly round and round in an endless spiral that carried them higher and higher.

"Oh, God, Jamey," Rue said softly at last, "I was afraid you wouldn't be here, afraid my restraint would mean nothing, after all." The pressure of his arms increased, pulling her to him so tightly that it seemed he wanted to pull her fully inside him, to meld two bodies into one.

"What restraint?" she questioned gently, burrowing closer yet to his male warmth.

Rue laughed, a happy-sad sound. "I knew you were here, in Nashville. Mac got the message to me as quickly as he could, and I flew straight home from Atlanta. We tore the town apart for two days, trying to find you," he said, the anguish of that search alive in his voice, "but when we finally learned where you were staying, I couldn't come to you. I'd let it go so far, I realized. Let you come this far by your own choice," he added wonderingly, "that I had to let you finish it in your own way."

"You knew where I was?" Jamey questioned, surprise lacing her words as she leaned back to look into his eyes.

He gazed down at her. "Yes," he confirmed. "Knew that, and knew you'd bought a ticket to tonight's concert. But when Mac sent word backstage that he and Meg hadn't been able to spot you, I was afraid you had gone back to Oregon again. That's when I added 'Raven's Flight' to tonight's program," he whispered. "I hadn't planned to sing it; I didn't want to feel the pain again. But I had to take the chance, in case you *were* in that audience. I had to risk everything on the thought that the song might have been partially responsible for bringing you to Nashville, the hope that it might bring you all the way home," he finished.

"Oh, Rue," Jamey whispered, a single tear escaping to slide down her cheek. "Love of you brought me home. Love of you, and the magic of our song. Steve was right, wasn't he?" she asked, a second tear joining the first. "Some songs *are* meant to have only one voice give them life."

Rue smiled tenderly as he lowered his head and let his lips erase the salty traces of her happy tears. He pulled her against him again as his mouth claimed hers.

Raven's song, a song that could be sung by only one man, had called her home.

Chapter Twelve

"Tell the truth, Jamey," Meg coaxed teasingly as she sipped at the herbal tea her friend placed before her. "You really weren't aware of any of us, were you? Didn't even think of that huge crowd when you were walking toward the stage?"

Jamey's eyes twinkled as she seated herself across from Meg, placing her own tea in front of her on the round oak table. She took a long sip of the relaxing liquid, her thoughts returning to a night more than six months past.

She had maintained that she had known exactly what she was doing on that night, that she had been conscious of every step that carried her closer to Rue, every eye that followed her progress, but that it had seemed at the time the best way to prove the depth of her love. To allow her return to be as public as Rue had made her escape with the release of "Raven's Flight."

Her return had been a nine-day wonder around Nashville, and she had been teased unmercifully about her abstracted behavior. Jamey had responded to the teasing good-naturedly, had always given the same story, and only Rue had known the truth behind her actions...until now.

"No," she confessed at last with a happy laugh, "you all might as well have been lumps of clay as far as I was concerned. To be honest, I think I was a little crazy. I'd had such a horrible three days—three *months,*" she amended, "that I'm not sure I was thinking at all. Just following my instincts," she added, smiling. "And the only thing my instincts were telling me was to get to Rue, to learn from him how he really felt."

"And now you know," Meg said, her eyes falling to the simple gold wedding band that circled Jamey's finger.

"And now I know," Jamey agreed. "But if you dare tell anyone what I just admitted, Meg, I swear I'll get even," she threatened mockingly, a laugh erasing any real meaning behind the threat.

Meg raised both hands, laughing herself. "I won't tell a soul ... promise! But Rue must know?"

"He knows," Jamey confirmed, a private smile softening her features. "I'm not sure there's much he doesn't know about me," she added, a tingle of anticipation stirring her insides at the thought that he would be home soon.

"Mmm, I know how you feel. I sometimes think Mac already has me thoroughly figured out too, especially since we're together so much," she said, thinking fondly of their sharing both at home and at work. "I'm really going to miss Tanasie Basin."

"Oh, but think what you're trading it for, Meg," Jamey sighed as her eyes traced the slight bulge at her friend's middle.

"I know," Meg responded happily, patting her tummy. "When are you going to join me?"

"Soon, I think. Every time we're together, I get a little more jealous of that precious life you're carrying," Jamey admitted. "Rue and I had talked about waiting two years, but I know he's held to that because of my career and, frankly, I'm beginning to wonder why I ever thought it would be a problem."

"Well, it *would* limit you, Jamey," Meg considered slowly, frowning.

Jamey smiled. "It wouldn't necessarily limit me at all," she contradicted, "and it could broaden my horizons considerably." She leaned forward, her eyes sparkling as she repeated the arguments she'd used when she and Rue had last discussed the issue. "I could stay on at Tanasie Basin until I was near term, and even continue my consulting, for a while, anyway, on the same limited basis I'm devoting to it now. Or I could begin work on the book on institutional education I've been thinking of trying to write. Then I could apply for a year's leave of absence to spend at home with the baby. And at the end of that year," she explained, "I'd have a decision to make—whether I should return to Tanasie Basin or simply continue my work indirectly by seeing where writing takes me."

"You've really given this a lot of thought, haven't you?" Meg's green eyes were alight with the admiration she felt for Jamey, admiration and deep affection.

"Yes," Jamey answered quietly, a faraway look in her eyes as her thoughts focused on images of that same small face, the one that blended the best of her and Rue.

She thought she understood now why Samantha was so happy. Her sister really did have the best of both worlds—a husband and child she doted on, and a career she enjoyed thoroughly, but kept in perspective.

Jamey believed she could have that too, though her perspective seemed to be changing. The idea of writing, of possibly reaching through the written word even more people who dealt daily with incarcerated delinquent youth, held more and more appeal. Funny, she thought, when the idea had originally been a spur-of-the-moment notion born of her fear at Rue's silence on that night so long ago. But she knew the power of the written word, and she was eager to test her command over that power. Almost as eager as she was to bear the child she and Rue could create through the power of their love.

"You know," Jamey said pensively, breaking the silence her thoughts had built, "I've never been happier in my life than I have these last six months."

"I know," Meg answered, an I-told-you-so look in her eyes as she grinned at her friend. "I haven't either! Would you say marriage agrees with us?" she asked impishly, twirling and showing off the slight swell that signaled the life she carried as she stood to carry her cup to the sink. "Say, how's the house coming along?" Meg turned back toward Jamey as she asked the question.

Jamey's eyes lit up with excitement and pleasure as she responded. "Great! We should be moving in within three months. Let me show you what we've been working on!"

Jamey placed her own cup on the counter and left the open spaces of the cabin's kitchen area. She returned quickly, her arms loaded, and beckoned for Meg to move across to join her in the living room.

The two women sat on the carpeted floor, blueprints and color chips and carpet and material samples spread around them. Jamey's hands flew as she matched chips and samples, explaining where they fit into the master plan for the home she and Rue were having built. Her eyes shone as she described the rustic look they planned, a look that would blend with the wildness of the Tennessee countryside, would complement the ever-changing backdrop of hills, valleys, trees, and flowers on the acreage they had bought.

Jamey and Rue had divided their time between the cabin and Rue's apartment in Nashville since her return, and the prospect of moving into the home they had lovingly designed together brought a bright shine to Jamey's eyes. She was absorbed in telling Meg of the log construction their home would have, in the memory of Rue's pleasure as he had looked over the construction site before he had left on this latest road trip. She could almost hear his voice as he swore that nowhere on earth was the grass greener, the sky bluer, or the pace of life more comfortable than right here in the simple, country atmosphere of middle Tennessee.

"Oh, Meg, it's really good to see you again. But must you leave so soon? I just got here." The deep, masculine voice was teasing as both women swiveled their heads toward the door to find Rue leaning casually in the doorway, his eyes alight with love as they rested on his wife's slender form, on the skimpy cutoffs and light green T-shirt she wore. His eyes swept hungrily from her bare feet to the tousled raven hair that hung free around her shoulders.

Meg laughed at Rue's teasing as Jamey rose and sped across the room to her husband, not even noticing the jeans and shirt he wore, or the slight stubble he hadn't yet taken time to shave away, as she launched herself into his arms and lifted her lips to him. He'd done it to her again—come home hours earlier than she expected him, long before she'd had time to make herself beautiful for him. But she was glad. How hungry she was for him!

"I think I can take a subtle hint," Meg teased back as she rose from the floor, smiling at the happiness reflected before her. Then she too was moving quickly toward the door, toward the other man who had just entered the tiny cabin.

"You giving my wife a hard time, Garrett?" Mac growled mock-menacingly as he slid his arms around Meg.

And suddenly they were all laughing. Jamey and Meg had only that second realized that Rue and Mac had arrived at the same time, had planned this scene as they watched their wives through the huge windows at the front of the cabin.

They talked for a few more minutes, the easy talk of close friends. Then Jamey and Rue stood, arms around each other, watching as Meg and Mac entered their car and drove away toward their own home.

"Come here, Jamey," Rue ordered huskily as he turned her into his arms and claimed her lips in a long, drugging kiss.

Long minutes later Jamey whispered up to him, "Oh, Rue, these are the best of the worst of times."

"What do you mean?" he asked tenderly.

"I mean," she said sweetly, a dimple showing beside her smiling mouth, "that I hate it when you're away, but I *love* it when you get back home."

Rue smiled lovingly at her implication. "Me too," he said feelingly as he lifted her in his strong arms and carried her slowly, his lips finding hers again, toward the double bed in the small room at the back of the cabin.

Finally when Rue lay sleeping contentedly beside her, Jamey turned to watch her husband. She loved these moments, she thought, loved the sight of this man, the sight and smell and feel of him. She loved being home with Rue.

Home. She smiled at the word. For her, home was Rue.

A lazy gray-blue eye blinked open, was followed by another, and Jamey blushed at being caught staring. Rue laughed and reached for her.

"I love you," he whispered as she snuggled into the haven of his arms, into the only home she would ever need.

ROBERTA LEIGH

A specially designed collection of six exciting love stories by one of the world's favorite romance writers—Roberta Leigh, author of more than 60 bestselling novels!

1 Love in Store	4 The Savage Aristocrat
2 Night of Love	5 The Facts of Love
3 Flower of the Desert	6 Too Young to Love

Available in August wherever paperback books are sold, or available through Harlequin Reader Service. Simply complete and mail the coupon below.

- -